PRAISE FC

"A magical blend of fact the author's understanding and love of this much maligned animal. This novel, revealing the true nature of the wolf— courageous, intelligent and loyal—will surely help to dispel the underlying fear or hatred that leads to their cruel persecution. It is a terrific book, and deserves to be read by many."

—DR. JANE GOODALL

"Imagine that wolves chose YOU to speak to. Now add time-travel, telepathy and shape-shifting, and you've got a rollicking good read. But *WOLF TIME* is not just a fun book, but an important one, a book from which people who care about animals and wilderness will draw affirmation, inspiration, and hope."

—SY MONTGOMERY,
Author of *The Soul of an Octopus*

"*Wolf Time* is storytelling at its best, complete with heroes and villains, unbearable tragedy, immense beauty and the magical inspiration of interspecies communication....the ultimate story of good and evil about the relationship between humans and wolves in America. It is a story richly populated by characters—human and wolf—the reader will fall in love with, shed tears for and cheer onward. I don't know which I relished more, the exquisite descriptions of the wolves' sensory perceptions of themselves, each other and the landscape they inhabit; or the straight-from-the-wolves'-mouths lessons on wolf biology and wolf recovery politics. In *Wolf Time*, Moritsch weaves a tapestry in which the reader begins to understand the design of nature, the solidarity of human and wolf cultures, and how we as humans have an opportunity to right an enormous wrong that was done to wolves and is still taking place today.

—AMAROQ WEISS,
West Coast Wolf Organizer, Center for Biological Diversity

"A story of the deep connection wolves once had with humans but lost. Through myth and fantasy woven together with facts, the truth about wolves is revealed. Barbara paints a picture of the dire challenges wolves face today and how the disconnection between humans and nature contributes to these problems. Her novel offers a glimmer of hope, inviting humans to listen to the voices of these incredibly important social animals, and to let go of their fears, so there can be space for people and wolves to share the land."

—JIM AND JAMIE DUTCHER,
Founders, Living with Wolves

"*Wolf Time* speaks to us, like a sweet, mysterious, sonorous howl emanating from distant mountains as dusk approaches. As a seasoned naturalist Barbara Moritsch has long given wilderness a poetic voice. Now, in this touching and deeply personal tribute, she does it again—honoring some of the most charismatic creatures on earth: the lobos of Yellowstone."

—TODD WILKINSON,
American environmental journalist
and author of *Grizzlies of Pilgrim Creek, An Intimate Portrait
of 399, the Most Famous Bear of Greater Yellowstone*

"Barbara J. Moritsch's heart swells with love for wolves. So does her new book, *Wolf Time*. Barbara has accomplished something remarkable. She has created a rich story filled with engaging characters—some of them wolves. She has spiced this work of fiction with plenty of accurate, valuable, and timely information about these essential predators. I'm glad to recommend Wolf Time, a book that entertains and educates and in the end leaves one filled with hope."

—RICK LAMPLUGH,
Author of *In the Temple of Wolves:*
A Winter's Immersion in Wild Yellowstone

"An endearing, if sometimes painful, read for animal lovers and a wake-up call for everyone else. Its dreamy prose and shocking statistics...will draw in teens and adults."

—KIRKUS REVIEWS

ALSO BY BARBARA J. MORITSCH:

The Soul of Yosemite: Finding, Defending, and Saving the Valley's Sacred Wild Nature

A portion of the profits from sales of this book will be donated to the Center for Biological Diversity for their continued work on behalf of wolves.

Wolf
TIME

A NOVEL

BARBARA J. MORITSCH

BEAR
CLOVER
BOOKS

EAGLE, IDAHO

WOLF TIME
By Barbara J. Moritsch

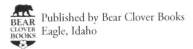 Published by Bear Clover Books
Eagle, Idaho

Cover design by: Jessa Tucker Riley | jessacat.com
Interior layout by: Yvonne Parks | PearCreative.ca

Library of Congress Control Number: 2020908649

Publisher's Cataloging-In-Publication Data
(Prepared by The Donohue Group, Inc.)

Names: Moritsch, Barbara J., author.
Title: Wolf time : a novel / Barbara J. Moritsch.
Description: Eagle, Idaho : Bear Clover Books, [2020]
Identifiers: ISBN 9780997986204 (Print) | ISBN 9780997986211 (Kindle) | ISBN 9780997986228 (ePub)
Subjects: LCSH: Wolves--Fiction. | Women biologists--Fiction. | Human-animal relationships--Fiction. | Shapeshifting--Fiction. | Time travel--Fiction. | Nature fiction.
Classification: LCC PS3613.O7543 W65 2020 (print) | LCC PS3613.O7543 (ebook) | DDC 813/.6--dc23

Dedicated to:
Cali, Angus, Kodi, and all the wild ones

If you talk to the animals they will talk with you and you will know each other. If you do not talk to them you will not know them, and what you do not know you will fear. What one fears one destroys.

—Chief Dan George

Prologue

2014

A sharp-tipped crescent moon cast its pale glow over a solo wolf, a well-used deer path, and a remote mountain lake in central Idaho. Snow had fallen intermittently over the past three days, and the large, fluffy flakes muted the sounds of the night and softened the edges of the pines and rock outcrops that framed the lake.

Moving at a steady trot, Tierra pushed easily through the soft blanket of snow that covered the path and wondered if the spring storm would ever end. The early spring conditions forced her to take the long way around the big lake; the ice was no longer thick enough to hold her weight. In a hurry, she'd travelled the better part of the day and stopped only for short breaks to catch her breath. Her family was waiting for her, relying on her to bring food.

The rendezvous with the other members of the Blackline Pack lasted longer than expected. She'd been surprised to learn most of the wolves in the area already were on the move to get out of Idaho, heading east and south to the region called the Yellow Stone, which was rumored to be safe.

As Tierra jogged, she reflected on how hard it had been to raise her litter without Redtail. The hunter's bullet had destroyed not only her beloved mate, but also her dreams of raising a family with him. Her older brother and two littermate sisters helped by bringing food to the den, but with all the killing, and the resulting changes in the family's structure, she was the pups' primary source of protection and sustenance. And they were still so helpless, less than two moons old.

The route descended as Tierra followed the course of a small creek that spilled from the lake's lower end. She picked up speed on the sloping terrain, her powerful body doing what it was built to do: flow like liquid around rocks and trees, leap with ease over downed limbs and small rivulets, and cover the miles seemingly without effort. There were fewer trees here than around the lake, and the snow was not as deep. A faint trace of campfire smoke floated past her nose, but she paid it no mind. She was focused on getting home.

She'd almost made it to the midpoint of the slope when a deafening crack, followed immediately by a searing sensation just above her right shoulder, threw her wildly off stride. The metallic odor of her blood coupled with intense pain almost overwhelmed her, but the image of six pairs of amber eyes watching for her, the knowledge of six empty stomachs trusting she would soon fill them, kept her moving.

Tierra's ears rang, her vision clouded, and the fire in her shoulder burned hotter with every stride. She crouched to leap over a downed log, but her body could not respond. A jagged limb caught a front foot and she flipped, rolled down the slope, and then slid on ice and snow. When she finally came to rest against the base of a large pine, Tierra's heart was still.

Chapter One
2018

Late one night, about a week before Christmas, I was surprised to hear an odd scratching sound at my front door. I was alone in a small log cabin built by my grandfather in the 1940s. Tucked back on a gentle slope a hundred yards or so west of a large meadow, the cabin was surrounded by a vast forest tract of mostly ponderosa pine and black oak that spread uphill to the east. Patches of red fir could be seen a bit higher in elevation. The land was part of a small private inholding in Yosemite National Park, on the west slope of California's Sierra Nevada. Only a few neighbors lived there year-round. Most of the cabins hosted summer people.

I'd been holed up in the cabin for the past two days as heavy snow fell from a featureless, steel gray sky. Using my solo time to catch up on my reading, I was immersed in narratives about the Battle of the Little Bighorn and Wounded Knee, which provided a welcome distraction from recent events in my life.

In November I'd come up to winter in the cabin. So much had changed so fast, I was hoping to make sense of it all. The cascade of trauma started in August, when I quit my job as a biologist with the United States Fish and Wildlife Service. Resigning had been heart-breaking; my life's dream had been to work to protect wildlife and wild lands. At the age of thirty-three, at long last, I realized that dream and went to work for the federal endangered species program. But the agency's pace was so slow that species were going extinct before they were even listed. After two years of hearing to too many excuses about how listing a species would cause financial harm to this rancher or that pipeline company, I'd had enough.

Right after I handed in my letter of resignation, I'd headed to South Dakota's Black Hills to explore a region that had been calling to me for a long time. While I was on the road, my grandmother was diagnosed with cancer. Unbeknownst to me, my mother was battling the same disease at the same time. They both passed in late October—Mom from melanoma and Grandma Rose from a combination of liver cancer, old age, and grief. I was devastated.

When I decided to run away to the embrace of the Yosemite cabin, I was worried about the farm in Davis where I'd been living for the past year. But I knew my friend, Angel, would take good care of the animals, and I desperately needed time to take stock and figure out what to do next with my life. Since Adam, my beau of sorts, was spending a sabbatical year up at Humboldt State, there was nothing holding me back.

I considered ignoring the scratching noises and not opening the door, pretending no one was home. But I glanced around the cabin and realized whoever was outside would have seen the flickering Christmas tree lights and heard Jewel's version of *O Holy Night* streaming forth from the stereo. With trepidation, I hauled myself out of my favorite chair, a maple rocker that I'd pulled up close to the fireplace. Dressed in white robe and beat-up slippers, I padded across the worn wooden floor to the front door and glanced down to be sure the large doggie door was securely fastened. I peered out through the peephole and my jaw dropped. Sitting side-by-side on the small front deck were two full-grown gray wolves.

My heart forgot to beat for several moments as I peered out at my unexpected night visitors. They were both very large, with thick, multi-colored coats. Their prominent, coal black noses glistened in the glow of the porch light. The wolf on the right had a sand-colored face, with white patches on both sides of its muzzle. Its shiny amber eyes were enhanced by black rings and eyebrows. The rest of its coat was a gorgeous swirly mix of pale gray and tan, with a few dark accents.

The second wolf was larger than the first. Its markings were similar, and it had the same liquid amber eyes. This wolf was darker, though, with a lot more black and red-gold hair mixed in with the gray. A light dusting of snow frosted their backs and shoulders.

A variety of creatures had shown up on my front porch over the years—quail, rabbits, raccoons, black bears, a weasel, a great gray owl, a grouse, a bobcat, and several smaller varieties of birds. Some of them needed help, were dehydrated, orphaned, or injured, but most were just passing through. Never before had I been so fortunate as to have wolves at my doorstep.

There was, however, one significant problem with these callers: Wild wolves did not exist this far south in California at that time. They had been eradicated in the state in 1924, and starting in 2011, a few solo wolves had begun to wander back and forth between Oregon and California. Eventually a few packs had become established up north in Lassen and Siskiyou counties. They had not yet come as far south as Yosemite—or had they?

Hoping I wouldn't regret it, I turned the lock and opened the door just a crack. "Hello," I said. I must tell you it was my habit to talk to animals. I'd done so all my life, but after Adam introduced me to Mary Beth Adelson a year earlier, I'd become a student of shamanism and animal communication. Much of the practice involved learning how to "talk" to animals, plants, and other nature spirits.

Peering around the edge of the door and holding the knob firmly in case the wolves tried to rush me, I saw them look at each other and then turn their gaze back to me. My eyes widened as the larger, darker wolf moved its jaw and yawned, exhibiting a set of very large, sharp teeth. Pulling myself together, once again I said, "Hello."

"Hi," said the smaller wolf.

Oh, dear, I thought. Did that wolf actually speak? No, its mouth hadn't moved. But I'd heard it plain as day in my head, and it was looking right at me. Had I once and for all truly lost my mind? Had I spent too much time out in the woods all alone? Nothing in my life or my studies prepared me for this. My past communications with animals had been subtle, and I was always unsure of my interpretations. This, on the other hand, was so clear. I was getting words, even though the communication was telepathic. I took three deep breaths to keep from passing out, and with great effort I asked, "Is there something I can do for you?"

"Yes, there is, as a matter of fact. For starters, can you please let us in? It's freezing out here. We may have warm coats, but we still get cold. We were okay until that wind kicked up. Oh, I'm Tish, and this is my brother, Issa." Tish stood up and shook the snow from her coat. She licked her lips and stared at me expectantly.

With great reluctance, I opened the door. Tish marched right in and looked around the cabin. Issa stayed where he was, sitting on the porch.

"It's okay. You can come in, too, I guess," I said to him.

"Sorry about my sister. She can be kind of pushy." Issa stood, shook off his snow coat, and walked past me. *"Thanks for not chasing us off. Sometimes people aren't very nice to wolves."*

"So do you have any food?" Tish had already completed a quick tour of the cabin's main living area, small bedroom, kitchenette, and bathroom, and was sniffing at the refrigerator. *"I could go for a big chunk of deer, or a bird, if that's the best you can do. And Issa has developed a fondness for pizza. Do you have any pizza?"*

My refrigerator was nearly empty, as the snow had kept me from making a run into the village, but I did, in fact, have half of a leftover pizza. I pulled it out, cut it in two equal pieces, and presented each wolf with a portion on a white dinner plate.

"Is this, um...." Tish wrinkled her nose as she sniffed at the pizza. *"Is this vegetarian pizza?"*

"Spinach and feta, actually," I answered, feeling a little silly.

"Hmph," Tish grunted as she leaned over and ate the entire piece in one bite, scattering bits of spinach across the kitchen floor. Issa, on the other hand, exhibited perfect manners as he ate his pizza slowly with no complaint.

"Got anything else?" asked Tish, as she let out a small belch.

"Tish, that's enough. We need to do what we came here to do," Issa said.

The hair on the back of my neck stood on end. Was the pizza just an appetizer?

"Okay," said Tish, licking her lips and staring at me.

I took a few steps toward the bedroom, without turning my back on the wolves.

"So, then, let's get started," Tish walked across the small room and lay down on the rug in front of the fireplace. "The sooner we get this over with, the sooner we can head back home and find ourselves some real food."

I took a deep breath when I realized they weren't planning to have me for dinner.

"Okay, here's the story," said Tish. "Sage, you just need to listen and type whatever we tell you. When we were seven-week-old puppies, our mom left us to meet with the rest of our pack, but she never came back. That was four and a half years ago." Tish's voice softened and trailed off. She stared at the fire in the rough cut stone fireplace, the flame's flicker reflected in her eyes.

"That's terrible. I'm sorry," I said, but I was unable to process anything other than the fact that not only could these wolves communicate their thoughts clearly and directly, this one also knew my name.

"How do you know my name?" I asked. "And why are you telling me this?"

"You're Sage McAllister, right? You're a writer, right?" The old Tish was back, her momentary sadness left behind.

"Yes, that's my name," I replied. "And, yes, I do write."

Tish stood up again and started pacing around the cabin. "Sage," she said, "we came to you because we need you to help us tell our story. We're hoping you'll write it for us. All you have to do is the typing and the publishing things. We'll tell you what to write." Tish stopped directly in front of me, and began lifting her front feet up and down off the ground as if she were running in place. "Please? Will you do it? Please?"

"Hold on, Tish," said Issa. "Sage might need to think about this. I don't think it's all that easy to write and publish a book."

"Oh, come on. How hard can it be? Will you, Sage?" Tish's furry head bobbed up and down in time with her prancing feet.

"Well," I answered slowly. "I think it's something I can do, but it's kind of late. How about if we get a good night's sleep first and talk about it in the morning?"

"But—"

"That's perfect, Sage." Issa cast a steady, be-quiet-now look at Tish as he cut her off. *"We're very grateful that you're willing to consider doing this. And I could use some rest, too. Tish, would you rather sleep out or in? Oh sorry, Sage, I guess I should ask first if you're okay with us sleeping here by the fire?"*

"That would be fine. Do you need anything before I go to bed?" My mind went first to towels and toothbrushes, and then jumped to large dog beds and bowls full of kibble. I shook my head to dispel the images.

"Some water would be good," said Tish. *"If you don't mind."*

"Oh, of course." I retrieved a large glass Pyrex bowl from the cupboard, filled it with tap water, and set it down on the kitchen floor.

"And Sage," said Issa, *"would you mind unlocking the wolf door? We may be moving in and out during the night."*

I nodded and went to do his bidding.

"I'll just be off to my room now," I said. "See you two in the morning."

I retreated to my small bedroom and closed the door behind me. I turned the small lock on the doorknob—just in case. After all, it's not every day one has two full grown wolves come to stay.

Chapter Two
2010

The boy was running late. The sun had just disappeared behind the jagged line of firs that topped the western ridge, and the temperature had dropped ten degrees. Blue wanted to be down the hill and home before it got really dark. Aunt Lois would worry, and the moon was waning. It would provide no light to guide him.

Chastising himself for tracking the big bull elk too far, Blue pulled his parka tightly around his body and pressed on, punching holes in the heavy, wet snow with every step. It was the second day of April, and daytime temperatures had risen high enough to initiate snowmelt.

Blue walked around the butt of a large fallen tree and stopped. At the far edge of a small swale, about forty feet away, a flicker of silver had caught his eye. He pushed a lock of straight blond hair out of his eyes and then stood very still. Barely breathing, Blue felt as if several minutes passed, but knew it was probably only a few seconds. He hardly dared to hope. His Uncle Marshal frequently told stories of his own encounters with an animal Blue had longed to see his whole life. Perhaps this was his chance.

Blue's left eye began to itch terribly. He wiped the eye with the back of his sleeve, trying not to move too much. As soon as his eyes refocused on a stand of stunted lodgepole pines at the edge of the swale, he saw it.

Even in the fading light, the animal seemed to glow—a pure white wolf, standing in snow, framed by dark trees. Blue held his breath again, but he knew the wolf had seen him. The animal turned to face the boy, and moved its head ever so slightly from side to side, as if working to focus on this stranger. Then the movement stopped and its eyes locked on Blue. Even from a distance, he could see the wolf's eyes were a brilliant green with just a hint of gold, orbs the color of Aunt Lois' peridot earrings. Blue blinked twice, and the white wolf was gone.

Once she was out of the boy's sight, the wolf trotted through the small patch of pines and emerged at the top of a rocky slope. Sniffing the air for signs of unwanted company, she dropped partway down the slope, picked up a barely discernible trail, and then stopped near a hole in the slope. She and her sister, and the three male wolves in their group, had cleaned out the den two weeks earlier, pushing piles of snow away from the entrance and clearing rocks, sticks, and soil from the interior passageway. The site was well concealed by rocks and brush and provided good views to the south. The two female wolves had been born in the same den three years earlier.

Tipping her head back, the wolf sniffed the air once more and then lay down next to a nearby log. She put her head on her paws and listened to the tiny squeaks, grunts, and squeals coming from inside the den. The six puppies were brand new, and their Auntie Aspen could not have been happier.

Blue arrived back at the cabin just as the light outside disappeared. He stepped through the front door into a rush of warm air. Uncle Marshal and Blue's little sister, Sunny, were seated at a small antique walnut table. Aunt Lois was leaning over the old Aga stove, stirring a pot of food that gave off gentle wisps of steam laden with one of Blue's favorite smells.

"Blue, you are lucky indeed," said Aunt Lois. "I was just about to send your uncle out to find you. Get in here and wash up for supper."

Once they were all seated at the table, and everyone had been served, Blue dug into his spaghetti and meatballs with gusto. Sunny pushed all her meatballs off to one side of her plate and focused on twisting noodles around her fork.

"So," said Marshal between bites. "Did you find your elk, Blue?"

"I did. He's really big this year." Blue considered telling his family about the wolf. He figured he could safely share his story with Aunt Lois and Sunny, but he wasn't sure if Uncle Marshal could be trusted. He decided to keep quiet.

"You're eleven now, Blue, almost twelve. I was twelve when I took my first elk, and so was your Uncle Grey. Maybe this will be the year you take your first elk. What do you think about that?" asked Marshal.

"Um, well," Blue stammered. "The season is a long way off. We'll just have to see." The last thing in the world Blue wanted to do was shoot an elk, or any animal, for that matter. He could barely stand it when his uncle brought home a deer that he'd shot. There was no way Blue was ever going to be a hunter, but he wasn't sure how to break this news to his uncle. So far, he'd managed to avoid the issue by being sick or absent when Marshal and Grey had gone off on their hunting forays. Blue was much more like his other uncle, Scott, who'd turned his back on the whole culture of hunting and trapping at an early age. Blue was afraid to tell Uncle Marshal how he felt, but knew the truth would come out eventually.

"Do we get to watch a movie tonight?" Blue asked, dodging the hunting issue. It was Saturday, and if they didn't go into town for dinner, they'd often watch a rented DVD.

"I think your aunt picked up two movies this week, so you'll have to choose," said Marshal.

"The new Harry Potter! Did you get it?" Blue felt as if he'd been waiting forever for the most recent installment of his all-time favorite series.

"I did," said Lois. "But I think the other movie might be a better choice for Sunny. It's *The Incredibles*."

"Harry Potter, Harry Potter, Harry Potter, I love Harry Potter," chanted Sunny. "Harry, Harry, we want Harry!" She'd risen from her chair and was circling around the table in a marching dance, her red curls bouncing around her narrow shoulders as she clapped her hands high in the air. Everything Blue liked automatically became Sunny's favorite, too.

"Well, then, *Harry Potter and the Prisoner of Azkaban* it is," said Lois. "But I need help with the dishes first."

Blue woke early the next morning, thought about his dreams of Sirius Black and werewolves, and then decided to sneak out before the rest of the family was up and moving. He crawled out of bed, slipped into fleece-lined jeans and a flannel shirt, and crept down the stairs from the loft where he and Sunny slept. Downstairs, he grabbed his small pair of Nikon binoculars—a treasured gift from his aunt and uncle the previous Christmas—and donned a down jacket and Sorel boots. He stepped out and closed the door carefully behind him. The thermometer's arrow pointed to 22 degrees.

A couple of inches of snow had fallen overnight, and the sun had not yet cleared the eastern horizon. Blue retraced his steps from the day before, back to the swale where he'd seen the white wolf. When he arrived, the sun was just cresting the ridge, and a dazzling scene unfolded as the first rays struck the fresh ice crystals. A swarm of tiny lights glimmered atop the blanket of new snow, sparkling and twinkling like the golden specks of glitter Sunny liked to put on her cheeks. It looked like the swale was lit by hundreds of miniature ice candles, their tiny wicks ignited by the sun's fire. Despite the beauty of the welcome, though, he was disappointed when the white wolf failed to appear.

On the trek back to the cabin, Blue pondered once again the movie from the previous night. He was having trouble associating the wolf he'd seen the day before, and the way his heart had swelled with happiness at the sight of the animal, with the frightening images of the werewolf portrayed in the movie.

Over the next few weeks Blue returned to the swale numerous times to try to see the wolf, but had no luck until almost a month later, when the land was beginning to swell with the energy of spring. It was Saturday, the last day of April. The snow had dwindled to scattered patches, the creeks were spilling over their banks, and large white trillium blossoms were at their peak. Aunt Lois had sent Blue off in search of watercress for their dinner salad. He thought it was too early in the season for watercress, but told Aunt Lois he'd give it a try. He decided to look for the plants close to the clearing where he'd first seen the wolf. Luck was with him. As he squatted down to pick plants from the edge of a slow-flowing section of Willow Creek, a sudden clatter of falling rocks caused him to turn around.

The white wolf stood on a small ridge about thirty yards away, silhouetted against a cobalt blue sky. Blue raised his binoculars and studied the wolf. Its coat was almost completely snow white, with just a slight whisper of gray around the muzzle and the tips of its ears. The wolf stared at Blue for a moment, and then turned its head to look back in the direction from which it had come. To Blue's surprise, a second wolf—this one dark gray—walked up to stand next to the first. A frisson of concern swept through Blue's body. He didn't think the wolves would hurt him, but he still felt vulnerable. He stood very slowly, and the wolves quickly spun away and ran off. With a sigh of mixed relief and disappointment, Blue turned back to his task.

"Happy Birthday, Blue!" Sunny was the first to greet him as he rolled over and opened his eyes the next morning. She was sitting on her bed, quietly looking at pictures in her favorite book, a well-worn copy of *Mr. Grabbit the Rabbit.*

"Blue," she said. "How old are you now?" Sunny couldn't ever remember his age, even though he'd told her at least ten times in the last two days.

"Twelve, Sunny." Blue rolled out of bed and slid his feet into slippers.

Sunny was almost eight years old, but most of the time she acted much younger. When people were first introduced to her, Aunt Lois usually told them in a low voice that her niece was "a little bit special." Sunny had been sitting on her mother's lap, with no seat belt, when the brakes on the old pickup failed.

Their mom, so the story went, curled her body around Sunny before they hurtled through the windshield. Their parents were both dead when the paramedics arrived, but a man named Sam found Sunny still alive, still held firmly in her mother's embrace. Frightened, but unhurt, the two-year-old toddler had never cried over her trauma and loss.

Blue worked hard to be patient that morning. His chosen birthday breakfast of waffles, fresh strawberries, and mountains of homemade whipped cream seemed to go on forever, and he was hard pressed to muster up enough enthusiasm while he opened his gifts. His aunt and uncle gave him a new pair of black dress shoes and a book on elk hunting, and Sunny presented him with a notepad covered with sunflowers that she proudly told him she'd painted herself. Blue was grateful for his family's generosity, but while he was pulling wrapping paper from his gifts, all he really wanted was to get back to the creek to look for the wolves. He bolted out the door as soon as he felt he could without being rude or raising suspicion.

Blue arrived at the creek and sat down on a large, flat boulder. The waiting seemed to go on forever. Every so often he'd get up to stretch and scan the terrain with his binoculars.

After about two hours, his patience was rewarded. A pair of erect ears crested the ridge above the creek, and the ears were followed by the rest of the gray wolf's body. As the animal turned to walk along the ridge line, Blue was stunned to see a very small wolf behind the first, and then another, and another. A total of six roly-poly balls of fluff—one white, one black, and four gray— paraded in a poorly-formed line behind their leader. The adult led the pups slowly, and looked back to check on them frequently. The big white wolf trailed behind the family, swatting the hindmost puppy with a soft paw every so often to keep it moving forward.

Beside himself with excitement, Blue watched the wolves walk about thirty yards along the ridge and then drop out of sight as they descended the far slope. He rose and headed for the spot where the wolves had disappeared. After climbing the gentle hill toward the ridge top, he crawled the last few feet up to the crest on hands and knees. When he peeked over the top, he saw the wolves had doubled back in the direction from which they had come.

Blue decided to be sneaky, and he followed the ridge away from the wolves, planning to eventually drop down the hill and circle back below the family. When he glanced over his shoulder, though, he saw the two adults were watching him. After a few more minutes of walking, Blue descended and looped back under the cover of a dense pocket of pines. As he drew closer to the wolves, he slowed and searched for a good vantage point. He found a gap in the trees that provided an unobstructed view, dropped to his knees, and watched.

The eight wolves were milling around on a narrow, rocky bench about halfway between the ridge top and a small, grassy meadow below. One of the pups attempted to nurse the gray adult, who sat watching the family, so Blue figured that must be the mama. Two of the puppies bit at her legs and chased her tail, trying to incite her to play. The white wolf, who Blue also thought was a female, was playing a mellow game of chase with two puppies, gently rolling them over when she caught them and then letting them catch her without much effort. The last sibling, a gray, sat at a slight remove from the others and chewed on a stick.

Blue watched the family for about fifteen minutes, and then, at some signal invisible to the boy, all the puppies looked up at the mama wolf. She let out a low growl and moved about ten feet farther along the slope. The puppies followed. At that moment Blue spotted the hole. He'd found their den!

The gray wolf stopped at the mouth of the den and carefully sniffed all around the entrance. Then she turned around and curled her lip at the trail of puppies behind her. The puppies waited while the gray went partway into the den. A few seconds later, she returned and seemed to tell the pups it was safe to enter. One by one, the puppies filed in, followed by their mom. The white wolf hesitated just outside the den and looked back over her shoulder at Blue. At that moment, a name flashed through his mind: Aspen. He smiled as he turned away from the den to start his walk home.

For the next three weeks, Blue took every chance he had to steal away from the cabin to watch the wolves. The youngsters grew quickly, and spent most of their time running up and down the slope that comprised their front yard, wrestling with one another and with Aspen and their mom—Blue had taken to calling the mom Sister—and napping in the sun. Sometimes when Blue arrived at his vantage point at the base of the slope opposite the den, the wolves were away. Blue liked to imagine they were off learning to hunt.

Late one afternoon, as he was preparing to go home after spending about two hours watching the wolf family, Blue was startled to see three new wolves trotting up to the den site. Two were large and solidly built, while the third, a black wolf, was a little smaller and leggier. Aspen and Sister had been lying down, watching the pups play, but they both rose to their feet at the sight of the new arrivals.

Blue was afraid for the puppies, but Aspen and Sister both held their tails high in the air, and they were wagging. When the five wolves were face to face, they all sniffed one another's front and back ends with no signs of aggression. Blue heaved a great sigh of relief. He watched as all the puppies ran over to the new arrivals and started to lick and gently nip at the big wolves' muzzles. Much to Blue's surprise, all three of the new wolves regurgitated a lot of nasty-looking stuff, which the puppies then devoured. The youngsters were getting their first taste of solid food.

Precisely three weeks after he discovered the den, Blue showed up one morning to see the puppies emerging from the small oval entrance into bright sunlight. He counted five, and then Sister emerged, carrying the sixth puppy in her mouth. She struggled with the large pup, half carrying and half dragging the limp body. Aspen followed Sister out of the den, and the two wolves pulled the puppy across the slope and out of sight.

With a sinking heart, Blue understood that the puppy, the only white one in the litter, and Blue's personal favorite, was dead. The boy sighed, but then quickly let go of his sadness. He knew this was the way of the world, the way of the wild, and of all living things. He thought of his twin brother Sean, and how, when the boys were only four years old, Sean just didn't wake up one morning. He hoped that Sean and the white puppy could play together on the other side.

Chapter Three
2018

After I closed and locked the bedroom door, I turned around, leaned back against the doorframe, and tried to slow my breathing. Unable to even think about sleep, I walked across the room and sat down at my desk. I lifted the lid on my laptop and pushed the power button.

I'd always admired wolves, but I really didn't know much about them. We never saw them at the ranch in Idaho where I'd grown up; almost all of them had been killed off decades earlier. I knew they'd been reintroduced to Idaho and Yellowstone in 1995, but in 1996 I'd moved to California. I'd heard of the ongoing wolf controversy in Idaho and Montana, but hadn't kept up on the news.

A quick Internet search led me to numerous gorgeous photos as well as articles about wolf hunting in Michigan and a recent clash between livestock owners and wolf advocates in Montana. A search for "wolf hunting" brought up a long row of images: a series of men in a variety of settings, many of them holding up the wolf they just shot, or standing next to long, furry bodies hanging from jowls or feet. Some of the hunters squatted next to a dead wolf, but held the animal's head up so it could look at the camera.

I studied a few of the photos, trying to understand why these men looked so proud of themselves. They all posed with shoulders squared and wore camo, or jeans, plaid shirts, and ball caps. Only one photo showed a woman with a dead wolf. She was dressed in a tight-fitting camo shirt, wore bright pink lipstick, and sported perfectly combed, shiny blond hair.

Are they proud of themselves because they've dominated these beautiful, wild animals? Do they think this makes them somehow superior to the wolves or to other men? I couldn't understand how killing a wolf with a high-powered rifle or a compound bow could be considered proof of manhood, or, in some cases, apparently, womanhood. If an individual engaged in hand-to-hand combat with the wolves and won the fight, that victory might say something about the person's relative physical prowess. But this annihilation of wolves using highly sophisticated weapons dropped my level of respect for these people to rock bottom.

I'd long been opposed to hunting in general, but had tempered my views somewhat if the hunter needed and ate the meat from the kill and showed a deep level of respect for the animal. Although I still didn't like hunting and would never do it myself, I'd come to almost accept some deer hunting. But trophy hunting, which is what wolf hunting was all about, was completely unacceptable. And then there was trapping animals for their pelts—a cruel and heartless practice I would never accept.

A Google search for "Idaho wolves" revealed the degree to which conflicts between wolves and humans had escalated in my absence. Idaho's governor declared that wolves constituted "a disaster emergency," and the town of Salmon was sponsoring a coyote- and wolf-killing derby at the end of this month.

With a deep sigh, I exited the Internet, and then stared at the computer's screensaver as it rolled through the random show of photos stored on the hard drive. Yosemite's Half Dome, a brown bear, horses grazing, and Adam's 30th birthday party passed by as I tried to pull myself together. Having two wolves in my cabin was unsettling, to say the least. But what had me most worried was: How did they know my name, and how had they found me?

I turned the computer off, stood, and stretched my back. I was surprised to find I was quite tired, even though it was only 9:15 p.m. I tip-toed across the bedroom floor, carefully opened the door, and peeked out, just to reassure myself I hadn't dreamt the whole thing.

Issa and Tish were curled up together in a tight ball in front of the fireplace. I thought they were sound asleep, but then, without any other movement, Issa opened his eyes and stared at me until I pulled the door closed once again. With a shiver, I crossed the rough-hewn wood floor to my single bed and crawled in under the fluffy down comforter.

It seemed as if my head had barely hit the pillow when I was startled awake by a very loud howl. The sound paralyzed me. I was quite sure one of the wolves was right there in the room with me. Had Issa and Tish changed their minds? Had they decided to eat me instead of rallying me to their cause, thereby reducing the human population by one? After what I'd seen on the Internet the night before, I could hardly blame them if they had.

Mustering my courage, I rolled over and switched on the bedside lamp. Finding myself alone in the room, I got out of bed, pulled the light lace curtain back, and opened the window to an inrush of icy air.

The storm had moved on. In the wake of the clouds a brilliant full moon had emerged to illuminate the landscape. Issa sat on his haunches in the small meadow south of the cabin. With his head thrown back and his muzzle in the air, he howled a second time, and then a third. With each howl, a plume of fine white mist rolled from his mouth like pale smoke. His bold notes echoed through my head, harmonizing with a deeply buried, but very clear, ancestral memory.

Suddenly Tish emerged out of nowhere. In a series of great, long leaps, she bounded full speed across the snow toward Issa. Just before slamming into him, she leaped high in the air and landed on top of him, rolling him over in the snow. Issa swatted at her with his big paws and Tish swatted right back. As snow flew in all directions, the wolves rolled and tussled, yipping, barking, and snapping. The wrestling match went on for several minutes, until Issa conceded victory to Tish and trotted back toward the cabin. The vision of these two beings, of black and gray and gold on white in moonlight, of linked lives rejoicing in wildness and unsurpassed beauty, was one I would never forget.

I met the two tired, grinning wolves at the door and welcomed them in for an early breakfast of eggs—note they prefer their eggs raw—and toast with loads of butter.

After the breakfast dishes were cleared, I sat down with the laptop at the dining table. Issa and Tish parked themselves on each side of me, ready to dictate. "Before we get started on this,"

I said, turning to look at them, "I'd like to know how you know who I am, and how you found me."

"*Oh, Sage,*" said Tish, as if I were asking a silly question. "*You're well known in animal circles. We all know you've been working on our behalf your whole life.*"

My head was suddenly filled with images, but I couldn't say where they came from. It was as if someone were telepathically relaying scenes from my life. I saw myself on a southern California beach burying under-sized clams that had been left on top of the sand by clam-diggers, feeding baby birds with an eye-dropper, and giving a bottle of formula to an abandoned baby deer. I saw our family cats and dogs, all of which we had rescued from some shelter or another, lined up in front of overflowing food bowls. And I saw myself seated at a desk in front of a computer, calculating how many small native grasses should be planted in a lodgepole pine forest to restore damaged habitat.

"*Yes, Sage,*" Issa broke in, "*we know all about you, what you've done on behalf of animals, and how deeply you care. Most humans have no idea how much we know, which is just as well. But, as you're probably aware, a time of reckoning is coming. That's why it's so important for us to share our story with the world now. We are deeply thankful that you're willing to help.*"

A shiver ran down my spine as Issa's words sunk in. I thought about how long I'd been waiting for something like this to happen. Somehow I'd known, almost since the day I was born, that at some point the more-than-human beings with whom we share the Earth—the animals, plants, rocks, rivers, and all of nature—would step up and hold humans accountable for their actions. This validation from Issa caused mixed feelings in my heart. I was overjoyed that the time had come at last, and relieved that the waiting was finally over, but I was afraid of the conflicts that could come from such an uprising. I decided I needed to stay with joy and relief, and not let myself fall into fear.

"Thank you," I said quietly. "Thank you for choosing me."

"*Um,*" said Tish. "*Can we get past all this touchy feely stuff and get to the story, please?*" She brought her right hind leg up to scratch vigorously at her chin.

"Yes, in a minute," I said. "You still haven't answered my question. How exactly did you find me?"

"*It was easy,*" said Tish. "*We did it through the Network.*"

"The network?"

"*It's a communication system, Sage. I'm surprised you don't know about it,*" Tish said. "*We went through the Raven Link, because ravens are always around everywhere we go. And the ravens agreed to use the Golden Eagle Link to help us find you. This wasn't exactly easy, because, well, you know, ravens and golden eagles are not the best of friends. But they knew this was for a good cause, so they helped us.*"

I leaned forward, put my elbows on the table, and dropped my head into my hands. This was crazy. I guess it shouldn't have been such a big surprise; after all, I was talking to wolves. Things couldn't get much crazier than that. The weird thing was that in all the places I had lived—California, Oregon, Wyoming, and Idaho—golden eagles had been abundant. I saw them all the time, hunting rabbits or ground squirrels, soaring high on thermal air currents, or just sitting somewhere on a fence post or tree limb. They'd perch on the rails of the arena where I worked my horses in Idaho, and I often wondered if they were watching me, making sure I did things right. And then, during my earliest shamanic experiences, the first spirit helper that had shown up was a golden eagle.

"So," I said, lifting my head. "Am I to understand that the eagles and the ravens share information? And that the ravens told you where to find me?"

"Yup," said Tish. "Just like that. It's pretty simple, really. The Network includes all the animals, and—"

"That's enough for now, Tish," Issa interrupted her. "Sage, it gets a little complicated at the higher levels. For now, it's enough for you to know we have lines of communication most people don't know about."

"You know, maybe I'm not the best person to write your story." I was feeling way out of my element. "I mean, don't you want someone who has had a lot of training in animal communications, or a full-on shaman, somebody more qualified than me?" I wasn't sure if I wanted them to say yes or no, but I had serious doubts about whether or not I was up to this task.

"Nope," said Tish. "You're the one. You've been tapped. It wasn't our decision. You were selected by the Council."

"The council? The council of what?" I asked, imagining a round table with high-backed chairs filled with wolves, bears, mountain lions, bighorn sheep, a few beavers, and maybe a humpback whale or a dolphin.

"No, this was the Council of Wolf Elders. There were no other species present," said Tish.

"Wait," I said, feeling a little dizzy. "Can...can you read my mind, too?"

"Oh, Tish," said Issa with a deep sigh. "Now you've done it."

"Oops," said Tish. "Sorry."

"I think I need some air." I stood and walked past Tish, heading for the front door.

"Wait, Sage," said Tish, as she rose to follow me.

"Let her go," said Issa. "She'll be fine."

I pulled a down jacket off the coat rack on my way out and slipped into the boots that sat just inside the door. I walked out and down the three steps. Clouds had coalesced once again and flurries of large snowflakes were falling, pushed in all directions by slight, shifting winds. About five inches had fallen since I'd shoveled the gravel walkway the day before. The wolf tracks made earlier that morning had disappeared.

I'd taken only three steps down the walkway when my feet slipped out from under me and I landed flat on my bottom on a rock hard layer of snow-covered ice. Terribly confused by all that had occurred in the last twelve hours, and with pain surging up my spine, I burst into tears.

The next thing I knew, Issa and Tish were by my side. Tish put her nose up next to my face and gently licked my wet cheeks.

"It's okay, Sage," she said. *"We're your friends. We're so grateful for this chance to meet you. And if you don't want to tell our story, that's okay. We will find someone else."*

"No," I said, wiping the remaining tears from my eyes. "I do want to write your story. I want to help you. It's just that this is all so...well, surprising. No, that's a huge understatement. This is overwhelming."

I stood and brushed the snow off my jeans and we all went back inside the cabin.

"I need a cup of tea." I announced as I removed my jacket. "I don't suppose you two like tea?"

"What's tea?" asked Tish.

"A wonderful hot drink that will warm your insides," I said. "And I usually add cinnamon and honey to it."

"Okay, if it's not too hot, then we probably love tea," said Tish.

I prepared one mug and two bowls of tea, and we sipped and lapped.

"Well," I said, after Tish had turned her bowl over with a paw to see if there was any remaining honey on the underside, "I guess we should get started."

"Okay," said Tish. She returned to her place by the fire and picked up where she'd left off the night before. Issa inspected his paws while I got ready to type.

"So, like I said," Tish began, *"our mom left us alone. She didn't return by the next morning. I suggested to the others that we look for something to eat. Issa and Seeker, our biggest brother, agreed, but the other pups didn't want to leave the den. They were too scared and hungry.*

"Finally, we decided three of us would go hunting, and the others would try to find someone from our pack. We knew we were part of a larger group, Mom told us they were our extended family. We'd only met one of our pack mates, an uncle who came to our den a few weeks earlier to guard the entrance while Mom went to look for our dad, who'd gone missing. Mom told us later that Dad had been shot and killed." Tish broke off and stared at her feet.

"Anyway," she resumed, *"we agreed to meet back at the den before dark."* She paused, and when I looked over at her, I could tell by her soft-eyed stare that she was deep in reminiscing.

"Tish," I said, stifling a yawn. "I'm sorry, but I think we need to take a time out. I know we've just started, but I'm at a loss as to how to go about this. We need to put our heads together and figure out how to make your story really come alive."

Tish and Issa exchanged glances, and I'm pretty sure I saw them nod to each other ever so slightly.

"Good idea, Sage," said Issa, as he rose to his feet. *"Let's think about this for a while, and maybe not get started until tomorrow. Can we go out and explore somewhere? I could use a good run."*

"Yes, we can do that," I said. "But you two will have to wear collars and be on leashes. We can tell people you're Alaskan malamutes or something."

"Nope," said Tish. *"No collars, no leashes. Never. Not ever. No way."*

Chapter Four

2010

Blue was halfway out the cabin's front door when Aunt Lois called him back. "Please finish building up the fire before you run off, Blue. And clean up the ashes around the hearth." It was the last Saturday morning in May, and Lois was kneading dough for the upcoming week's bread, a ritual as old as Blue, maybe older.

"And don't be gone too long," Lois continued. "I need your help this afternoon. Lunch will be ready in about an hour, and then I want you to look after Sunny while I run into town for groceries."

Blue's face fell. He already had plans for his afternoon, and now this. It occurred to him that he could take his sister with him. Sunny would love the wolves, but she wasn't too good with secrets. In fact, Sunny wasn't like anyone else he'd ever met. She had a hard time making friends because she said whatever came into her head, whether or not it was something the other person wanted to hear. In lieu of human companions, she had a lot of imaginary animal friends with whom she carried on lengthy conversations, and she was a virtual magnet when it came to living, breathing animals. She didn't talk much to people, but Blue was pretty sure she could communicate with animals. She seemed to understand what they were thinking, and, from the way they looked at her and behaved in her presence, they seemed to understand her, too. Sunny's teachers and psychologists thought she'd probably hit her head in the car crash, and the shock of the accident, and losing both of her parents, was just too much for her to cope with. Blue just figured she'd gone someplace else in her mind when the accident happened, and parts of her had decided to not come back.

Blue had wanted to take Sunny to see the wolf puppies ever since he'd discovered them, but he was afraid she'd forget they were a secret and tell someone. He still hadn't shared his knowledge of the wolves with anyone. He knew that would put the animals at risk.

Lunch consisted of venison stew loaded with potatoes and carrots. Sunny carefully picked out every piece of venison, and, much to Aunt Lois' chagrin, fed them to Angus, the blue heeler that had wandered into their lives about six months earlier.

After lunch, Blue's desire to visit the wolves overrode his concern about Sunny's difficulty keeping secrets. "Aunt Lois," he announced. "Sunny and I are going to take a little walk up the hill while you're in town."

"That's fine. Just be back by dark, and keep her out of the creek. That wind is still carrying a chill." Lois carefully laid the pale ball of dough in a large bowl, covered it with a moist towel, and set it in the warm oven to rise.

"I get to go, too, Blue, really? Where are we going?" Sunny could barely contain her excitement. A walk in the woods with Blue in the spring was her idea of heaven.

"What will we see? Will we see deer or elk? Will we see a family of wolves?" Blue turned and stared hard at Sunny. Was it possible she already knew about the wolves? No, it couldn't be. On the other hand, he wouldn't be surprised if she were reading his mind.

"I don't know what we'll see, Sunny. Let's get you into your boots and coat and we'll go find out." Blue pulled Sunny's pink parka off the coat rack and held it out to her.

Sunny was a slow hiker, but Blue had learned a long time ago to be patient. He recalled a day two years earlier when they'd gone to the county fair. Walking the midway, they were surrounded by carnies cat-calling at them to toss the rings or throw a dart, to try to win a giant stuffed SpongeBob SquarePants or a live goldfish, or to guess the fat lady's weight.

The crowd was thick. The sun beat down without mercy. Sunny was delighted to be at the fair. She'd walked slowly, holding tight to Blue's hand as she looked at everything and everyone. Blue had been in a hurry. He'd agreed to meet his buddies, Cal and Denny, at noon at Uncle Billy's Corn Dog stand next to the Ferris wheel. He'd tried to pull Sunny along, but she dragged her feet. "No, Blue. I have to see everything. I just love it all so much."

"Okay," said Blue. "But can't you hurry a little? We can come back after we eat lunch."

The next thing he knew, Sunny's small hand had slipped from his grasp. His view was blocked as a large group of women in red sequined dresses and two people of unknown gender wearing clown suits pushed past him, accompanied by a dense cloud of beer fumes. By the time the crowd cleared, Sunny was nowhere to be seen.

Blue's heart skipped a beat just recalling the incident. He'd found Sunny about ten minutes later—it had seemed like ten hours—sitting just outside a small corral filled with goats of all shapes and sizes, several hundred yards from the midway, near the big livestock barns. It had been the longest ten minutes of Blue's life. He'd realized, when he spotted her sitting in the dirt, petting the nose of a white baby goat, that Sunny would always come first in his life.

As he watched her now, stopping to sit next to a large patch of bright yellow sunflowers, it dawned on him that his ability to take care of Sunny made him feel good about himself.

It took almost two hours to make the trek from the cabin to the den site, nearly four times as long as it took when Blue traveled alone. Sunny insisted on stopping and greeting every new species of flower they encountered, including white trilliums just past their peak, fresh new Indian paintbrush, scattered lupine beginning to show purple and white, and lots of arrowleaf balsamroot with flowers still firmly encased in large buds. Sunny also spoke to each of the dozens of birds they sighted, and complimented them on their loveliness.

"Blue, wait!" They'd almost made it to the den area when Sunny's voice rang out.

Blue turned back to see what Sunny was up to. Following her gaze, he saw a squirrel perched on a rock just above the trail, holding a Douglas-fir cone half shredded by the animal's efforts to find seeds. He watched as girl and squirrel silently conversed, and then was shocked to see the squirrel jump off the rock and scurry over to Sunny. It stood up on its hind feet and offered her the cone. Sunny accepted the gift, put her hands together in front of her chest as if she were praying, and bowed to the squirrel. Blue shook his head in wonder as the squirrel ran off into the forest. Sunny looked at Blue and grinned.

They continued down the trail for a few more minutes, and as they neared the den site, Blue stopped. "Sunny," he said. "I have a surprise for you, but you have to be really quiet."

"Oh, Blue, are we getting close?"

"Close to what?" Blue was afraid he already knew what her answer would be.

"The puppies' home, what else? Silly Blue, did you think it was a secret?" Sunny danced a little circle and then reached down to touch the ground for no apparent reason.

"How did you know?"

"Oh, that's easy. You've been carrying pictures of the wolf family in your head for weeks. Let's go see them now. I was afraid you'd never get around to showing me." She continued down the trail toward the creek.

Sunny reached the vantage point below the den ahead of Blue and was the first to see the wolves. The five adults were lounging, and the puppies were busy wrestling with something on the ground. Blue pulled his binoculars from his pocket and saw the something was a large haunch, most likely from a big deer or an elk. The puppies were ferocious in their eating. Every so often, one would emit a high-pitched growl or squeal when a competing sibling tried to take the best looking bite.

"Do you know their names?" asked Sunny after they'd watched the feeding frenzy for a few minutes.

"Just the two adults on the far left. The gray one is the puppies' mom, and her name is Sister. The white one is Aspen." Blue looked at Sunny, worried she might tell him he was wrong.

"And what about the puppies?" she asked.

"I don't know."

"Hmm," said Sunny. She peered up at the clear, deep blue sky. "Let's see. What does Uncle Marshal call those lovely, wispy clouds that we see sometimes? Serious clouds?"

"Cirrus clouds," said Blue.

"That's it!" said Sunny. "The smallest gray one—her name is Cirrus.

"And, Blue, what kind of grass is this?" Sunny held up a thin-stemmed blade.

"Grama. Why?"

"Because that's the larger gray wolf's name, the boy with the black on his legs. I think he's the biggest of them all."

She sat quietly and seemed to drift away for a few minutes. Blue watched the only black pup, which had prominent white tips on its ears, leap on top of Cirrus.

"That black one is Cinder," said Sunny. "And the other two gray sisters are Goldenrod and Tierra. Look closely and you'll see Goldie has a little more red and brown in her coat, while Tierra looks more like a beautiful puff of pale gray smoke. See how Tierra has one white ear, her left ear? And, the little white one who died, her name was Cloud. Don't you think they have lovely names, Blue?

"And the brothers," she continued before Blue had a chance to answer. "The two big grown-up wolves are brothers, Arctos and Asher. Arctos is the father of these puppies. The younger male, the black one, is Lonestar. He got his name because of that white patch on his right side. See how it looks like a star with six points? He's only a year old. Arctos and Sister are his parents, too. So he's a big brother to the puppies."

"Who's telling you the wolves' names, Sunny?" asked Blue as he chewed on the end of a piece of grass.

"Auntie Aspen. Why?"

"Oh, just curious," Blue said. Inside, he was ecstatic to know he'd gotten Aspen and Sister right. Sunny was so much better at this than he was.

"Can't you hear her, Blue? Her voice is as clear as the wind when it talks to the pine trees. How did you know the names of Sister and Aspen?"

"I don't know. I just did, I guess," said Blue.

"Well, there you go."

That night, Sunny lay in bed for hours thinking about the wolves. Unable to sleep, she crept out of bed to find a flashlight and a notebook. She returned to bed, crawled all the way under her covers, and wrote a short poem.

<u>Aspen Wolf</u>
I love you Aspen Wolf
And those baby puppies, too
Rolling around in the sun
And smelling the pink flowers
Never hurting anyone
You are so beautiful
I love you Aspen Wolf

Sunny read her poem over and over to herself until she fell asleep.

The next morning, Blue woke first and noticed the notebook on the floor next to Sunny's bed. He smiled. His sister was known to stay up all night doodling and drawing pictures, usually of dinosaurs, flowers, and mountains.

Sunny's eyes popped open when she heard Blue moving around the loft. "Blue," she said quietly, "we have to go back to the den today. We have to."

Blue thought about all the homework that was waiting for his attention. "I don't know, Sunny. Maybe this afternoon, but only if I can get enough work done first."

"No, Blue," Sunny insisted. "We have to go soon. We have to go this morning."

Blue knew there was no reasoning with Sunny when she was this adamant about something.

"Why?" he asked.

"I can't tell you," said Sunny, casting her eyes downward.

"What's going on, Sunny?"

"I can't tell you. We just have to go."

After breakfast, Marshal rose from his chair and said, "Well, I'm off to town. The clothes dryer has quit heating, so I'm on a mission to find a new heating element. Anybody want to come with me? There could be ice cream afterwards."

"No, thanks," said Blue. "I've got homework."

"Me, too," said Sunny.

"Well, that's mighty unusual," said their uncle. "Passing up ice cream to do homework? I think this must be a first. All right then. See you all in a while." He donned his red plaid cap and stepped out into the morning.

As soon as the drone of the departing truck faded into silence, Lois stood up from the table and said, "Okay, you two, just who is Aspen Wolf?"

Her question was met with silence. Blue looked at Sunny, and Sunny cast her eyes in all directions, except toward Aunt Lois.

"Is this why you've been disappearing so often lately, Blue? And, Sunny, is this why you were so happy when you two got back yesterday?"

"Yes, Aunt Lois," said Sunny. "Yes, that's why. Aspen is the auntie."

"And I take it you've found a den?" Lois was rubbing her face as she spoke, wondering whether or not she really wanted to know.

"Aunt Lois, how did you find out? How do you know her name? You can't tell anyone about this, please!" Blue was frantic. He was sure Uncle Marshal would feel obligated to kill the wolves if he knew about them, as there were so many ranching operations in the area, and the section of forest where the wolves had chosen to den was leased for cattle grazing.

"Well, your sister wrote a sweet little poem called Aspen Wolf, which I happened to see when I went up to get your dirty clothes."

"She's beautiful, Aunt Lois," Sunny said. "She's whiter than snow, with a few soft ashy streaks. You'd love her, too."

"Oh, Sunny," sighed Lois. "I'm sure she is beautiful, and yes, I probably would love her, too. But you know how your uncle feels about wolves. It's not that he has any real hatred for them, but he wants to be a responsible neighbor. And he has his job to consider."

"Then you can't tell him about them," said Sunny, as if it were that simple. "It will be our secret, yours and mine and Blue's."

"Okay, but if the wolves cause any trouble, any trouble at all, you're going to have to tell your uncle everything."

"We're going to see them this morning. Do you want to come, too?" asked Sunny.

"No, the less I know about them the better. And be sure you're back here in time to get all that homework done." Lois rose from her chair and swept a few crumbs off her blue sweatshirt. "Wash up these dishes before you leave, please."

Once they managed to escape from the cabin, Sunny marched down the trail at a much faster pace than she had the day before. She stopped only once, to say good morning to a bobcat that was heading down the trail toward them, but which then veered off and disappeared into the trees.

"Blue," she said when they were several hundred yards from the den site. "Something has happened. It feels bad."

"What?" asked Blue. "What do you mean?"

"I don't know exactly."

"Oh, Sunny, you're imagining things. Is this why we had to come out here this morning? You just couldn't wait to see the puppies again, could you? Nothing has happened."

But as soon as Blue rounded the next turn in the trail, he saw that Sunny was right. Something very bad had happened.

Chapter Five
2018

I opened the rear door of my silver pickup and Issa jumped easily onto the narrow backseat. Tish insisted on riding shotgun, and sat up straight and tall as she gazed out the window—a queen surveying her domain. Both wolves winced when I started the truck and the Pat Benatar CD woke up and the speakers blasted: *"Hit me with your best shot."* I reached to turn the volume down, but not before Pat belted out, "*Fire away!*"

I ejected the CD, and we all sat for a few moments without speaking.

"Um, Sage," Tish finally said. *"What was that all about?"*

"I'm sorry," I said. "It's a little hard to explain. The words in songs, the lyrics, can mean everything or nothing, and they're often symbolic. I honestly have no idea what that song is about. I just like the beat and the singer's voice."

"Why was it so loud?" asked Tish.

"I like it loud," I said. "I'm sorry if it hurt your ears."

I put the truck into four-wheel drive and we rolled along the narrow, snow-covered road. Deer Meadows, the small enclave that included our family cabin, was composed of about fifty dwellings of various styles spread out over many acres. The area had been subject to two large wildfires within the last twenty-five years, resulting in a patchwork quilt of burned and unburned habitat. The black skeletons of hundreds of trees stood like silent sentinels as we drove up the icy hill to the Big Oak Flat Road. At the junction, we turned right and headed down toward the Merced River and Yosemite Valley.

"So," I said, after we made the turn. "Let's talk about the book. Who do you want to read it? What age group? Have you thought about this?"

"Hmm," said Tish. *"I guess I'd have to say everyone. I want everyone to read it."*

"Okay, I agree. That would be great. But it can be difficult to write a book for everyone. It helps if you can define your audience," I said.

"Who do you think is most likely to take our message to heart?" Issa leaned forward and put his big furry feet up on the console between the front seats.

"Young people," I said, without hesitation. "And maybe older people who have seen and experienced a wide slice of life, who have opened themselves up to being compassionate. It seems to me that many people in between young and old can be pretty dogmatic in their beliefs. If you want to influence or change people's attitudes and feelings about wolves, people in that middle range will be the most difficult to convince."

"What's compassionate?" asked Tish.

"Whoa," I said. "That's a biggie." I thought about it for a few moments. "In my mind, it's having the ability to imagine oneself in the position of another person, to feel the pain or sadness of another's misfortune, and to want to alleviate their suffering. I'm not sure if that's a complete answer, Tish. I might have to ponder this a bit more."

Lost in feelings of inadequacy because I couldn't clearly define compassion, I failed to see the doe before she stepped out onto the road in front of us.

"Oh, crap, not again," I said, as I simultaneously hit the brake, flashed on an image of Marta and Greg's wedding picture, and threw my right arm out to the side to prevent Issa and Tish from crashing through the windshield.

I felt the rear end of the truck skid to the left. My defensive driving instructor's voice filled my head as I tried to turn into the skid to keep from spinning completely out of control. I kept the truck straight, but we kept moving, sliding on a diagonal across the opposite lane and smashing into the snowbank on the far side of the road. Luckily, we were on a fairly long, almost straight stretch, so the odds of getting hit by an oncoming car were low. The doe turned around and trotted nonchalantly back in the direction from which she had come.

I looked over at the wolves, hoping against hope no one was hurt. Tish was on the floor in front of the passenger seat. She'd flown off the seat when I hit the brakes. Issa had been jolted forward, and then was sandwiched against me when we collided with the bank. Both of them stared at me.

"Are you two okay?" I asked.

"Yes," said Issa. "Tish?"

"I'm fine," said Tish. "But Sage, does this kind of thing happen often when you ride in a car? When we started our trek to the Yellow Stone, our uncle told us cars could be dangerous and we should stay far away from them, but I had no idea." She shook her head and untangled herself from the pile of leashes and collars I'd tossed on the floor when we got into the truck. Issa carefully maneuvered himself back onto the rear seat.

Just as my heartbeat began to slow, a park service patrol vehicle pulled up behind us, lights flashing. It was too late to send the wolves off into the woods.

"Okay, you two," I said. "You're dogs, got it? Dogs. Malamute crosses. You belong to a friend who—"

I turned in response to the knock on my window and pushed the button to open it. "Hi, Mike," I said, with what I hoped was a sheepish look. "It was a deer. What can I say?"

"Hi, Sage," said the towering, solidly-built, dark-haired ranger. "Well, you're not the only one today. We've pulled three cars out of snowbanks already this morning. Hey, those are really big dogs. They look like wolves. Are they yours?"

"No, they belong to a friend who had to leave town for some family stuff. He asked me to take care of them. I think he said they were a Malamute cross of some sort. They're pretty good dogs." I was learning to be a good liar again, something I thought I'd outgrown after I left my parent's home to go to college. I looked over at Tish. She rolled her eyes and turned her head away to look out the window.

"Well," said Mike. "Why don't you get out while I pull your truck out of the snow bank and check to see how much damage you've done? The dogs can stay inside." He turned to walk back to his pickup.

As soon as Mike was out of hearing range, Tish looked over at me and said, *"Gotta pee, Sage. Gotta get out right now."*

"Oh, Tish. Okay, but come right back, please." I leaned over and let Issa and Tish out, hoping Mike wouldn't cite me for having dogs off leash in the park.

The damage to the truck was minimal, just a few small dents where the otherwise soft snow had hidden large rocks. I waved to Mike as he drove off to his next motor vehicle accident, which, according to the park radio, involved two large motor homes. We continued on our way toward Yosemite Valley.

"If we can return to where we left off, Sage, can you tell us what dogmatic means?" Tish wasted no time getting back to the book conversation.

"Hmm, let's see," I said, collecting my thoughts. "Someone who is dogmatic has an idea or a belief about something that they won't or can't change. They'll assert their opinion as if it were the absolute truth, even if it isn't, or can't be proven."

"So it has nothing to do with dogs?" asked Tish.

"Nope, sorry about that," I said.

Ten minutes later we arrived at the junction of the El Portal Road, swung east and drove into Yosemite Valley. I pulled off the road at Fern Spring.

"Okay, we're heading into the busy part of the park now. After this stop, I'm going to have to put you two on leashes. I'm sorry, but that's just the way it is. We can't afford to get in trouble." I reached over to the floor in front of Tish and grabbed two large blue nylon collars with leashes. I'd found them in the storage shed behind the cabin, and they brought back memories of my grandpa's two best friends: a pair of German shepherds named Molly and Moses, who always stuck to Grandpa like glue.

"Why do we have to do this leash thing?" asked Tish.

"Because all dogs have to be on a leash in the park," I said.

"Why?"

"Lots of reasons. Dogs harass wildlife like squirrels and birds by chasing them. Dogs leave poo wherever they feel a need to go. Dogs can carry diseases that can be transmitted to wildlife. And the scents from dog's pads, poo, and urine aren't natural to this place, and can disrupt wildlife behavior." I was proud of my comprehensive answer.

"But we're not dogs. Wouldn't we be the wildlife those rules are designed to protect?"

"Tish, give it up. We're dogs as long as Sage says we're dogs. Do you want to get out and move, or not?" Issa was ready for some exercise, although he didn't sound thrilled about the leash idea either.

"Hey," I said. "I'm not even supposed to take you guys on trails in the park, but I'm going to anyway. And if you promise to stay close to me, I'll let you off leash once we're out of sight of roads and people. Do you want to get a drink here? This spring water is the best."

We all exited the truck and Issa and Tish took a long drink from the pool below the spring, while I filled up two large water bottles to take back to the cabin. Just as the wolves finished satisfying their thirst, a trio of ravens sliced through the air from the east and perched on a maple branch overhead. Issa and Tish were immediately at full attention as the glossy black birds settled their feathers and started to squawk and chirr. Entranced, I watched the two wolves listen carefully and periodically nod their heads.

Issa took advantage of a break in the ravens' conversation and let loose with a series of vocalizations that weren't barks, but were more like a continuous stream of low, non-threatening, growly noises. His apparent question prompted another long narrative from the ravens, and then the birds once again took wing, disappearing behind a long row of leafless cottonwoods.

"They said things are getting worse up in Idaho," said Issa, in response to my questioning look. *"It's been bad for quite some time,*

and now that the state is supposedly managing wolves, things are really falling apart."

"Managing?" I said. "Based on what I saw on the Internet last night, it seems more like wholesale slaughter. I don't think that's what most people would call management."

"Maybe we should go for that walk now, Sage," Issa suggested. *"And talk about this later."*

We got back in the truck, continued on to the chapel parking lot, and parked the truck before heading down a section of trail that skirted the base of the valley's steep south wall. I unclipped their leashes and the wolves ran off down the trail at top speed, turned around and ran back to me, and then ran off again. They repeated this routine for the entire mile-and-a-half walk.

The high point of the day for Issa and Tish came when they spotted a coyote about fifty yards off the trail, nosing around in a pile of twigs. I saw the two wolves freeze and stare at the thick-furred coyote. The smaller canid looked up from his task and stared right back.

"Don't even think about it," I said quietly.

Tish was dancing in place, eager for the chase. Issa looked at her and then swatted her on the head with a heavy paw, which broke her focus. Tish was quick to return the smack, and the two wolves were soon fully engaged in play mode, jumping, twisting, and rolling in the slushy mixture of snow, pine needles, and oak leaves that covered the ground. The coyote watched the show for a few moments with wide eyes, and then slipped away when the wolves weren't watching.

Tired and happy, we returned to the truck and settled in for the drive home. On our way out of the valley, we drove past the developed areas of Yosemite Village and Yosemite Lodge. The truck windows were rolled down partway so the wolves could sample the smells.

Tish thrust her nose out the window until we passed the lodge and entered undeveloped forest. She pulled her head back in and looked over at me.

"Sage," she said, *"Your world is so much more complicated than ours, and not in a good way. It's overwhelming. How can you ever hear anything, or smell food, or sense another's mood with all this stuff around? Your world is so full of noise, and big machines and buildings, and foul odors from cars and trucks. How can you possibly know what's going on around you?"*

"Believe me, Tish, I know what you mean," I said. "And this is just a small village, although it does get really busy in the summer. Heaven forbid I should take you to a city, to someplace like Los Angeles or New York."

"Please don't," said Tish.

"You two don't know how many times I've wanted nothing more than to leave the so-called comforts of civilization behind," I said. "To go off and live in the woods, or in a cave somewhere. The problem is I've become so ill-equipped to do that. I'm not in super great shape, and I don't know how I'd secure food and water in the wild."

"Oh, you'd remember quickly. You're hard-wired to survive, Sage. You'd be fine," said Tish.

The world was shifting to shades of blue and gray when we turned north away from the Merced River canyon to head back home. We climbed in silence, and I thought about the plight of the wolves, the need for humans to embrace them instead of persecuting them. That thought spun off to all the other species that were in trouble because of humans—elephants, rhinos, polar bears, and so many others. It made me very sad, and I wondered how we could turn these destructive trends around.

Just after we made our final turn down toward Deer Meadows, I spotted a large, dark animal crossing the road about a hundred feet ahead of us. I slowly pressed my foot down on the brake pedal.

"What is that?" asked Tish.

"Probably a bear," I said, peering through the windshield into the darkening world. "No, wait, it's not…Wow, I think it's a wolverine," I said. "I've never seen one before. They're really rare, and are said to be pretty tough."

"I'll say," said Issa. *"Everything about him says 'I dare you'. It reminds me of badger energy, but bigger, way more imposing. We've never met a wolverine before, either."*

The animal picked up its pace and stepped off the road and out of sight behind a stand of trees.

"I'm not sure you'd want to meet up with one, Issa," I said. "But it's great to know they're here."

As soon as we got back to the cabin, I stoked the fire and set the teakettle on the stove to boil. Still curious about definitions, I went to the table and sat down at the computer.

After a few minutes of Internet surfing, I turned around in my chair and said, "Okay, you two. Here's the best description I can find for compassion. In the words of a woman named Crystal Maddox, 'Compassion is a quality that comes from having an open heart, where intelligence and emotions can converge and support each other in effective action to alleviate the suffering of another.' Does that make any sense to you?"

"Not really," said Tish. *"Sounds like a human thing. But, if you think it's important, I'll go along with it. How does a human get compassion?"*

"Well," I answered. "I think it has to do with overcoming fear. A person needs to have enough knowledge, information, and experience to be able to move past being afraid of the things they encounter in life, or imagine they might encounter. A lot of what people are afraid of doesn't even exist. We're good at imagining things that might occur in the future, and being afraid of them right now, even though they might not ever happen. I think once fear moves out of a person, compassion can move in."

Issa and Tish looked at each other. I couldn't quite read their reactions, but I sensed confusion. And, maybe I imagined it, but I also thought I saw sadness in their eyes.

"So," Issa said. *"Your point about wanting compassionate readers stems from a hope that those readers will learn to care about us and then speak up on our behalf to help alleviate our suffering?"*

"Exactly," I said.

"But where does the fear part come in?" asked Tish.

"In lots of places," I said. "You already know many people have irrational fears about wolves. Sadly, those fears have been perpetuated through the stories humans tell each other, and the stories we tell our children. People need to learn the truth about wolves—that you're not cold-blooded killers out to eat small humans. That you do kill prey to eat, but that's necessary for you to live."

"It seems a lot of the trouble comes when wolves hunt animals that humans claim to own, like cows and sheep," said Issa.

"That's a really tough problem," I said. "Somehow we need to keep the wolves and the livestock separated."

Dinner that night consisted of chicken breasts I found buried in the back of the freezer, and several cans of organic corn, which Tish declared was barely edible. After dinner, we all took our places around the fireplace. I picked up my notebook, opened it, and found my notes from the night before.

"Last night, I did some quick research on wolves and found information I think we should include in your story. It might not mean much to you, but it will help the readers understand you better. Remember, knowledge helps alleviate fear."

"Like what information?" asked Tish, as she licked bits of corn from her muzzle.

"Like the fact that wolves once were the most abundant predator in all of North America," I answered. "Biologists think there were more than two million of you spread across the continent from coast to coast."

The wolves gazed at one another in silence. I was glad to see they were impressed. They unlocked their gaze and turned to look at me. *"What's North America? And how many is two million? And why is this important?"* asked Tish.

Oh dear, I thought. This could be more difficult than I'd anticipated.

"Okay," I said. "I'll explain anything you want me to, but for some of this you'll just have to trust me. North America is a very big piece of land called a continent. It's the land we live on. And a million is a very large number. This is important because people need to know that wolves were abundant all over North America in the past, but humans managed to kill almost all of them."

The silence that followed was thick enough to cut with a knife.

"Issa," Tish finally said in a quiet voice. *"Let's sleep outside tonight."*

Chapter Six
2010

Sister lay on her side next to the trail, near the base of a large tree. All around her, in a circle, the earth had been churned up by her scrabbling feet as she'd tried to escape. Her glassy eyes were wide open, and her tongue hung from the corner of her mouth. A thick line of saliva ran from her lips to the ground.

Blue was frozen to the spot. He stared at the wolf, unable to comprehend what was happening. Sunny pushed past him and walked slowly toward Sister, stopping just outside the circle. A thin, steel cable was looped tightly around Sister's neck, while a line tied high up in a nearby pine secured the deadly snare.

"Is she...is she still alive?" Blue asked. "Can we help her? Oh, be careful, Sunny." Blue was deeply ashamed that he was unable to do anything, not even move.

"She's alive, Blue. Just barely," said Sunny softly. "I think we're too late to save her. But we're here now, and we can send her off with love." Sunny crawled on hands and knees through the dirt and patches of foam and spittle to get closer to Sister, murmuring something Blue couldn't hear.

"Sunny, don't get too close. She could bite." Blue watched in stunned silence as his little sister continued to move toward the snared wolf.

When she got close enough, Sunny extended her right hand to let Sister smell her, but the exhausted animal didn't move. Blue could see Sister didn't have the strength to lash out. After lightly touching the wolf's dry, dirt-encrusted nose, Sunny crawled right up next to Sister and gently lifted the wolf's heavy head to cradle it in her lap. She stroked Sister's forehead and muzzle and spoke to her.

"Sister dear, Sister wolf, your time has come." From where Blue stood, it looked like Sunny had entered some sort of trance, with her head tipped back slightly. He could hear her clearly now. Her words were a soft chant.

"We are here, Sister dear, we are so sorry this happened. We know you are brave and strong and good, and your spirit will carry all of this goodness with you to the other side. Go in peace, Sister dear. We love you. Goodbye for now."

Blue was so focused on Sunny and Sister he didn't realize they had company until he heard a soft sneeze.

"Sunny!" he whispered. "Sunny, look!"

Sunny turned and followed Blue's gaze to the east, in the direction of the den. Aspen stood in the middle of the trail, about thirty feet away. She looked at Blue, then at Sunny, and then strode toward the girl and the dying wolf. Sister's puppies were right behind Aspen, following single file. No one was acting out now. They were all silent and wide-eyed. Lonestar was behind the puppies, and Arctos and Asher brought up the rear. Aspen walked to the right of the circle of churned-up earth and looped around to sit next to Sunny. The trailing wolves followed her and created a circle around Sister.

Blue realized he was holding his breath. When he exhaled audibly, Arctos turned to look back at the boy. While Blue watched, the big male wolf moved closer to Asher. Arctos then patted his right foot on the patch of ground he'd just vacated. Hoping he had read the signal correctly, Blue accepted Arctos' invitation to join the group, and took his place in the circle.

Blue gazed around at all the wolves and realized one of the puppies was missing. He cast his mind back to the previous day, when Sunny had recited all their names. He recognized Cinder, the black pup, and Grama, the large male with black legs. The small gray one, Cirrus, was on the far side of the circle. And one of the two females that were the hardest for Blue to tell apart, Goldie and Tierra, sat next to Aspen. The other one, the one with the white ear tip, was missing.

Before Blue could ask Sunny which wolf was not in the circle, three ravens soared into the clearing. They flew over the circle several times, barely clearing the heads of those gathered, and they cawed repeatedly and loudly. Blue expected the wolves to be angered by the raucous ravens, but everyone just watched the big, black birds swoop back and forth. At first, their flying appeared erratic, but Blue soon recognized a pattern. The birds swooped on a north to south line, and then curved around to do the same on an east to west line. The third pass was more like a dive; the birds flew up about fifty feet, and then swooped straight down directly over Sister, pulling up just before they would have crashed into the ground. After repeating this pattern three times, they landed on a series of pine branches that hung above the circle. The birds shook their heads and shoulders vigorously, and ruffled their feathers before settling down.

As soon as the ravens were quiet, Arctos lifted his nose into the air and let loose a long, low-pitched howl. He was immediately joined by all the other wolves. The collective mourning howl was very loud. Blue felt as though an iron band was squeezing his chest impossibly hard, and a few tears slid down his cheeks, followed by a torrent. This was the first time he'd really cried in more than five years, since the night Aunt Lois told him his parents had been killed in a car accident.

The howling lasted for at least five minutes, and then trailed off, leaving the group in a deep chamber of silence. Blue stared at the ground, letting his tears water the soil below him. When he finally looked up at Sunny, he saw her gently run her hands over Sister's eyes, as if closing them. Sister had left them during the howling. The wolves had been singing her home.

The circle stayed intact for a few more minutes, and then the ravens each cawed once and took flight, winging their way east. Aspen stood and nodded at Sunny. Then Arctos rose, turned away from the circle, and led the procession of wolves back down the trail toward the den.

After the wolves departed, Sunny got up and wiped dirt and pine needles from her pants. She stared down at Sister's body for a moment, and then put her hands together and bowed over the wolf, the same way she had bowed to the squirrel with the pine cone. After completing the bow, she walked over to Blue, who was still sitting on the ground. She reached out to take his hand and helped him to stand. Blue was still weeping and shaking slightly from head to toe. Sunny reached up and put her arms around him and held him in a tight hug until he stopped shaking. Then she took the lead down the trail toward home.

"Why are you so down at the mouth, Blue?" Uncle Marshal asked as he dove into his lunch of hamburger and barbecued potato chips. "You should have come into town with me. I ran into Sidney and his boy Barry. They're planning to go after bear in the fall, asked if you and I wanted to join them. That would be something now, wouldn't it?"

"Hmm," answered Blue. "Yeah, something."

"Oh, come on, now. Cheer up. Whatever it is can't be all that bad," Marshal said. "What's a boy like you got to worry about anyway? Leave the worrying for when you're all grown up." He rose from the table, walked to the refrigerator, and pulled out a jar of dill pickles. Returning to the table, he pulled a large pickle from the jar and laid it on Blue's plate. "There, that should cure whatever ails you," he said with a grin.

"Thanks, Uncle Marshal," said Blue. "I'm just tired, I guess."

"Are you feeling ill?" asked Lois.

"No, I'm okay. Just tired."

"Well," said Lois, "if you're sure. Maybe you should take a little nap this afternoon."

"Yeah," said Blue, staring at his uneaten lunch. "Maybe I will. Can I be excused, please?"

"Of course," said Lois. "I'll come wake you in an hour or so."

"I'm going to nap, too," Sunny announced. Lois wasn't surprised. Sunny had been particularly attached to Blue these past few days. The girl would go through phases like this every so often. Lois figured there was no harm in it, as long as Blue didn't mind.

"Don't be sad, Blue," Sunny said as she climbed the stairs behind her brother. "The puppies will be okay."

"I know they will. It just makes me so mad that someone would put a trap out like that. I hate trapping. And I hate hunting, too. I'm never going to hunt, no matter what Uncle Marshal says."

"I'm glad about that, Blue. I don't like trapping or hunting, either."

Sunny lay down on her bed, crawled under the covers, and fell fast asleep. Blue envied her ability to do this. He lay on his back in his bed, stared at the ceiling, and wondered if life would always be this painful.

An hour later, Sunny rolled over and said, "Hey, Blue. We need to go back to the den tomorrow after school."

"No way. It's too depressing."

"Really, Blue. We have to. We have to see how everybody is doing. It'll be okay," said Sunny.

"No. I don't want to see them again."

"Oh, yes, you do, Blue. Wait until tomorrow, you'll see."

Sunny was right, as usual, thought Blue as they made their way down the trail on Monday afternoon. The weather had changed since the day before. Dark clouds were massing overhead, and the air smelled like rain. Blue hoped the wolves would be at the den. He needed to know they were okay without Sister.

When Blue and Sunny approached the den, they saw Aspen seated near the entrance. Arctos and Asher were stretched out part way down the slope, on a secondary bench formed by an old river terrace. Four of the puppies were piled on top of Asher, pulling on his ears and tail, and licking at his muzzle, hoping to get him to regurgitate a meal for them. Lonestar was nowhere to be seen. The three adults all looked up at Blue and Sunny, and then looked at one another. Blue had the feeling the wolves had been waiting for them.

"Hey, where's Tierra?" asked Blue, when he noticed she wasn't with the others.

As if to answer him, Aspen looked to her left at a rock outcrop about fifteen feet away. Tierra lay next to the rock. She appeared to be asleep.

Blue and Sunny sat down on the ground about twenty yards away from Aspen to wait and see what would happen next. The wolves seemed relaxed, and Blue suspected they had eaten recently and would soon be napping. He was surprised to find himself content, even happy, to be there, despite his earlier misgivings.

"You know, Sunny," he said, as he played with a small piece of obsidian he always kept in his pocket. "I feel better than I thought I would, being here with the wolves again. I'm still sad and everything, but, for some reason, the wolves give me a sense of comfort. Even though they've lost Sister, their lives go on."

"That's true, Blue," said Sunny. "I think animals are better about death than humans are. The animals seem sad and all, but it's an okay sort of sad."

She paused, and gazed at the wolves with a small smile on her face.

"And Blue," she continued, "even though they lost their mama, those puppies still have the rest of their family. Like you and I have Aunt Lois and Uncle Marshal. And like you and I have each other."

Blue sat silent and still, listening to the wind fingering the needles of the pines overhead, acknowledging the truth of Sunny's words. This was as close as Sunny had ever come to talking about their parents' death.

As brother and sister drifted along in their thoughts, Aspen stood up, stretched, and yawned. The other adults quickly followed suit. Aspen walked over to the puppies and they all gathered around her. She barked softly two times and then walked down the slope to the east. The rest of the wolves lined up behind her in the same procession they'd formed when they came to mourn Sister. Without looking back, Aspen crossed the creek and started to climb the far bank.

"Wait, Aspen," cried Blue. "Wait, you've forgotten Tierra." As Blue and Sunny looked on, the lone gray puppy struggled to her feet and watched her family walk away. She took a few unsteady steps to try to follow them, then stumbled and fell.

"She's sick, Blue," said Sunny. "She can't go with them. We'll have to take her home with us."

Blue had no response. He knew that wasn't possible. There was no way Uncle Marshal would let them keep Tierra.

He looked again at the far slope where the departing wolves were about to cross the ridge and drop over to the other side. Aspen stopped at the top and looked back. She barked once, and then, one by one, the wolf family crested the ridge and disappeared.

Chapter Seven
2018

Before the sun had emerged from behind the eastern ridge, I sat down at the dining table, ready to dive into scrambled eggs and a bagel smothered in cream cheese topped by two fresh figs. Before I could begin, though, I heard the patter of dog feet on the deck and then watched the doggie door pop open to admit Tish. Issa was close on her heels. The two wolves walked over and sat down next to me. I cringed at the sight of the blood smeared all over their muzzles.

"Sage, you should have been there!" said Tish, panting hard. *"Issa was magnificent."*

"Tish played her part, too," said Issa.

"It was a small deer, but we took her so easily," Tish said. *"She wasn't even afraid of us. It was like she'd never seen a wolf before."*

"I'm sure she hadn't," I said, feeling sad for the unsuspecting doe. "So, I guess this means you're not hungry."

"No, we're good," said Tish. She walked to the fireplace, sat down, and carefully cleaned the blood from her muzzle and front paws. Issa got a big, noisy drink from the water bowl and then went to join her.

I turned my attention back to breakfast, but just as I was about to lift the first steamy bite of eggs to my mouth, Tish jumped up, walked across the room, and sat down right behind me. My fork dropped to the plate with a clatter when Tish reared up and planted her still wet front feet on the back of the chair.

"Sorry, but this is easier on an empty stomach," she whispered. My gut clenched and my shoulders grew rigid as her meaty, warm breath flowed across the back of my neck. Before I could react, her sharp teeth made light contact with my skin.

My mind told me to fight back, but my body went completely limp. I felt no pain. Instead, I was suffused with a delicious warm feeling, as if I were submerged in a hot springs pool somewhere, instead of facing imminent death. I closed my eyes, surrendered to the warmth, and wondered if death felt like a return to the womb. And then I was falling backwards and spinning downward, slipping away.

I was groggy when I opened my eyes. It seemed as if no time had passed, like waking up after being under anesthesia. The scene before me was unfamiliar, and it certainly was not a hospital. I was standing outside, on a moderately steep, rocky slope. A jagged, snow-covered mountain range rose up on the eastern horizon. A faint yellow pre-dawn glow outlined the ridgeline. Despite the low light, I could see clearly. I took a deep breath and was almost knocked over backwards. That one cold breath was filled with the strongest, most overwhelming set of odors I'd ever experienced. I smelled pine trees and damp soil, the reek of dead things, stale urine and feces, wood smoke, and a host of other things I couldn't name. As I tried to make sense of it all, Tish's voice cut through my sensory overload.

"Don't worry, Sage." I heard her clearly, but I couldn't see her.

"Tish?" I said. "Tish, where are you? Where am I? What's happening? Why should I be worried?"

"Everything's okay," said Tish's voice. *"You're fine, I think. It's kind of hard to explain. Let's just say, for the moment, that you've entered Wolf Time. It'll make sense soon, at least...oh, never mind. Trust me. Everything's fine, better than fine. Issa was right."*

I had no idea what she was talking about, and was concerned that her usual confident demeanor seemed to be wavering. I looked around to try to find her. The glow to the east had brightened. The ground was covered with fresh, unbroken snow, and the sky was streaked with clouds. The air was still, and cold enough to freeze the moisture in my nose. Tish was nowhere in sight.

About a hundred yards downhill from where I stood, the rocky slope gave way to an open, grassy meadow fed by several creeks flowing down from the mountains and coalescing into one larger stream near the center of the meadow. My eyes were drawn to movement around the meadow's edges. Three small herds of deer and a lone bull elk were feeding at different places, all close to sheltering stands of conifers. A family of raccoons was busy at the edge of one of the feeder creeks, and dozens of small birds as well as a few bats flitted over the central stream. I was drawn in by the richness of the place, and surprised I could see everything so clearly. But where was I? And how did I get here?

A series of high-pitched yips laced with intermittent growls cut through my wonderings, and I turned toward the slope behind me to see a large, roughly triangular hole, maybe two feet at its widest point. At that moment, the sun cleared the ridge, and I realized with a shock that I was looking at a wolf den.

"Um, Tish," I whispered. "Where are you? Please tell me what's going on."

"We've merged, Sage, you and I. Your spirit is with me in my body. You're seeing the world through my eyes, smelling through my nose, hearing what I hear. And we've stepped back in time."

I closed my eyes. Part of me was thrilled by the possibility that what Tish said was true, but mostly I just wanted to open my eyes and be back in my cabin, safely wrapped in a fuzzy blanket, with a hot cup of tea and my scrambled eggs, reveling in the afterglow of the most amazing dream ever. But when I opened my eyes, I was still standing on the snowy slope.

"No, Sage," said Tish. *"It's not a dream, at least not a sleeping dream. It's more like a waking dream. Look down."*

With some hesitation, I did as instructed. The ground was much closer than I'd expected it to be. I was looking at a pair of heavily furred, cream-colored paws, each with a set of hard, black claws. Tish was not kidding; we were merged. I was in her body, but not the body she'd had when she showed up on my doorstep. I was in the body of a wolf puppy.

"Oh, Tish," I said. "What have you done?"

"It wasn't all my doing," said Tish. *"Issa suggested it. You were primed and ready, Sage. You just didn't know it. With all the shamanic training you've done, and your Grandmother Rose's influence, you were just waiting for this opportunity. I'm sorry I had to bite you, but the first few times we initiate the merge, we have to take you by surprise. Otherwise, your survival instincts would kick in and cause you to resist, and the merge wouldn't happen."*

"Tish, dear, come back in. I need to give you puppies the ground rules for today." I looked up at the sound of this new, deeper voice.

A full-grown wolf towered over us. The big gray took a quick look around at the land and the sky, and said, *"Ah, finally it stopped snowing. Perhaps now we can have a successful hunt."*

"I'll be right in," said Tish.

"That's Mom," Tish said as the big wolf turned back into the den.

"Wow," was all I could say. Then it occurred to me that I didn't know anything about how this merging thing worked. "So, do I need to be silent?" I whispered. "Will the others hear me?"

"Nope, not a problem," said Tish. *"Since you're in my body, you can't vocalize except telepathically to me. And I'm not speaking to you, I'm thinking to you. No one else will even know you're here. Mom might suspect something, but she's no stranger to merging. She won't mind."*

Tish stood and walked to the den's entrance, ducked her head slightly, and entered a narrow, dark tunnel. The walls looked like mostly clay soil, embedded with scattered rocks of many sizes, some smooth and some sharp-edged. Here and there, thin, pale plant roots dangled from the ceiling. But once again, what I noticed most were the smells. Outside, the odors had been strong, but in here they were intoxicating, overpowering. I smelled dank, rich earthiness, as well as meat and milk, all wrapped up in a dense cloud of puppy.

"Oh, by the way, Sage," said Tish as we moved farther into the den. *"You needn't worry about getting hurt or killed or anything while you're in Wolf Time. I mean, think about it. I showed up at your cabin as an adult wolf, right? And now I'm just a pup, which means I survived. So, you'll be fine. Trust me."*

Her words did little to make me feel better.

After we'd walked into the den about twelve feet or so, the tunnel opened up into a large chamber. The big mama wolf was crouched on a narrow shelf slightly above the den's floor, and a bunch of puppies took up the rest of the space. I wasn't sure how anyone was able to sleep in there, it felt so crowded. One pair of pups was wrestling, rolling on the floor, growling and snapping. Within the space of a few seconds, one of them bit the other on the ear, which elicited a loud, shrill yelp. The victim retaliated by yanking its sibling's floppy tail. A second pair was curled up together next to the far wall, one puppy stood near its mom, and one pup sat alone.

"There are seven of us puppies," said Tish. *"The two snoozers over there are Seeker, the big, black one; and Rusty the runt, the smallest gray. You already know Issa, off by himself, as usual. The two wrestlers are Harley, the black one with silver highlights; and Marley, who is dark gray like Rusty, but larger. And that beautiful white puppy sitting by Mom is Snow, my only sister."*

"Okay, gang." Mom's voice carried over and suppressed the noisy players. *"This is the first day we will travel away from the den, so stay close together. Don't wander off. Your auntie and uncle should be meeting us with food."*

Tish and I emerged first from the den behind Mom. The sun had climbed above the mountains, but was caught behind a stunning display of clouds. Just above the ridge, multiple layers of gold fleece supported a massive fan-shaped sunburst of pink and pale violet topped by dozens of horizontal thread-like cirrus clouds the color of cotton candy. The line of wolves stopped to witness the show, and then we struck out for the meadow, traveling downhill over fresh snow.

Rusty, the smallest puppy, trotted behind Tish and me. We hadn't gone more than ten yards before the combination of cold air and young dog caused a minor eruption. I felt Tish's body lower into a crouch and then she launched straight up, reaching high with both front paws. She spun like a dancer in mid-air and landed on Rusty's head. Rusty dropped his left shoulder and tumbled Tish into the snow. Marley, next in line, couldn't resist the impulse and jumped on both of his siblings with a ferocious growl. Tish tried to wriggle out from under the pile, but Rusty's right paw was solidly planted on her left ear, and her mouth and nose were filling with snow. Summoning all of her strength, she rolled sideways and managed to escape the melee. She stood and shook a blizzard of snow from her coat and sneezed twice. And then we went down again as Harley and Marley pounced on Tish's head and hips, respectively.

The next thing I knew I was back in my cabin, sitting in my chair in front of my breakfast. A wisp of steam rose from the eggs. I glanced over at Issa. He was still curled up by the fire, watching me intently.

"Congratulations, Sage, for being able to do this," Issa said. *"We know every human has the ability to do it, but, so far, there are very few of you who trust the world enough to allow the merge to fully manifest. In time, though, we hope it will become commonplace, second-nature."*

I felt a gentle, wet touch on my arm as Tish gave me a soft lick. *"You okay?"* she asked.

I was silent for a moment. "Yes," I said. "I think so." I knew, though, that it would be a while before I was really okay. Wolf Time would take some getting used to.

Chapter Eight
2010

"Aspen asked us to help this puppy, Blue. We have to try. Can I use your jacket? We can wrap her up to carry her home." Sunny dropped to her knees, hunched over Tierra, and began stroking the puppy's soft face. The young wolf's nose was dry and cracked, and a nasty yellow-green discharge seeped from her nostrils.

"Sunny, this is impossible. We can't take her home. What will Aunt Lois and Uncle Marshal say? Most likely, Uncle Marshal will take her to the creek and drown her. You know how hard it was to get him to let us keep Angus, and he's just a dog." Blue stayed back a bit from Tierra. He knew if he touched her, he would immediately become attached, and then they'd have to take her home.

"Come on. Let's go." Blue turned away from Sunny and the pup and walked a few steps down the trail.

"We can't just leave her here, Blue. She'll die."

Tierra was weak, and offered no resistance when Sunny wrapped Blue's jacket around her body. Blue picked up the bundle with a soft grunt and they headed down the trail.

They stopped to take a break about halfway to the cabin and Blue wiped sweat from his face. He laid Tierra down on a soft patch of grass near the trail. She looked up at him, but made no move to get up. "Okay, we need to make a plan. Where are we going to put her when we get home?"

"Our room," said Sunny.

"No way. We'll put her in the shed."

"She'll get lonely and howl. She's never been alone before."

"Sunny, this whole thing is a very bad idea."

"No, Blue," said Sunny. "It's the best idea. It's the only idea. Tierra will die if we leave her. If Uncle Marshal wants to kill her, we'll talk him out of it. If we can't, then at least we tried."

When they reached the bottom of a small clearing below the cabin, Sunny waited with Tierra while Blue went ahead to figure out how to get the pup inside. As soon as he stepped into the cabin, Blue saw the handwritten note on the table: *Your uncle's truck broke down. Gone to get him. Do your homework.*

Well, thought Blue, maybe we will get away with this. He called for Angus, but got no response, so Blue figured the dog must be with Aunt Lois. Not knowing how soon their aunt and uncle would return, Blue ran back to Sunny, and they hurried to get Tierra settled in upstairs. Sunny put together a bed from an old wool blanket, while Blue collected bowls and a few cans of Angus' food. He also grabbed several of Aunt Lois' old cleaning towels; things were likely to get messy. He carefully placed two faded blue-and-white checked towels on top of the blanket, and they laid Tierra in the makeshift bed. She immediately put her head down and closed her eyes.

All through dinner, Blue prayed the puppy would keep quiet. Fortunately, Angus was outside and couldn't betray Tierra's presence. As soon as the meal was finished, Blue stood up and said, "Well, we're off. We still have more homework to finish."

"Boy, they're really piling it on," said Marshal.

"They are. Probably because it's almost the end of the year," said Blue, wiping his face with his napkin and heading for the stairs to the loft.

Upstairs, Tierra refused the food they offered and was unwilling to drink. Sunny wet the end of a towel and dripped water into the pup's mouth. "She could die if we don't get her to a vet soon. You know that, don't you, Blue?"

Blue was trying hard not to retch as he finished cleaning the watery diarrhea off Tierra's hind legs. "And how do you suggest we do that? We don't have any money, and the vet will tell on us."

"We have to tell Aunt Lois," Sunny said. "She'll help."

"If you say so," said Blue. "But right now, I really do need to get this homework done." He sat down at the work desk their uncle had fabricated from cinder blocks and a sanded piece of plywood, and pulled books and notebooks out of his daypack.

"Don't worry too much about homework, Blue," said Sunny. "I don't think we'll be going to school tomorrow."

"Mrs. Morrison," said the vet. "You do know this is not just a dog. Right?"

"We do," said Lois. "We think she might be one of those crosses between a wolf and a dog. It's kind of a long story. Will you help us?"

Blue flashed back to the scene in the kitchen earlier that morning, when Sunny had used almost those exact words on Aunt Lois. By the time their aunt agreed to help, all three of them were in tears. They were united in their desire to help Tierra, but none of them wanted to be at the receiving end of Uncle Marshal's anger.

"She's pretty sick. We'll have to run some tests to see what it is, but it looks like distemper. What does your husband think about this?" Dr. Carleton knew Marshal and couldn't imagine the man would accept a wolf in his home.

"Please don't tell him, Dr. Carleton." This was the first time Sunny had spoken since they'd arrived at the vet's office.

"We'll tell him when the time is right." Lois chimed in to support Sunny.

Tierra was stretched out on the stainless steel table in the middle of the vet's examining room. Her eyes were closed, and her tail drooped over the edge of the table.

"Can you help her?" Sunny asked.

Both Lois and Blue were surprised by Sunny's interaction with the vet. She was usually very reluctant to communicate with anyone outside of the immediate family.

"There isn't much we can do if it's distemper. It's caused by a virus, so antibiotics won't help. You need to keep her warm, keep her eyes and nose as clean as possible, and be sure she stays hydrated. Is she drinking at all?"

"No," said Sunny. "But we can use a baster or something to get her to drink."

"That might not work, Sunny," said Dr. Carleton. "If she gets too dehydrated, she'll have to come back here to be sedated and put on IV fluids. Right now I think she's okay and can go home, but if she doesn't start drinking again in two days, you'll need to bring her back."

Blue carried Tierra out to the car, and Sunny opened the door of the blue Subaru and helped get the pup settled. Lois stayed behind in the office to pay for the visit.

"I'm not going to charge you anything for this, Lois," said Dr. Carleton. "And let me know if you need any help with Marshal."

While his family was driving home from the vet's office, Marshal was traveling down a dirt road riddled with potholes and long washboard sections. He and his partner, Joe Cramer, were on a mission to locate and destroy a wolf den that had been reported on the Abel grazing allotment. The den may have been abandoned for the season, but the men planned to set a number of traps in the area, in case the wolves were still close by. Marshal and Joe worked for Wildlife Services, a federal agency in the Department of Agriculture. Joe had held his job for about twelve years, but Marshal was a newbie—he'd taken the position with the agency about six months earlier, after the funding for his job with Idaho's fish and game department had dried up.

"Joe, can't you drive any smoother?" asked Marshal. "Those doughnuts haven't quite settled yet."

"Blame it on the U.S. Forest Service," said Joe. "It's their road."

"No, I think we're on Abel's ranch, now, aren't we? Have been ever since we crossed that last cattle guard."

"Same difference," said Joe. "I can't imagine old Abel spending precious dollars on road maintenance, either."

A sudden movement on the right shoulder of the road caught Joe's eye, and he quickly shifted his foot from accelerator to brake. In one smooth movement, Marshal grabbed a rifle from the rack behind his head, opened the door of the truck, and swung his body partway out. Before Joe could even bring the truck to a full stop, Marshal fired off several quick shots and the big animal dropped dead in the middle of the road.

"Good one," said Joe, looking over at Marshal. "Wow. Are you fast or what? That's a beauty. I've never gotten one myself. But, Marshal, we're not in season, and if you're right, we're on private property. I hope you at least have a tag."

Marshal was silent. One part of his brain heard the kudos from Joe and swelled with pride, but the other part was stunned by his action and overwhelmed by an unfamiliar sadness. This was his first lion kill. He'd hoped for this day most of his life, ever since his dad had first taken him hunting, when Marshal had been so excited to shoot his first chukar. But now his dreams of taking a mountain lion, of making his dad in heaven so proud, and of admiring the huge pelt on the wall of his cabin all evaporated as he faced the reality of what he'd done. This once magnificent golden animal, so gorgeous and strong in life, now lay dead on a dusty road.

Marshal felt tears well in the corners of his eyes. He looked away from Joe and coughed to mask the unexpected flood of emotion. He felt like he couldn't breathe.

Joe looked at Marshal and said, "Aren't you going to check it out?"

Without a word, Marshal stepped down from the truck and walked the few paces to where the lion lay stretched out on the ground. Just as he was about to lean over to touch the animal's fur, the lion slowly lifted its head and turned to look at Marshal with its large golden eyes. Marshal leaped back, almost falling over his own feet as he hurried to return to the truck. But when he turned to look at the animal again, he saw the lethal wound behind its right shoulder. He knew it would die soon.

"Do you need to shoot it again?" asked Joe. "Maybe not, huh? It doesn't look like it's got much life left in it. That was a great shot. Should we get a photo?"

Marshal's head was spinning, and a strong wave of nausea washed over him. He took a few steps away from the truck, turned his back to Joe, leaned over, and vomited.

"Hey," said Joe, as he climbed out of the truck to check on Marshal. "You okay? Was it the doughnuts?"

Marshal pulled his truck up next to the cabin and turned off the ignition. As late as it was, he figured Lois would have dinner ready soon. Instead of getting out and going inside, though, he sat in the quiet and thought about the lion. He had mixed feelings about giving it to Joe, but couldn't stomach the idea of bringing it home and skinning it out. He knew it would upset Sunny, although she tried to hide her feelings about his hunting. As for Blue, Marshal knew full well the boy would never be a hunter, would never take his first elk. And while Lois always supported Marshal no matter what he chose to do, he knew she was squeamish about killing animals, too. And the truth was, since he'd taken this new job, which was all about killing all the time, Marshal had kind of soured on the whole deal himself. He'd asked Joe to not mention to anyone that Marshal had shot the lion. Joe could take credit for the kill himself. As a brush of cool evening air crept in through the truck's open window, Marshal decided he wouldn't mention the lion to his family. When he finally left the truck and headed for the cabin, he saw Sunny holding the door open just a crack, peering out.

"He's coming in!" Sunny spoke in a voice just above a whisper, but Marshal heard the announcement and wondered if there was some sort of surprise awaiting him. Sunny loved to celebrate and would find any excuse to do so. Birthdays, holidays, anniversaries, even the dog's adoption day, were suitable occasions for a party.

He stepped inside and was surprised by the odors of steak and what he thought was asparagus. Had he forgotten some special occasion? Sunny ran over to give him a hug, but there were no signs of cakes or party favors.

"Hi, Uncle Marshal!" Sunny said. "Did you have a nice day at work?"

"Hi, Sunny. Hi, Blue," he answered. "Oh, it was just another day." He gave Lois a quick kiss on the cheek, then flipped through the day's mail, which sat in a pile on the kitchen counter.

"Anything new around here?" he asked.

No one answered. Marshal looked up at Lois. It must be bad news, he thought. If it were good, they'd be competing with each other to tell him.

"Honey," said Lois, "we do have some news, and we hope it's okay with you."

Marshal remained silent, looking one at a time at the three tight faces.

"Sunny and Blue found a sick animal, and they brought it home," said Lois.

Marshal wasn't too surprised. This wasn't the first time this had happened. A small parade of animals and birds, including a fawn, a family of orphaned deer mice, and even a loon, had been rescued by Sunny and Blue over the years.

"Well," Marshal said, "as long as it's not a wolf, it's probably okay."

The glances exchanged among Sunny, Blue, and Lois told him everything he needed to know. With a deep sigh, he said, "Okay, tell me what's going on."

Marshal refused to go upstairs to see Tierra for four days. During that time, when they weren't at school, Sunny and Blue took turns keeping the pup clean and coaxing her to drink. Lois took over the tasks during school hours. By Wednesday morning, Tierra was starting to lap at water in her bowl, and was showing limited interest in the baked chicken and boiled potato mixture that Lois had prepared for her.

On Saturday morning, Marshal finally broke down and let Sunny convince him it was okay for him to just look at Tierra. He followed Sunny up the stairs while Blue and Lois stayed behind in the kitchen.

Sunny kept silent as she led her uncle across the loft's worn wooden floor to Tierra's blanket, which was tucked up right next to Sunny's bed—a single-sized mattress she'd moved off its frame onto the floor so she could be closer to Tierra.

Marshal winced when the sour smell of the sick puppy hit his nose. Suddenly, he was ten years old again, kneeling by the bed of his beloved golden lab, Smiley Joe. The dog had been very ill, poisoned when a neighbor had put out beef laced with strychnine to kill coyotes and Smiley Joe took the bait. On the long trip to town, Marshal tried to keep Smiley Joe from hurting himself as his best friend's body was wracked repeatedly by seizures. Dr. Holley sedated Smiley Joe, and administered fluids for three days, but the poison was too much for the pup. Smiley Joe took his last labored breath in Marshal's arms.

A small shiver ran down Marshal's body, and he felt the wrench of a sob start deep in his chest. He pushed the urge to cry back down, irritated with this new propensity. He walked over to Tierra and stared down at the puppy, while Sunny hung back and watched. Tierra looked up at him without raising her head from the bed, and asked him with her eyes if she could please stay with the family until she was well. How can I say no? Marshal wondered, as he turned and looked at Sunny's wide-open, hopeful face. He reached out to scratch the top of Tierra's head. She sighed and closed her eyes.

Chapter Nine
2018

"*Well, how was it? How did she do?*" Issa stood and stretched. He circled three times and then lay back down on the red and black Afghani rug that covered the oak floor of the cabin's main room.

"*Pretty good, I think,*" said Tish. "*Considering it was the first time for both of us. It was easy for me. Sage was upset at first, and confused, but she relaxed into it pretty quickly. I wonder when she'll wake up.*"

"*Soon, I hope,*" said Issa. "*I'm famished. I hope there's still some meat left on our deer. I think we need to stay here, though, until she wakes up.*"

I was laid flat out on the futon couch that constituted my only piece of family room furniture. I could hear Issa and Tish, but their voices seemed to come from far away, drifting in and out. The last thing I remembered about the morning was finishing my breakfast. I was so tired after I ate I could barely drag myself from the kitchen table to the futon, where I'd immediately fallen into a deep sleep. I'd shifted out of that sleep state quite a while ago, but I'd been unable to completely cross the thin veil that separated sleep and wakefulness. I would start to open my eyes, and they would close again. This happened at least half a dozen times. With a struggle, I forced myself to sit up and open my eyes all the way.

"Hey, there she is," said Issa. *"Did you have a nice nap?"*

I rubbed my eyes and glanced at the clock above the front door. It said 5 p.m. I rubbed my eyes and looked again. How could it be 5 p.m.? That couldn't be right. I glanced out the window and the pale gray light confirmed evening was upon us.

"How do you feel?" asked Tish.

"Pretty good," I said. "But I'm not used to sleeping all day."

Tish took that moment to yawn. As soon as I saw her teeth, I remembered feeling her soft bite on the back of my neck, and the journey into Wolf Time. It was a great relief to realize I'd been sleeping. The whole experience had been a really strange dream.

"Oh, no," said Tish with a little laugh. *"It wasn't a dream. Sorry about the bite, that's just how it works. You might be a little bruised."*

I'd forgotten the wolves could read my thoughts.

"If it's all right with you, Sage, Tish and I will be off to revisit our deer carcass. We didn't want to leave you alone while you slept, but we're both really hungry." Issa nodded at Tish, and the two of them walked to the door and pushed their way through to the outside.

As soon as the flap dropped behind Tish's hind end, I stood up, rubbed my eyes, and went to my computer to type up the strange experiences of the past two days. Dream or not, I didn't want to forget a single thing.

Issa and Tish returned two hours later, having finished the last tasty bits of their deer. Once again they spent about ten minutes cleaning blood and gore from their muzzles. Tish took a long drink of water and dribbled all over the kitchen floor, and then wandered back to the fireplace and lay down.

"If it's okay with you two, I think I'll get a little rest." She curled up and tucked her nose under a big front paw. I took that as a cue, said my goodnights, and went to bed.

The wolves were gone again when I woke up the following morning. I did some stretches and yoga poses and started preparing breakfast. A few minutes later, Tish shoved her head through the dog door and said, *"Hey! That smells good. What is it?"*

"Turkey bacon," I answered. "Found it in the back of the fridge. But I'm going to need to make a grocery run soon. I'm running out of food."

"A grocery run," said Tish. *"Is that like chasing down a deer?"*

"Well, not exactly. I don't really have to run, and the food is already dead and packaged up for me at the store."

"Hmm," said Tish. *"Sounds boring. But that stuff you're cooking smells great."*

The three of us shared bacon and eggs, and then I sat down with the laptop. "I assume you'll want to do some story-telling this morning?" I said, while I waited for the computer to boot up. "Can you start by telling me your mom's name, so I can use it in the story?"

"Our mom's name was Tierra," Issa said softly. I turned around quickly to look at him, because it sounded as if he were standing right behind me. He was. And then I felt his teeth on my neck. My last thought was that Issa was much gentler than Tish.

I tried to pay closer attention to the transition this time. It felt as if I descended a long distance, but slowly, like floating backwards down a spiral staircase. I landed softly, and regained my senses more quickly than I had during my first tumble into Wolf Time.

When I opened my eyes, I saw we were just below the mouth of the same den Tish and I had visited the last time. The sun was high in the sky and there was a trace of warmth in the air. The snow cover was thinner, revealing open patches of rocky, reddish-brown soil. I heard the call of a chickadee from a small stand of conifers upslope of the den, and then the shrill cry of a golden eagle overhead. I looked up in search of the big raptor, wondering who or what it really was, but my attention was quickly pulled back to ground level.

In stark contrast to the quiet scene I'd encountered at the den when I'd merged with Tish, Issa and I landed in the middle of pure puppy pandemonium. The three gray and two black pups were all running pell-mell after a covey of quail that must have landed in the wrong place at the wrong time. Tierra sat calmly at the den's mouth, yipping directions to the pups on how to catch the birds. The white puppy, Snow, sat off to one side, away from the frenzy of activity. With her nose in the air, she was looking off to the north, away from her siblings' lesson.

Issa and I leaped into the fray with the pack of hunters, even though it was obvious none of the pups had any chance of actually catching a quail. After the last bird disappeared down the slope amidst a great whirring of wings, the puppies turned their attention to tackling each other. Stopping to catch his breath, Issa turned to look at the spot where Snow had been sitting a moment earlier. She was gone. Just as he opened his mouth to tell Tierra, an ear-splitting shriek followed by a long, terrible howl split the air.

Tierra leaped up and raced off in the direction of the cries. *"Pups,"* she ordered. *"Follow me, but stay behind."*

We all ran in a line behind Tierra, who was moving fast. It was hard to keep up with her on our short legs. We were already tired, and we were running uphill. As we loped, I noticed a very distinctive odor. It smelled like tuna fish left out on the counter all night, and it got stronger with every step.

Tierra stopped short in a small clearing in the middle of a cluster of tall pines. Issa and I were so close behind Tish that we ran smack into her, and we all fell down in a heap. As we were untangling ourselves from one another, we heard Tierra's quiet gasp.

"Oh, Snow. Oh, no. Not my little Snow."

Snow was laid out flat on the ground, her small right foreleg crushed between the jaws of a steel coyote trap. Blood stained her soft white coat and soaked the ground beneath her. By the time we caught up with Tierra, Snow's shrill cries had turned to whimpers.

Tierra ran to Snow's side and bit at the trap repeatedly, and then grabbed it between her teeth to try to pull it off, but her actions only caused Snow more pain. After working for what seemed like hours to free Snow from the trap, Tierra finally gave up and lay down next to her injured daughter. She gently licked Snow' head and the injured leg. Several times she looked up toward the sky and whined.

The rest of us lay down in silence and waited for Tierra to tell us what to do. After what seemed like more hours, she finally stood up and said, *"Okay, pups. We need to get something to eat."*

In silence, we followed her back to the den. Once we were all inside, Tierra said, *"I'm going to get you some meat from the elk your aunties took down yesterday. Stay here, all of you, and keep quiet."*

We sat in the den and looked at each other for a few minutes. Rusty finally broke the silence. *"How are we going to get our Snow out of that nasty trap?"*

No one had an answer for him.

Tierra returned a half hour later and regurgitated a pile of partially digested elk parts that the puppies lit into with gusto. I was on the verge of throwing up myself when Issa got close to the yucky mess, but I held my breath. I knew he was going to eat it, whether I liked it or not. Tierra left and returned with food two more times, and then we all settled down to rest.

Just before Issa and I drifted off to sleep, I whispered, "Issa, won't Tish be worried about us being gone for so long?"

"Don't worry, Sage. Time stands still when you're in Wolf Time. She won't even have a chance to miss us."

The only two who slept soundly that night were Marley and Harley, who, according to Issa, could sleep under any circumstances. It seemed like the longest night of my life, but eventually morning light filtered into the den. Tierra stood up, stretched, and said, *"We need to go back now."*

When we arrived at the edge of the clearing, we all lined up next to Tierra and peered through the trees. The trap and little Snow were gone. Scuffed up dirt and blood-stained leaves and soil were the only signs that she'd been there. Tish took a few steps into the clearing to look for Snow, but Tierra hissed, *"Stop, pups! I smell humans!"*

We ducked down and huddled together as two men stepped into the clearing, no more than thirty feet away from us. The larger man, dressed in full camouflage, held up the trap. Snow's limp body dangled in the frigid air, held fast by the trap's savage jaws. The man spat on the ground and said, "This is just a stupid cub. No one will pay anything for the pelt."

"No," said the second man. "But that's one less wolf we've got to worry about. The den must be close. Didn't Joe say he was going to come up here and search this area for dens as soon as he could get away from the office?"

I felt a potent mix of rage and sadness emanating from Tierra's body as she slowly and quietly herded us away from the clearing and back to the den. When we were all safely inside and curled up next to her, she said, *"We're going to have to move away from here, pups, and soon. Before the man called Joe comes looking."*

Chapter Ten
2010

"You two do know we eventually have to return her to the wild, right?" Marshal was sitting on the floor, brushing Tierra's heavy winter coat. "She could probably survive quite well on dog food, and the mice you've been trapping for her, if she was going to live with us forever, but I think she'll be much happier in the wild."

Tierra lay on her back, all four feet in the air, exposing her tan, gray and white belly for Marshal's ministrations. Angus, seeking equal time with the brush, lay on his back behind Marshal, nosing him every so often on the leg to ensure a fair distribution of attention. The dog and the wolf had become good friends; they'd had only one major altercation over a marrow bone. Angus had won the battle, with Tierra losing a corner of her left ear in the scuffle.

"I don't know," said Sunny. "She looks pretty happy to me."

"I think it's time to tell them, Marshal," Lois said from her rocking chair, where she was knitting a Christmas sweater.

"Tell us what?" asked Blue, his forehead furrowing into two small creases.

"Well, it looks like we're going to be moving come spring. I've got a new job starting next summer, down near Jackson, Wyoming. I'll be working as a guide. We're going to live on a dude ranch. Doesn't that sound great?"

"A guest ranch, dear," said Lois. "Not a dude ranch."

Uncle Marshal sounds pretty happy about this, thought Blue. His uncle seemed upbeat for the first time in a long time. For the last several months he'd been withdrawn and distant, ever since he'd quit his job with the government, soon after Tierra arrived. Blue knew the unemployment checks that came every two weeks were small, and he'd already prepared himself to not expect much in the way of Christmas presents. But he didn't want to move. He'd lived in Idaho his whole life.

"Will there be horses for us to ride?" asked Sunny.

"I'm sure there will be," said Marshal. "And plenty of things to do. The place is called the Lazy G Ranch. There's a river for rafting, and rock climbing nearby. There's plenty of room to ride and camp. It won't be too much different from here, except there will be more things to do."

"What about school?" Blue had just started seventh grade. The extra work had been a struggle for him at first, but in the last few weeks he was starting to feel better about things. Two weeks earlier, he'd entered a writing contest and was waiting to find out if he'd won.

"We won't go until school is done for the year. Your uncle will go down first, probably in April, to start settling in," said Lois.

Blue realized this move was going to happen, regardless of how he felt about it. Then he remembered his uncle's comment about Tierra. "Can't we take Tierra?" he asked.

Lois took that moment to get up to check on the soufflé in the oven. On her way to the kitchen, she flipped on the overhead light in the living room. Outside, autumn's bright golds and yellows were transitioning to the gray and blue hues of evening.

As Lois leaned over to close the window above the kitchen sink, a distinct four beat *hoo-h'HOO-hoo-hoo* broke the silence outside. A few seconds later, the great horned owl was echoed by another of its kind some distance away. Such a lonesome sound, thought Lois, as she pulled open the oven door to a warm cloud of air suffused with the aroma of cheese and onions. She tried to be quiet as she worked, so she could hear the conversation in the next room.

"We can't take her, Blue. She's a wolf, and she's likely to get in big trouble around a lot of people and other animals. The ranch owners said we can bring dogs, so Angus is fine, but I have a lot of concerns about Tierra." Marshal knew this was going to be hard on the kids, and on him and Lois, too, but he'd already made up his mind.

While Marshal broke the news, Sunny stared out the window that faced the mountains to the northwest. Did she even hear me? Marshal wondered. "Sunny—" he began.

"Okay, time to eat," announced Lois. "Wash up first, please."

Marshal gave both Tierra and Angus a last belly scratch and stood up. Without a word, and without looking at his uncle, Blue went to the bathroom to wash his hands. Sunny remained on the floor, her gaze still locked on the window. It was completely dark out, save for the light of a few emerging stars.

"Sunny," Marshal said. "Dinner's ready."

"What?" said Sunny, with a slight shake of her head. "Oh, okay. We're done. It'll be fine." Marshal had no idea what Sunny was talking about, but he had the sense she'd been far away. She checked out like this occasionally, and it always had an unsettling effect on Marshal.

Blue was silent through dinner, and asked to be excused from the table as soon as he finished his meal.

"We've got strawberry shortcake for dessert," said Lois. "Surely you have room for that?"

"No thanks," said Blue, as he stared at his lap. "I just want to go upstairs."

"You're excused then," said Marshal.

After Blue had disappeared into the loft, followed by Tierra, Marshal looked at Sunny, who was, as usual, eating her dessert in order: all of the whipped cream off the top first, then the strawberries and residual juice, and then the yellow cake at the bottom, which she cut carefully into eight even-sized pieces before taking a bite.

"How do you feel about all this, Sunny?" Marshal asked.

"About what?"

"About the move to Wyoming."

"The ranch sounds nice. I like horses."

"And how about Tierra?" said Marshal. "How does that feel?" Lois and Marshal made it a habit to ask Sunny about her feelings, as opposed to her thoughts. When asked what she thought about something, Sunny often became confused and was unable to answer. She had no trouble, though, expressing her feelings.

"It's okay. It'll be fine," she said, echoing her earlier statement. She used her last bite of shortcake to sop up the dabs of sugary juice from her plate, and then carefully licked her fork, as well as the plate. She looked up, sent a big smile across the table at Marshal and Lois, and said, "You'll see."

When Sunny climbed up the stairs, she saw Blue curled up on the floor with Tierra lying inside the curve of his body. He was crying. Sunny walked over and patted Blue gently on his shoulder, and then she changed into her flannel pajamas, which sported a colorful pattern of several types of fruit and numerous rabbits. She descended the stairs again to brush her teeth in the cabin's only bathroom. When she went back up to the loft, she saw Blue had fallen asleep, and Tierra had returned to the cabin's ground floor. Sunny opened the window on her side of the room, and crawled into bed with her notebook and a pen. She lost herself in thought for several minutes, and then wrote a poem.

<u>Goodbye, Dear Tierra</u>
You were sick,
We brought you home.
Now you are well,
And it's time for you to go.
Part of you will always be with us.
We wish you a happy life.
We love you.
Goodbye, Dear Tierra.

Sunny leaned over to turn off the lamp on her milk crate nightstand, dropped her head to her pillow, and fell asleep. She awoke a few hours later to the sound of scratching downstairs, at the cabin's front door. Either Tierra or Angus had a need to go outside, and Sunny heard Aunt Lois getting up to open the door. Before the door closed again, though, Sunny heard the howls. At first there was just one voice, deep and low. Then another joined the first, this one with a slightly higher pitch. And then a third, and then Sunny lost count.

"Oh, Tierra," she said softly. "I didn't think it would be so soon."

At the sound of the howling, Blue sat up from his nest on the floor. "Where's Tierra? Where'd she go?" He stood up and stumbled toward the stairs.

Before he could set his foot on the first step, Tierra came bounding back up to the loft, almost knocking Blue over in her haste. She stood in the middle of the room, looked at Blue and Sunny in turn, then tossed her head back and howled. The hair stood up on the back of Blue's neck as Tierra howled in concert with the wolves outside. The chorus lasted for several minutes, and then was over as quickly as it had begun.

At a loss for words, Blue changed into his pajamas and got into bed. Angus climbed the stairs and peered into the room, checking to see if it was safe to enter. He slipped past Tierra and jumped into bed with Sunny. Tierra went back downstairs to take up her usual sleeping position by the front door.

The two children and the dog lay in silence for several moments, the howls still echoing in their heads. "She'll be leaving us soon, you know," Sunny finally said. "They'll take good care of her. They've been waiting for this time."

The next morning, just after sunrise, Sunny opened the front door to let Tierra out. Blue hurried down the stairs to stand in the doorway next to Sunny. Tierra loped off across the gravel driveway, aiming for the trail into the mountains. Just before she disappeared from sight, she stopped and turned back. The wolf looked at Sunny and Blue, and then bounded back down the hill to stand at their feet.

Tierra looked up at Sunny, stared deep into the girl's eyes for several seconds, and then licked her hand. She repeated these gestures with Blue, and then looked toward the kitchen window where Lois stood watching. Finally, with a big wag of her tail, Tierra turned, ran up the trail, and disappeared.

Chapter Eleven
2018

"We won't be traveling in Wolf Time today, Sage. We all need to take a break. It can be pretty hard on the body." It was Sunday morning, and I felt a twinge of disappointment when Issa made his announcement. Even though the merge to witness the loss of Snow had been traumatic and emotionally draining, I'd begun to look forward to my strange travels through time, and, unbeknownst to the wolves, I'd been writing everything down for inclusion in their story.

"Also, Tish and I talked about it last night and decided it would be best if you didn't tell anyone about Wolf Time for now. It needs to be our secret." Issa lay in a patch of sun on the wood floor near the front door. Tish had decided the day before that the futon was the best place in the cabin for wolves, and was enjoying her new found comfort.

"That's fine," I said. "I don't know who I would even be able to tell. Everyone would think I'd gone completely bonkers."

Tish glanced at Issa and raised an eyebrow. *"Bonkers?"* she asked.

"Nuts, crazy, you know, people would think I had lost my mind."

I expected her to ask for a better explanation, so her next words caught me off guard. *"Who's Adam?"* she asked.

"Adam?" I said. "Um, oh, well, he's my boyfriend. How do you know about Adam?" The words spilled out before I remembered. This mind-reading business could be very inconvenient.

"When is he coming here?" asked Tish.

"Well," I said. "I don't know. I was supposed to fly up to Eureka and stay with him to celebrate Christmas and New Year's. I need to call him and tell him I can't come. But I've been stalling because I don't know how to explain the reason for my change of plans."

"It's okay if he comes here," said Issa. *"We will act like ordinary malamutes. Tell him what you told that ranger, that you're caring for us while our owner is out of town."*

"Okay," I said. "I guess that works. What are you going to do today?"

"Hunt," said Tish, licking her lips. *"We can only survive for so long on eggs and sandwiches and the other things you've been feeding us. Not that I don't like your food. I do. It's just, well, you know, we prefer things raw and, when possible, freshly killed."*

"Stay away from roads and buildings while you're out. And don't let anyone see you," I said. "It would be best if you went uphill in that direction." I pointed to the northeast. "Just be careful when you cross the road."

"Will do," said Tish, stepping through the dog door.

"See you in a while," said Issa as he followed Tish's lead.

I welcomed the quiet that descended on the cabin when the wolves left, but was surprised to feel a twinge of loneliness. I was growing accustomed to having them around. To ease the silence, I pushed a CD into the player and relaxed into the mesmerizing sounds of R. Carlos Nakai and his Native American flute. Reclining on the futon, I promptly fell asleep and slipped into a dream.

I was in a stuffy, windowless basement with a single wooden door set into the far wall. A bare light bulb hung from the ceiling, illuminating the empty space. I walked to the door, pushed it open, and faced a set of stairs leading up. I ascended the stairs and emerged into bright sunlight when I reached the top step. A sawdust path ahead led me into a flower garden. I spotted a stone bench and took a seat. A woman approached from the far end of the garden, passing under an arbor crowned with wisteria in full flower. It was my Grandmother Rose. She carried a broom. It was broken at the midpoint, but was not completely severed. She walked up to me, and without a word or a smile, or any sign of emotion, she handed me the broom. And then I woke up.

I lay on the futon and considered the dream. My maternal Grandmother Rose, as I mentioned, had passed away a few months earlier. She was born on October 31st, and many family members speculated that she was, in fact, a witch. I thought that was funny when I was young because witches were old and wrinkled, and not always very nice, which kind of described my grandmother. But, with the recent turn of events in my life, I wondered if being a witch held greater significance. Had my grandmother just passed me the broom?

I got up and made lunch. The wolves hadn't returned by the time I finished eating, so I took the opportunity to drive down to the village to buy groceries. The cabin was still empty when I got back, and I used the quiet time to do some writing.

I glanced up at the clock several hours later. The wolves had been gone for at least seven hours. I knew it was fruitless to worry, but I did anyway. I ate a small bean and cheese burrito without tasting it, and had just washed my plate when Tish came crashing through the dog door.

"Wow, what a day," she said. *"What a beautiful place this is. And the deer are so easy to catch! After we ate, we took a nap a little ways away from the kill, by a creek."*

Issa stepped inside and looked around. When he spotted me in the kitchen, I noticed his brow appeared furrowed. Wow, I thought, I'm learning to see furrowed brows on wolves; who knew? On the other hand, facial expressions on dogs are easy to read, if one pays attention, so why not wolves, too?

"Did you tell her yet?" asked Issa, looking hard at Tish.

"Um, no. Do I have to?"

"Yes, you do. We're guests here, and I don't think what happened was acceptable."

I held my breath and waited for the bad news.

"Well," Tish said. *"After our little nap, we walked back to the deer carcass, and there was this coyote pulling at it, and well, I chased the coyote away, and, um, caught it, and killed it."* I began to breathe again, and was deeply thankful it had been a coyote and not a park visitor.

"I know wolves kill coyotes," I said. "But the coyotes and other animals around here aren't familiar with wolves, and that gives you an unfair advantage. One coyote is not a big problem, but maybe you could refrain from doing that again?"

"I'll try," said Tish. *"So, what did you do all day?"*

"I've been doing some research and writing, and I found some good information for the book. It's depressing, but important." I picked up a page of my notes. "Listen to this: Since federal endangered species act protections were taken away from wolves, which started happening in 2011, over 6,000 wolves have been killed. And that number doesn't include the ones taken when wolf haters 'shoot, shovel, and shut up.' It also don't include wolves killed by government employees because of conflicts with livestock. Now the U.S. Fish and Wildlife Service is proposing to take wolves off the endangered species list altogether. That's flat wrong. What they need to do is re-list wolves nationwide, and stop this carnage."

Neither of the wolves responded right away, but, as they stared at me, I thought I could see sadness in their amber eyes, underlain by a strong current of anger. Then Issa said, *"Why are they doing this, Sage?"*

"I'm not exactly sure, Issa," I said. "But I'm finding a lot of propaganda out there on the Internet about how terrible wolves are."

"What's propaganda?" asked Tish.

"Information that people spread around," I said. "Information that's often not true, used to support some cause or another. For example, the people who want to kill all the wolves try to convince other people that wolves are dangerous to humans—to make people afraid of wolves. But the facts don't support this. In the last hundred years, I could only find records of two incidents in all of North America, one in 2005 and one in 2010, where wolves supposedly killed a human. Both times were near illegal garbage dumps that attracted wolves, bears, and coyotes. One of the deaths was in Canada, and one was in Alaska. There are no records of wolves killing humans in the lower forty-eight states.

"To put this into context, in North America, since 1990, black and grizzly bears killed eighty-one people, and cougars killed twelve. And in the U.S., domestic dogs kill between twenty and thirty people every year. And, even more telling, hunters kill nearly a hundred people in the U.S. and Canada every year and injure around a thousand. Wild wolves are simply not dangerous to people."

"Humans are weird creatures," said Tish. She curled up near the fire and closed her eyes.

"Thanks for taking the time to find all this information, Sage," said Issa. *"People need to know the truth."*

"You're welcome, Issa. And now I think I'll be off to bed. See you two in the morning." I carefully pulled the screen away from the fireplace, pushed the low burning coals to the back, and stacked three more large oak logs on top of the embers. Since I was now pretty sure the wolves weren't going to eat me, I left the bedroom door ajar to benefit from the heat of the burning wood.

The next bite came while I was sleeping. On his well-padded feet, Issa crept in silently while I slept, and took me away once again. We were inside the wolf den when we landed, lying on the low bench at the far end of the space. I could see young Tish stretched out on the den's dirt floor. Rusty was curled up next to her, while Marley and Harley were both sound asleep just below Issa and me. The puppies were still just babies, maybe a bit older than the last time I'd seen them.

Seeker stood at the southeast-facing entrance of the den, peering out at the forested slopes. Looking past him, I saw the landscape once again covered with several inches of new snow. The dying rays of the sun cast a pearly incandescence over everything.

The air was still. A squirrel chirruped repeatedly from a tall fir not far from the den.

"Where could she be?" Seeker asked. *"Mom's never left us alone for this long before."*

"She'll be back soon," Tish replied. *"She won't leave us alone after dark."*

"Ooooh, I'm so hungry I think my stomach's going to die," whined Rusty. *"I'm afraid Mom's never coming back. I have this really bad feeling."* He sighed and rested his head on his paws.

"What if we have to hunt for ourselves?" Rusty asked a moment later. He snuggled closer to Tish, looking for reassurance.

Issa chewed at his right front paw, where a wild rose thorn was embedded in the large middle pad. I felt a tense knot in his chest.

"I wish Snow were here," Rusty whimpered. *"She was so smart. She'd know what to do."*

"And I wish you'd stop talking about her. It makes me too sad." Tears welled in Tish's eyes, and I saw images flash through Issa's head of Tish and Snow playing tug with a stick and pulling on each other's ears.

Darkness descended quickly. I looked around at all the long faces and wondered where Tierra had gone. *"She went to a pack meeting early this morning,"* Issa answered. *"She said she'd be back before dark."*

I heard a chorus of stomachs growling and felt a gnawing pain run through Issa's body. A minute later, as if by some unspoken agreement, one by one, the puppies stood and stretched, and we all made our way to the landing just outside the den. Issa and I were last to emerge. The sky was a dark canopy of blue velvet, and a bright crescent moon stood like a sentinel in the southern sky. A soft breeze gently played with the furry tips of Issa's ears.

The hungry pups were quiet as they remembered their sister, and I knew they all wondered what was keeping their mom away for so long. They looked at one another in silence, coping with their fear as best they could. After a few more silent minutes, we all filed back into the den and curled up together in a tight ball.

The night passed slowly, but peacefully. Just after sunrise, the puppies stood and stretched, and headed outside to do their business. Accompanying Issa during his morning constitutional was one of the more unusual experiences I'd had so far in Wolf Time, but we'll just leave it at that.

When Issa and I got back to the den, Tish was standing by the entrance. The rest of the family had gathered around their new, self-appointed leader. I wasn't surprised that Tish had stepped up.

"Water and food," she said. *"Those are the two things we can't live without. We've got water close by at the spring, but getting food is going to be harder. I think we should divide up into two groups. One group will look for food, and the other will try to find someone from our pack who can help us."*

"Seeker," Issa said. *"Can you take Harley and Rusty to look for pack mates? Tish and I and Marley can try to find something to eat."* The teams set out on their respective missions, and gathered back at the den about two hours later.

"Well," reported Issa. *"We didn't get anything to eat. We tracked a rabbit for a short distance, but it was too fast, we couldn't keep up. And we weren't able to follow its scent once it crossed the creek."*

"And we didn't find anyone from the pack," said Seeker. *"We saw a solo wolf on the second ridge to the east, and we all howled as loud as we could to get its attention, but it didn't even look our way."*

No one knew what to do next, so we all went back into the den to rest. I could feel the gnawing pain of Issa's empty stomach, and knew the puppies would have to find food soon, or they would starve to death.

"Well," said Seeker, once everyone had settled into their favorite resting places. *"I guess we'll just have to try— "*

His sentence was left hanging as a loud, deep howl rolled across the valley. A few moments later, a full-grown black wolf shoved his head inside the den. *"Hey pups! What's up? Where's your mom?"*

The puppies instantly jumped all over the newcomer, each trying to make contact with him at once, crawling on his back, biting at his legs and neck, and whimpering. *"Uncle Lonestar, she's gone. She left yesterday, early in the morning. We were alone all night. She never came back. We're so hungry. We tried to hunt. Was that you on the ridge?"* All six voices clamored at once.

"Whoa, hold on a minute, one at a time." Lonestar stepped further into the den and gently pushed the cubs back so he could look at them. With a puzzled look, he asked, *"Where's your sister?"*

The pups looked at one another and cast their eyes away from Lonestar, not wanting to talk about Snow. I felt Issa's heart flutter.

"Oh," said Lonestar. *"Okay, I get it. I'm sorry. Maybe you can tell me about it later. First, we need to get you pups fed. I just left part of a deer not far from here. Let's go. Follow me and stay together."*

"Wow," said Rusty, after he'd spent several minutes chewing on a small piece of deer leg. *"I've never been so happy to eat in all my life. I'd rather have it all chewed up soft by Mom first, but this will do."* Everyone ate their fill, and then we made our way back to the den and fell into a deep sleep.

When we emerged from the den later that afternoon, two more adult wolves were resting outside, near the entrance. Lonestar introduced the puppies to their aunties, Cinder and Goldenrod, and then told us he had some bad news.

"Pups, we have to leave this den and travel a long distance. All the wolves in this region, about one hundred and fifty of us, have to go. If we stay here, we're in great danger. The humans want to kill us all. Cinder, Goldie, and I will travel with you."

"Where are we going?" asked Rusty, at the end of a mighty yawn. *"Shouldn't we wait for Mom? She'll be back soon, I think."*

"Rusty, my friend, we have to move south. We have many miles to go, to a place called the Yellow Stone, which will be our new home," Lonestar said.

"But will Mom know where to find us? I guess she will, because she's a great tracker. But I still think it's better if we wait for her. You guys can go on ahead. I'll wait for her, and then we'll catch up with you," Rusty looked up at Lonestar for approval of this plan.

Lonestar dropped his head. Judging from the way the other pups kept silent, they already knew what he was about to say.

"Rusty, I'm afraid your mom isn't coming back," said Lonestar. *"I'm sorry. We all left the rendezvous site at the same time. If she were alive, she'd be here by now."*

"Well, maybe she's sick or hurt and can't get back. Maybe we need to go look for her." Rusty stared up at Lonestar with wide, bright eyes.

"Okay, I guess I need to tell you all of it." Lonestar said. *"Cinder and Goldie went all the way back to the rendezvous site and tracked your mom's scent out from there. Just this side of a large lake they found the place where her life ended."*

Cinder delivered the next piece. *"This is so hard."* She stood for a minute and turned her head to the sky, as if searching for the right words. She ended up taking the direct approach. *"We figure she must have been shot, because there was no evidence of traps or snares. We followed the trail of her blood down the hill, and then we saw where she had passed. There was no sign of her body, and we could smell human and see boot tracks. They took her body. But, pups, remember, her spirit is strong, and she will be with us always."*

I felt a long, deep shudder start in Issa's chest and ripple out to the end of his nose, the tip of his tail, and all four feet. It felt as if his heart collapsed, became smaller. He looked at Lonestar, and then at each of his other siblings and pack members.

Rusty stared at Lonestar for several minutes. Then the pup tipped his head back as far as he could and let out a long, quivering howl. Before Rusty's lament ended, the other wolves raised their muzzles to the sky and let loose with disconsolate howls of their own.

Five minutes later, we were moving south at a steady trot through slushy snow, our bodies warmed by the climbing sun. We were heading for the land called the Yellow Stone, where wolves were supposed to be safe.

Chapter Twelve
2011

"I like it here, Blue. Don't you?" Sunny untied the lead rope and led Rowdy, a shaggy blue roan gelding, from the hitching rail to the corral fence. She steadfastly refused to employ the wooden mounting block, which most of the dudes needed, and all the wranglers took great pains to avoid. At 4'10" tall, Sunny couldn't quite stretch her foot up to the stirrup to climb into the saddle on the 15-hand-tall gelding. So, she led her willing mount up to the fence and touched his right hip gently to urge him to step closer to the rails. She climbed to the top rail, slipped her foot into the stirrup, and threw her leg over Rowdy's rump, sliding easily into the saddle.

It was almost the end of June. Sunny, Blue, and Lois had arrived at the Lazy G a week earlier, after packing up their belongings and giving the old cabin a thorough cleaning. The day after they arrived, the Lazy G ranch foreman, Bobby Reed, had given each of them a horse to ride and care for. Blue and Sunny had ridden out every day since then, exploring the ranch and adjacent national forest lands.

"Oh, it's okay here, I guess," said Blue, as he swung into the saddle on Barberry, a sorrel mare with four bright white socks and a shiny flaxen mane and tail. She switched her tail and tossed her head, sensing her rider's mood.

"What's wrong, Blue?" asked Sunny. "It's nice here. The people are friendly, we have our own horses, and it's so beautiful." She swung her arms wide, taking in the broad view of emerald green pastures flanked by massive, snow-capped mountains. Rowdy turned his head around to look at his passenger, as if to determine if anything more than standing still was required of him at the moment.

"Oh," said Blue. "There's nothing really wrong, I guess. I just miss our old place. And I miss Tierra." Even though the wolf had not been part of his life for almost eight months, Blue still thought about her almost every day. He had hoped she and her pack would return to their old den site, and that they all would be reunited, but he hadn't seen any sign of the wolves after Tierra rejoined her pack the previous October.

"We've all moved on, Blue," Sunny said. "You and me and Aunt Lois and Uncle Marshal. And Tierra and her pack, too. It wasn't safe for them to go back to their old den after that new sheepherder moved in. They had to go higher up into the mountains."

Blue stared hard at Sunny. Even though she'd been doing it for years, it was still unsettling when she read his thoughts.

"There are wolves here, too, you know," she said.

"How do you know that? I haven't seen any." As soon as Blue asked the question, he realized it wasn't worth asking. Sunny knew all kinds of things about which normal people didn't have a clue.

"I hear them at night sometimes," Sunny said. "They sing to the moon and stars."

"How come I haven't heard them?" asked Blue, who was by far the lightest sleeper in the family. Then it occurred to him: the strange click.

When they arrived at the Lazy G, Sunny and Blue were thrilled to learn they would each have their own rooms. Part of Uncle Marshal's employment package included use of a spacious four bedroom log cabin. Sunny's room was downstairs, across the hall from the mudroom, which had a door that led outside. Blue's space was upstairs, right above Sunny's room. Several times since they'd moved in, he'd been awakened when he heard Sunny get up in the middle of the night. He'd thought she was just using the bathroom, but several times he'd heard a funny click before he drifted off to sleep again.

That night Blue kept himself awake by reading *Stuart Little* for the fourth time. He was determined to find out if his hunch about the clicking was correct. Sure enough, at about 12:10 a.m., he heard the unmistakable sound of a door latch. He descended the stairs and tiptoed to the laundry room, shushing Angus when the dog tried to follow him. Blue peered into Sunny's room—empty. He crossed the hall to the mud room and stepped outside into a night lit by an almost full moon. Sunny was heading across the parking area toward the main barn. He barely heard the crunch of her feet on the gravel over the serenade of cicadas and frogs. Blue tried to be quiet as he tracked her, walking on the outer edges of his boots like Uncle Marshal had taught him, but Sunny's hearing was too acute; she turned back and spotted him before he'd gone ten feet.

"I'm just going to the barn, Blue," she said when he caught up with her. "I like to sleep with the horses. They tell me things. You can come, too, but just this once."

Sunny led Blue to the far end of the barn, and up a ladder to the hay loft. From this vantage point, they had a view of the twelve horses stabled below, including Rowdy and Barberry. The Lazy G was established back in 1896, and had grown haphazardly over time. Numerous barns and sheds were used to house animals and equipment. This structure, the main barn, and Bobby's house were the two oldest buildings on the ranch.

Blue fell asleep in the hay nest Sunny had prepared in one corner of the loft. Several times in the night he woke and saw that Sunny was wide-awake, listening to the horses quietly munching their hay.

About a half hour before the sun had a chance to rise, Sunny shook Blue awake. "Blue, it's time to go back to the house. I don't want them to worry. And I don't want them to know I sleep out here. Please don't tell them."

They climbed down, greeted Rowdy and Barberry with strokes on their velvety noses, and stepped out into the pre-dawn light. Blue was a few steps ahead of Sunny, and as soon as he passed the barn's threshold, he stopped short with a sharp intake of breath.

"Sunny," he turned to her and whispered. "Look!"

Sunny pulled up even with Blue and watched as five leggy, lean wolves—three gray and two black—ambled across the gravel barnyard, headed toward the north pastures.

"Holy crap," said Blue. At his words, all five wolves turned their heads in unison to look at Sunny and Blue. Unconcerned, they turned back and continued on their way.

"Leave this place, brothers and sisters," said Sunny in a low voice. "It's not safe for you to be here." The wolves broke into a trot, ducked below the bottom wire of the pasture fence, and headed toward Snow Creek, which tumbled down from the mountains and kept the north pastures lush.

"Blue," said Sunny. "We must tell no one about these wolves. No one."

Later that day, Blue and Sunny were enlisted to help Bobby and the ranch hands prepare for the first guests of the season, who would arrive the next day. The weekly schedule involved a new group of guests arriving every Monday afternoon, and then departing the following Sunday morning. The only time off between groups was Sunday afternoon and Monday morning.

The first week of dudes flew by, as everyone adjusted to the new schedule. It wasn't until after lunch on Saturday that Blue and Sunny were able to slip away for a ride. The weather was perfect, about 75 degrees, with a light breeze and a few bright white cumulus clouds over the western ridge. They led Rowdy and Barberry out of the barn, mounted up, and headed toward the north pastures and Snow Creek. A full week had passed since they'd seen the wolves near the barn, and Sunny had spent every night since then in the loft. She wouldn't let Blue join her. She told him she needed to be alone, and Blue could almost respect that.

"I hope those wolves cleared out of here," said Blue as they rode through the first pasture gate.

"Me, too. You know, Blue, they're all young. There are no leaders in that pack. Somehow they lost their alphas."

"Does that matter? Won't one of them step up and take charge?"

"I don't know," said Sunny. "But I don't think it works that way. They didn't seem at all scared of us, and they looked pretty skinny."

"All the more reason they'd better steer clear of this place," said Blue. "Even though they don't talk about it, I'd guess everyone here at the ranch, Bobby and them, would be quick to kill a wolf if they saw one hanging around."

When they got back to the ranch, the week's guests were assembling around a cluster of picnic tables set up behind the main barn, and three barbeques were fired up and ready for burgers and hot dogs. The Saturday night barbeque was the last hurrah for the guests, and according to Bobby, the event usually involved consumption of a great deal of alcohol.

"Do you want to go to the barbeque tonight?" Sunny asked as they unsaddled and brushed down the horses.

"I do," said Blue. "I'm already a little tired of the dudes, but I have to beat Carter at horseshoes. It's getting embarrassing. I've lost so many games to him." Carter, the same age as Blue, was Bobby's eldest son, and the two boys were developing a friendship laced with a large dose of good-natured rivalry.

"You always win when you play with me, though," said Sunny.

"Yeah, that's different."

After polishing off his burger and a huge pile of potato chips, Blue wandered over to the horseshoe pit. Sunny stayed behind at the picnic table, slowly finishing her baked potato and a large helping of salad. She and Lois and Marshal were sharing a table with Bobby and his two head wranglers, Keene Stewart and Macklin Rodgers. After filling her plate at the buffet table, Sunny sat down near Keene and immediately regretted it. The man gave off a powerful sour odor, and had a disturbingly pock-marked face. A black mole resided on his chin, just below his lip on the right side. Sunny caught herself staring at the man's face; every time he said something, the mole shifted up and down like a tick that hasn't quite settled into its dog.

Macklin, on the other hand, was the first man Sunny considered cute. His curly black hair twisted down to the collar of his blue plaid western shirt, and every hair in his handlebar moustache was positioned perfectly. Sparkling blue eyes under heavy dark brows finished the picture. He sat at the opposite end of the table from Sunny, which allowed her to adore him without attracting anyone's notice.

"Woohoo! I finally did it! I finally beat Carter!" Everyone's attention was drawn to the horseshoe pits as Blue strutted around in the sand, pointing at the stake where he'd just thrown a ringer.

His victory celebration was short-lived, though, as all eyes turned to a horse and rider loping toward them. Rick Bennett, one of Bobby's wranglers, pulled his flea-bitten gray gelding to a sliding stop just shy of Sunny's table.

"A colt," stammered Rick, out of breath, "at the far end of the northwest pasture." He slipped from his saddle to the ground and bent over at the waist to catch his breath. "I was just checking fence," he panted. "And, and..." He paused for a moment. "I think it was wolves."

As soon as the words were out of his mouth, Bobby, Keene, Macklin, and Marshal were on their feet.

"Keene," said Bobby in a steady voice. "Run up to the house and get the thirty-aught-six and the Winchester. And make sure we have enough rounds."

Keene ran for the house and the other three hurried off toward the main barn. Within five minutes, all four were mounted and riding.

When they returned an hour later, the evening campfire had been lit. Bobby's wife, Cameron, was sitting on one of the benches nearest the fire, strumming her guitar. Most of the guests had stayed in the area, eager to hear what had happened to the colt, and whether or not the men had seen any wolves.

After the horses had been unsaddled and put back in their stalls, Bobby approached the group. "Well," he said. "There's not much to tell. Dusty Legs was killed by something. We won't know for sure what did it until the wildlife guys come take a look. Cami, can you call them and see how fast they can get here?"

Blue cringed when he heard which colt had been killed. He knew the liver chestnut yearling was Bobby's favorite up-and-coming horse. He'd bred his Doc Bar mare, Daylight Dust, to a racing Quarter Horse stud called Legs Like Steel. When that foal was born, Keene said Bobby did a little dance in the foaling stall. He had big plans to start the colt racing as a three-year-old down south at Rock Springs. Blue remembered Bobby's exact words when he'd brought the colt out of the barn to present him to Blue and Sunny: "This time I've got a winner, just you wait and see."

Bobby sat on top of a picnic table and picked up Cami's guitar, slipping right back into his entertain-the-guests persona, starting with a song about an old strawberry roan, and progressing through a few Willie Nelson tunes. The guests settled back down, sitting at the tables and in the row of folding chairs near the fire.

Blue had returned to the horseshoe pit, and Sunny hadn't moved from the picnic table where she'd eaten dinner. Lois watched her niece closely, as she appeared to be in a trance of some sort. Lois attributed Sunny's periodic lapses to the car accident, and perhaps some damage to the girl's brain. She always seemed to snap out of this state with no apparent ill effects, so Lois just accepted it as part of Sunny.

When Marshal, Keene, and Macklin returned to the campfire area, they all sat down at a table behind Sunny. They carried on an animated, but quiet conversation, clearly making an effort to not be heard by the guests sitting closer to Bobby and the fire. Sunny was close enough, though, to hear snippets of the conversation, most of them coming from Keene, who had a distinctive high-pitched voice.

"...the way it used to be."

"...kill all the wolves we see."

"Shoot, shovel, and shut up."

"...four or five packs running around."

Sunny shivered and her concern grew for the five wolves she and Blue had seen—the wolves she thought of as Midnight's Children. It was likely they had killed the colt. Once again she sent mental messages to them to go away, to leave the ranch far behind.

On Sunday morning, while Marshal, Lois, Sunny, and Blue were at breakfast, a white pickup truck with government plates drove past the cabin and up to the main house. Marshal stood and pushed his chair back from the table. "That's probably Wildlife Services. I'd better go see if they need me. Working on a Sunday; they won't be happy about this."

A few minutes later, Blue watched Marshal and Bobby climb into the red Ford ranch truck and lead the two men in the white truck out across the pastures to Dusty Legs' body. By now, Blue figured, lots of different animals had probably eaten off the carcass and it would be a real mess.

By the time the two trucks and their passengers returned to the ranch house, the guests were all assembled in front of the house saying their goodbyes. Bobby and Keene walked up to the group and the white pickup drove out toward the highway, leaving a thin plume of dust in its wake.

"What did they say?" asked Cami. Everyone present seemed eager to learn what had happened.

"I'm not so sure we should—" started Bobby.

"They said the evidence was inconclusive," Keene said with a snarly undertone. He spat a long stream of brown tobacco juice toward the dirt near his feet. "Said they couldn't say for sure that wolves did it, which to me means they aren't any good at their jobs. That colt was killed by wolves, and we're not going to let it happen again."

"That's enough, Keene," said Bobby. "We'll keep an eye out, and if we see any wolves here, I'm sure those fine gentlemen will come out and remove them for us." He turned to his clients. "Folks, it's been a fabulous week. Sorry for the disturbance last night. We hope you all enjoyed your stay and will come back and see us again soon." After a lot of handshakes and a few hugs were exchanged, the guests loaded up and headed for home.

Sunny and Blue lounged around the house for the rest of the morning, and took a short ride in the afternoon. According to The Weather Channel, the high temperature was supposed to reach 85 degrees, prompting the two to ride out to Bishop Creek to look for a swimming hole Carter had told them about. They failed to find the pool, but had a good time cooling off in the creek. On their return trip, they flushed a mama black bear with two small cubs from a dense willow thicket. The horses held their ground, and the bears meandered off with no harm done.

Conversation at dinner that night was limited. Everyone was tired, and the next day was Monday, which meant the arrival of a new group of guests. Sunny and Blue had been hired to work part-time for Bobby. Their main responsibility was to keep the grounds tidy around the barn, the guest cabins, and the common areas like the barbecue site and horseshoe pits.

After taking the last bite of her chocolate sundae, Sunny said, "Uncle Marshal, do you know if it was wolves that killed Dusty Legs?"

"Oh, Sunny," sighed Marshal. "I think we need to accept the Wildlife Service guys' judgment. The colt was real torn up. There were coyote and bear tracks, and even what might have been cougar. Yes, there were wolf tracks, too, but it's critical that we not blame wolves unless we're sure it was wolves that did it. Otherwise we'll just make a mess of things."

After dinner, the family sat down to watch *Jeremiah Johnson*, Marshal's favorite movie. Sunny fell asleep about twenty minutes into the film, and Blue was out at halftime. Marshal turned the TV off, and sent the two kids to bed.

Just after midnight, Sunny crawled out of bed, and walked across the hall and through the mud room. She stepped outside and before she could take two steps toward the barn, the big halogen lights above the barn door flickered and then slowly brightened to full strength. She sat down on the small wooden deck by the cabin, silently waiting and watching. A few minutes later, Keene and Bobby rode out of the barn and turned their horses to the north.

Chapter Thirteen
2018

I slept soundly after Issa and I returned from our travels. When
I awoke the next morning I stayed in bed for quite a while,
thinking about the wolf puppies losing their mom to a hunter,
and their sister to a trapper, and how lucky they were to have
other pack members come to their aid. If not for Lonestar and
the aunties, would the man named Joe have found the puppies?
And what would he have done to them? I shuddered, and hauled
myself out of bed.

The fire from the night before had settled down to a quiet
burn. A red bed of coals glowed under charred remnants of pieces
of my favorite old black oak, which fell the previous spring after
a heavy snow. Issa and Tish were still curled up on the rug. I sat
in the rocking chair near them and said, "I thought a lot about
your book while I lay in bed this morning, and I'm ready to put
everything I can into it. We need to figure out how to get more
people to understand that wolves are people, too." I was surprised

to hear these words slip out of my mouth. Where had they come from? I wasn't used to referring to animals as people, but it seemed like the thing to say.

Issa and Tish both stared at me. I fervently hoped I hadn't insulted them. Tish finally broke the silence. *"That's a bit weird, but if that's how you want to look at it, that's fine. I've never thought of us as 'people,' but maybe it's a useful way to put us on a more equal footing with humans."*

After breakfast, the three of us took a short walk, and then returned to the cabin to work on the story. *"We were on the move for several days after we left our natal den,"* said Issa. *"Our route took us south for many miles, and we had to make wide detours around areas of human development. Lonestar was deathly afraid of people, and kept us completely out of sight."*

"We crossed over a high pass," Tish picked up the story. *"And then headed down a long valley dotted with a few small towns, a lot of cars, and hundreds of cows and sheep. For most of the length of the valley, we stayed to the west of all the buildings and roads, but eventually we had to cross a big highway in order to go farther east, toward the Yellow Stone. Lonestar and the aunties were able to get us rabbits, small deer, and once even an antelope, and they were teaching us to hunt things like mice and gophers. We were all doing pretty well, until—"* Tish broke off.

Issa gave Tish a sharp look when the conversation flagged, and said, *"Sage, do you think you could fill up the water bowl?"*

"Oh, ah, sure," I said, puzzled by his request as I'd filled it earlier that morning.

I stood and stretched my back, picked up the half-full bowl, and went to the kitchen to fill it. As I leaned over to put the bowl back on the floor, I had a strong sense we'd be traveling again soon. Sure enough, Tish's sharp teeth caught my neck and we were off.

When I came to, Tish and I were curled up with Issa next to a large rock. I heard what sounded like a large river, and the rustle of cottonwood leaves from a row of trees not far from our rock. Issa was asleep, as were the rest of the pack members. Rusty was curled up with Goldie, and was snoring softly. All the puppies were quite a bit larger than when I'd last seen them. *"We're in southern Idaho,"* Tish whispered. *"Lonestar's been telling us stories about the Yellow Stone. He said the wolves and the humans have a pact there, and wolves are safe from hunting and trapping."*

The puppies started to stir, and the adult wolves rose to stretch and yawn. Before everyone had come fully awake, the breeze strengthened and shifted and a strong odor suffused the air. It was moist and rich. I felt Tish's mouth fill with saliva.

"What is it, Tish?" I asked.

"It's the smell of birth," she said. *"And newborns."*

The delectable scent quickly penetrated the nostrils of all the drowsy wolves, evoking dreamy images of finding enough food to satisfy their deep hunger. It was the sounds, though, the grunts and soft bleats that co-mingled with the smells that pulled the wolves fully out of sleep and into the new day.

"Wow," Rusty was the first to voice what they were all thinking. *"That smells too good to be true. Let's go find out what it is."* He rose from his bed of conifer needles and cottonwood leaves near the base of a stout tree, and stretched his neck, shoulders and back in one long rippling motion.

Lonestar stood up quickly and shook all over, sending dust and twigs flying. *"Not so fast. Sometimes such good smells can bring trouble."*

I saw an image of Snow struggling to pull free from the leg-hold trap as the memory flashed through Tish's head. Her heart pounded and I tasted the bile that rose in her throat. And then Tish's latent anger shot through her body like a white-hot laser. Through all of her inner turmoil, though, we remained curled up in a ball next to Issa, who waited to take his cue from Lonestar. Both Seeker and Rusty were up on their feet, also watching their uncle.

Marley and Harley, on the other hand, were already up and running toward the smells. The gorgeous black Harley, with his silver-tipped ears and tail, took the lead, but his solid gray streak of a brother was not far behind. These two seemed to me to be the tricksters of the pack. Good-natured and always looking for fun, they were the first to pounce on their siblings, find a butterfly to chase, or grab a stick to play tug-of-war. They reminded me of Fred and George Weasley, the prankster brothers of Harry Potter's close friend, Ron. Of course they would be the first to check out the enticing aromas.

"Boys!" snapped Lonestar. *"Wait! It may not be safe. Let me check it out first."* He leaped over a pile of rocks and a downed log, and took off after the brothers.

"Should we go help?" asked Goldie.

"You go," said Cinder. *"I'll stay here with these guys."*

Goldie loped off after Lonestar and the errant pups. They didn't have far to go, for the source of the smell was only about a quarter of a mile from where the wolves had been slumbering. The carcass lay on the far side of a barbed wire fence.

Marley and Harley had stopped at the fence, and were working out how best to get to the other side of it. The fence was about five feet high and tightly strung.

"We can jump it," said Marley.

"Or squeeze through it." Harley was pushing his head through two of the lower strands when Lonestar and Goldie caught up

with them. By now, the smell of the dead animal was making everyone salivate.

"Quiet," said Lonestar. He tipped his head slightly to one side and listened, trying to determine if it was safe to cross the fence and investigate the carcass. He also sniffed the air for danger, but his nose was no help; he couldn't smell anything beyond the reek of birth and death.

Harley couldn't wait. He pushed his way through the fence, leaving sizable clumps of thick black hair on the barbs, and ran to the carcass. Marley was right on his heels.

"No, wait," Lonestar called. He and Goldie watched as the two pups approached the carcass, and then started pulling pieces of meat from the body. The rest of the pack, unable to wait when food was involved, joined Lonestar and Goldie at the fence.

"Is it safe?" asked Rusty. *"Can we go, too? What is it?"*

"It's a sheep, Rusty," said Lonestar. *"It's an animal that belongs to a human. It just had a baby, that's why it smells so good. The mama may have died while giving birth. And, no, it doesn't feel safe at all."*

"But—" Before Rusty could air his protest, the sound of three gun shots exploded in our ears. Marley was flipped sideways by the force of the first shot. Harley tried to run, but was hit by one of the successive shots. His body rolled head over heels and came to an abrupt stop.

"Run, pups!" barked Lonestar. *"This way. Run for your lives. And don't look back."*

Chapter Fourteen
2011

Sunny was unable to sleep after watching the two men depart. She lay awake in the hay, whispering her prayers to the wolf guardians, pleading for the safety of Midnight's Children.

A strong wind picked up almost immediately after the men rode away, causing the branches of the large cottonwood adjacent to the barn to scrape across the eaves. Intermittent stronger gusts set up high-pitched whistles around the edges of the barn doors. The combination of screeching and whistling flushed a large barn owl past Sunny and out through the open barn doors. A full moon that missed no detail traced its way slowly across the sky.

Several hours passed before the clatter of hooves on gravel alerted Sunny to the men's return. She peered over the edge of the loft and watched Bobby and Keene lead the horses back into the barn. They didn't speak to one another while they hurried to unsaddle and put the horses in their stalls. Bobby threw each gelding a flake of alfalfa, and he and Keene left the barn. Minutes later, Sunny heard the ranch truck's tires spinning on the gravel. Once again, the men were heading north.

As soon as the sound of the truck's engine faded, Sunny climbed down the loft ladder and crossed the barn aisle to the stall where Snip, the brown and white paint gelding that Bobby had been riding, was housed. The big horse raised his mostly white head from the feeder and looked at Sunny with a pair of sky blue eyes. She saw sadness in his look, and a heavy, tight sensation arose in her own chest. She knew the tightness had originated with Snip.

As far back as she could remember, Sunny had been able to communicate with animals in numerous ways. Horses and dogs were the easiest to read. Messages came to her through body language, like the look in Snip's eyes; in pictures or words in her head; or as a direct transference of a physical feeling. As she felt Snip's deep sadness, she recalled a conversation when she'd tried to explain to Blue how she was able to understand the animals.

"I've never thought much about it before," she'd said. "It just sort of happens. I try to clear out my own stuff first. I breathe deep before I get close to the animal, and I find my own feelings and emotions. They all live somewhere in your body, you know. If I'm upset, I look for that feeling. I usually find it right below my ribs. Then, I ask my feelings to go away for a little while, so I can be open to any messages the animal might want to share."

Sunny sighed as Snip's images of wolves and men and guns washed over her, and wordlessly she told the horse she was sorry he had to see such terrible things. She was about to walk over to Keene's horse, Renegade, a sturdy, solid black gelding, when she heard the truck's engine again, and the sound of a gate latch closing. She slipped quickly into Renegade's stall and crouched down, out of sight. The black horse took a moment away from his hay to nuzzle her back.

Sunny listened to the truck roll around to the back of the barn and stop. She eased her way out of the stall and tiptoed to the rear barn door, staying close to the stall walls to keep out of sight. As she peered around the corner of the door, her heart contracted, and she dropped to her knees on the sandy barn aisle in a silent wash of tears. She swiped her eyes with the back of her hand and forced herself to watch the proceedings.

As soon as the men got back in the truck and drove off toward the main house, Sunny, with great effort, climbed back up to the hay loft. She waited until just before dawn to return to the house. After quietly closing her bedroom door, she sat on the floor until she heard movement upstairs, then she climbed the stairs and knocked on Blue's bedroom door. Leaning in close to the door crack, she said quietly, "Blue, it's me. I need to ask you something."

Blue, dressed in blue plaid pajamas, opened the door so Sunny could enter his domain. She rarely spent time up here, and she noticed Blue's posters were not the images of horses and cowboys that had graced the sleeping loft in Idaho. Those had been replaced with posters of pretty blonde cowgirls.

"What is it, Sunny?" Blue asked, rubbing his eyes.

"I was wondering," she said. "Can you look something up for me on Uncle Marshal's computer?"

"Well, I guess so. What do you want to know?"

"I want to know what happens to someone who kills a wolf."

"What do you mean?"

"Like, do they pay a fine, or go to jail?"

Blue stared at Sunny. Her jaw was set and her eyes were puffy and red.

"Yes, I'll look it up," he said finally. "But I don't think I want to know why you're asking."

"Thanks, Blue." Sunny turned to go downstairs. Back in her own room with the door shut, she lay down on the bed and closed her eyes. Although what she'd seen the night before was terrible, she needed to remember every detail: the men pulling five dead wolves, limp and bloody, from the bed of the pickup, stuffing the wolves into large black plastic bags, putting the bags in the storage shed behind the barn, and then rinsing copious amounts of blood from the truck bed, all clearly visible under the open gaze of the big moon.

"How many eggs do you want, Sunny?" Lois used a spatula to turn the bacon in the big cast iron skillet and started breaking eggs into a large blue bowl. Blue and Marshal sat at the table, waiting to eat and working together on a crossword in the morning paper.

"None, thanks," said Sunny. "I don't want anything to eat this morning."

"Are you feeling okay?" asked Lois, looking at Sunny's swollen eyes.

"I'm fine. Just not hungry."

"Okay, let me know if you change your mind," said Lois. "If you're not going to eat, you can get started raking the barnyard. It's a mess out there after that wind last night."

Three hours later, Sunny and Blue finished cleaning up the areas they were responsible for, and were picking up a few remaining pieces of trash near the hitching rails in front of the barn. The next group of dudes was due to arrive that afternoon.

As Blue dropped a bubble gum wrapper and a coke can into the trash bag Sunny was holding, he said, "I went into Uncle Marshal's computer before breakfast, while he was out feeding horses. If you kill an animal that's protected under the federal Endangered Species Act, you can get fined up to $100,000, and serve a year in jail."

Sunny absorbed this information as they walked to the dumpster behind the barbeque pit. "Maybe now you should tell me why you wanted this information," Blue said, as he lifted the lid on the big dumpster.

"I can't tell you yet," said Sunny. She dropped the trash into the bin and turned to face Blue. "I needed to know because I saw something. I think it's best if I don't tell you about it right now. But can you take me to the library this afternoon? Maybe when Aunt Lois goes grocery shopping she could drop us off there."

"Sure, Sunny. Whatever." Blue was curious about what Sunny had seen, but he let it go for the moment and allowed her this convenient change of subject. She could be very stubborn. But she was still bad at secrets. He knew she'd let the story slip if he was patient.

"The guest list for this upcoming week is completely full," said Bobby to the assembled staff right after lunch. "This means there will be thirty people here for us to look after. Blue, if you think you're ready, I'd like to have you ride out with us on Tuesday during the cattle drive, and on Thursday, when we take the guests up for their mountain ride." Bobby glanced over at Marshal, who was seated at the far end of the facility they called the Last Chance Saloon, which doubled as the Lazy G's meeting room. Marshal gave a nod of agreement.

"Okay, then, let's get back to it. They'll be here soon." Keene met Bobby as they were leaving the saloon. The two men exchanged a few quiet words and then both of them looked over at Sunny. For a moment Sunny was afraid they'd seen her in the barn the night before, and she prepared to defend herself.

"Sunny," said Bobby. "You're welcome to join us on the rides this week, too, if you'd like."

Sunny looked at Keene, and then at Bobby, still wondering how much they knew. Keene's face looked tight, and his mole twitched as he sucked hard on the tobacco tucked inside his lower lip.

"Okay," she finally said. "Thank you for asking me."

"It'll be fun, you'll see," said Keene with a chuckle.

As soon as the staff meeting ended, Blue and Sunny rode into town with Lois, who wanted to run her errands before everything closed the next day, in observance of the July 4th holiday. She pulled the Subaru into the library parking lot and said, "Okay, you two, I'll be gone for at least two hours. I need to get groceries, stop at the bank, and mail these books to your Aunt Abby. I'll be back at eleven-thirty. Will that be too long for you?"

"No," Sunny piped up. "That will be just great."

Blue looked at Sunny. He thought she was acting stranger than usual. He knew Sunny loved the library, but something was different today. He shook off his concerns, figuring it was just part of his little sister's unusual character.

Blue and Sunny entered the library together, and in keeping with their usual pattern, they went in separate directions. Blue headed for the young adult science fiction section, while Sunny went off to see if there were any new books about animals.

As soon as Sunny saw Blue settle in at one of the library carrels with a small pile of books, she slipped back out the front door to the street. A dark gray bank of cumulus clouds had amassed rapidly over the mountains, and a strong wind blew Sunny's hair every which way. She crossed the street, walked several blocks, and stopped in front of a large wood building near a plaza that sported large animal sculptures, including a bronze grizzly bear. The building housed a visitor center used by several federal agencies to provide information on the area's parks and forests, as well as the nearby elk refuge, which was managed by the United States Fish and Wildlife Service. Sunny was sure someone in the center would be interested in her story. Fifteen minutes later, Sunny left the center, and the tall, dark-haired woman working at the center's information desk picked up the phone to call her supervisor.

Outside, the storm had moved in. At the precise moment Sunny's feet hit the sidewalk in front of the visitor center, she heard a faint sizzle and then an intense *crack* as lightning struck the top of the bronze grizzly bear's head. The force of the strike threw Sunny to her knees on the cement walkway, and the roar of thunder that followed caused her to crouch down in a fetal position with her hands over her ears. Repeated peals of thunder kept her shivering on the ground for several minutes, and then she was hit by a downpour of cold rain followed by hail the size of peas. When the hail started, she took cover under an awning in front of a nearby art gallery. Within minutes, the storm passed and the clouds overhead broke up to reveal small patches of blue.

Sunny returned to the library before Blue even noticed her absence. She stepped into the restroom and tried to dry her hair with several wads of paper towels, but succeeded only in making a frightful mess of her curls. After leaving the restroom, she pulled an old Nancy Drew mystery from the shelves and found a seat at an unoccupied table, but she was unable to focus on the story.

Promptly at 11:30, Lois walked into the library and tracked down Sunny.

"Hey," Lois whispered. "Are you ready to go?" She took a closer look at her niece and said, "How did you get all wet?"

"Oh, Aunt Lois," said Sunny. "I'm sorry. I just had to go outside when the storm came, to watch and listen." Sunny was not a good liar; she felt a wave of stress and guilt as soon as the words left her mouth. Luckily, Blue joined them before she broke down and confessed all.

The three of them returned to the Lazy G and ate a quick supper of sandwiches, chips, and root beer. Blue headed upstairs to his room with his new stack of library books, and Sunny took off to the creek with Angus. A half hour later, Sunny returned to the house and went up to find Blue.

"Blue," she said through his open door. "The new dudes are here. Do you want to go out and watch them meet their horses?"

"In a few minutes," said Blue, without looking up from his book. "Let me finish this chapter."

When they got to the corrals, a deeply tanned blond boy who looked close to Blue's age was in the arena talking to another boy who could have been his identical twin, except the second boy looked several years younger. The older boy was mounted on Gameboy, a black and white paint gelding known for his cranky disposition. "Watch this," the boy said as he lifted his legs far away from Gameboy's belly, and then slammed them down on the horse's sides with a loud smack. The gelding leaped forward. The offensive rider was thrown way back in the saddle, but didn't lose his grip on Gameboy's mane.

"You might want to tone that down a bit, Jamie," said Bobby, who watched from the far end of the arena. "If you want to stay on, that is."

Sunny and Blue leaned up against the arena fence, appreciating the live entertainment. A group of five boys belonging to two families were all trying to be the center of attention, while their parents struggled to climb into their saddles. Two of the boys had already fallen off, much to their cohorts' amusement.

"Those wild boys are like Midnight's Children," said Sunny. "Blue, do you remember when I told you those wolves were all young?" Sunny's voice rose in pitch, but lowered in volume, so Blue had to lean in close to hear what she was saying. "They were all boys, all just two years old. That's why they killed Dusty Legs, because they didn't know any better. Someone killed their parents and they had no one to teach them how or what to hunt. They had to fend for themselves. That's what they do, Blue. They do whatever they need to do to survive, and if that means killing a horse, then that's what they do."

"Wait, Sunny," said Blue. "What do you mean they *were* young? And how do you know they killed Dusty Legs? I thought the Wildlife Services guys said they couldn't be sure."

"Oh, Blue. Those beautiful young wolves are all dead! They're all dead because someone killed their parents. This is wrong, Blue. It's just wrong. This crazy killing has to stop."

Blue stood in silence while he processed Sunny's words. Then he spoke his thoughts, trying to sort out what she was telling him. "So, you think the wolves we saw killed Dusty Legs? And now those wolves are all dead? How do you know this? Who killed them?"

"Blue," said Sunny. "This is a big secret, and you must keep it. It was Keene and Bobby. I saw them come back with the dead wolves. And this morning I told the lady at the elk refuge office all about it."

"Oh, Sunny," said Blue, covering his mouth with his hand. "You didn't."

"I had to, Blue," said Sunny. "It was the right thing to do."

Chapter Fifteen
2018

Tuesday morning was clear and cold. The last of the fluffy cumulus clouds trailed away with the sun's arrival. I stood by the kitchen window with a large mug of tea, and watched a light show produced by the interplay of tree, sun, and snow. Seconds after the sun's rays hit a clump of snow perched on a pine branch, the snow began to melt and lose its hold, falling to the ground in a breathy white cloud. Individual flakes of snow descended slowly in freefall, catching the sun's rays and lighting up like tiny fireflies.

Simultaneously, the sun provided another light show inside the cabin. Beams coming through the living room window illuminated a large citrine sphere on the coffee table. Tish was sitting on the futon, staring at the orb, mesmerized.

"I especially like the rainbows inside," she said. *"Did a human make this? I've never seen anything like it before, except sometimes the way the sun makes little sparkles on the surface of new snow."*

"No," I said. "Nature made it. And then a human shaped it perfectly round and polished it smooth."

"It's fabulous," said Tish. *"I'm glad to see humans can work with the earth to do good things."*

I finished my tea and made my way to the living room floor, where I sat for a moment, and then stretched out on my belly on the rug. I had planned to do my usual yoga routine, but was afraid of what the wolves might think. I decided to start with the downward-facing dog pose, figuring at the very least we would all get a good laugh when I tried to explain.

I raised myself up onto my hands and knees and was ready to push my rear into the air when I felt those now familiar wolf teeth make contact with the back of my neck. Tish was still standing by the golden crystal, so I knew the bite came from Issa.

Once again, I felt myself falling backwards and spiraling down. This time I tried to stay conscious the whole time, to fully experience the transition. When we stopped falling and spinning, I felt myself being squeezed through a small hole, and I noticed a tiny purple gate on the far side of the hole. Then I lost track of myself.

We were running when I emerged from the fuzziness. The snow on the ground was in patches, broken up by fresh, emergent clumps of grass. Scattered cottonwoods were sending forth resinous new leaves, and I heard the splash and gurgle of water somewhere out of sight.

"Hi, Sage," said Issa. *"How did it go? Sorry we have to be off and running so soon, but we're on our way to a kill, and time is of the essence. Uncle Lonestar and the aunties took down an old, crippled bison cow last night and we're all going to feast!"*

"I'm okay." I was unable to say anything more. Running with Issa was without a doubt the most exhilarating experience of my life. In Tish's body, I had felt flexibility and fluidity, and an almost reluctant softness in the way she interfaced with the world. Issa was all about strength and power. He loped easily across broken terrain, around rocks and small trees, and over downed logs. He never broke his stride, never seemed stressed or pressured, or the least bit tired. It felt as if Issa could run like this forever. Mentally, he seemed to be in a mild trance, completely relaxed, yet aware of everything in the landscape: the twitchy nose of a wide-eyed cottontail hiding behind a fallen log, the freshly turned soil near a big boulder where a badger had been digging minutes earlier, and the sudden shift of the wind, which assailed us with the faint, but now familiar, smell of death.

I was acutely aware of Issa's feet as he ran. The large pads on his toes, lined with long, dense fur, cushioned the impact as he touched down with each stride. His feet played with the surface of the ground. It didn't seem to matter that the surface was constantly changing. Issa's flow was seamless whether he was breaking through a light crust over soft spring snow, sliding on patches of invisible ice formed in the shade cast by tree canopies, or being caressed by small patches of soft, new grass.

Through Issa, I was graced with a feeling of connection to the earth I'd never before experienced. I'd been a runner since I was eighteen and had sometimes felt deep rhythm and connection with the land when I ran, but never anything like this: so strong, so fluid, so right. It felt as if Issa and the rabbit, the rocks and the snow, and all the rest, were one connected body. Issa's feet knew the earth, and the earth knew Issa's feet, and their relationship was an ancient one.

"I thought you might like this." Issa's voice pulled me out of my reverie.

"Oh, Issa. You were so right. Thank you."

"This next part might not be as much fun. I'll try to be mindful."

As I heard his words and wondered what was coming, I detected a strong new odor. A shiver ran through Issa's body. It didn't feel like fear, more like a heightened level of awareness. It also didn't feel like it originated in Issa. He turned to look back at the rest of the pack. We were fourth in line, behind Lonestar and the aunts. As I watched the wolves behind us, it seemed as if the new smell created something like an electrical current that ran through all the wolves. I assumed it had started with Lonestar and was quickly relayed to all the other wolves. Everyone slowed simultaneously.

"We must be close to the kill site," said Issa. He pushed his nose into the air and took a slow, deep breath. *"I've smelled dead bison before, but this is different."*

Lonestar stopped, and the rest of the wolves gathered up next to him and followed his gaze. As the puppies' noses took in the scents, their minds worked to process this new, but somehow familiar sensory information. The bison carcass appeared tiny in their field of view. It was still several hundred yards away.

"Bear," said Lonestar, answering everyone's question. *"And she has three cubs."* He paused for a moment and appeared to consider the options.

"Okay," he said finally. *"This isn't what I was expecting, but it could be fun. These are grizzly bears, pups. We don't interact with them very often. More commonly we run across black bears, which are smaller. This big, fat mama bear can run pretty fast, but we're more agile. She'll be testy because of the cubs, so be careful. It might be best*

if you all just watch from a distance, and come in to feed after we've driven her away."

Issa couldn't focus clearly on the bears yet, but I detected movement on the far side and on each end of the bison. Every once in a while the dead animal itself would move, which was kind of creepy.

We crept forward a few dozen feet. I could see that the bison's back was to us, and the massive, chocolate-brown mother bear was sprawled out on her belly on the far side of the carcass. Her head and shoulders were inside the dead bison's body cavity, so when the big bear moved her head, the carcass moved, too. The three small cubs were settled in at different places around the bison, pulling at bits of meat from the dead animal's hips and shoulders. The click of teeth, the smack of wet lips, and the crunch of small bones carried well across the level ground as the bears fed. I was surprised by how clearly I could hear the mother bear's soft *chuffing* sounds when she took time out from eating to communicate with her babies. The cubs responded with snorts and high-pitched growls. About twenty feet west of the kill, five ravens and two magpies observed the proceedings from the branches of a dead cottonwood.

As we watched, one cub grew bored with the carcass and darted off toward a small copse of willows in an adjacent draw. The mother bear was on that baby in an instant. She chased it down, turned in front of it to cut off its path, and gently clubbed the baby with a huge forepaw, sending the cub rolling. A few loud grunts convinced the youngster to return quickly to the bison.

"That gives you an idea of how fast she is," said Cinder.

After the mama bear resumed eating, two of the ravens made a bold move and flew down to the bison. As they were about to land on the carcass, the big sow let out a deep growl and swung a paw up to swat them away. They cawed in unison, then leaped up and flew off, landing on the ground a few feet away.

Lonestar, Cinder, and Goldie conferred in low tones, too quietly for me to hear. A moment later, they told us they thought three adults and four young wolves could take on this family of bears.

"Pups," Lonestar directed. *"Stay about fifty feet behind us, and stop when we stop. Don't come any closer until I give you a signal. If the sow makes a serious charge, run away, but don't lose sight of each other. Go back to the place where we slept last night and we'll meet you there."* The three adult wolves trotted off toward the carcass, fanning out to come at the bears from slightly different angles.

"I don't like this one bit," said Rusty. *"That bear is huge. She could eat any one of us in one bite. I'm going last."*

"Oh, no, you're not," said Seeker. *"Lonestar asked me to bring up the rear. You can be second to last. Issa, can you take the lead?"*

So off we went, with Issa maintaining the specified gap between us and the adult wolves. I have to admit I felt the same way Rusty did. I was very uncomfortable getting closer to the bear. It was a grizzly, for heaven's sake, and everyone knew grizzlies were bad tempered.

"It's okay, Sage," said Issa. *"Remember what Tish said when you travelled with her. You've seen me as an adult. I survived this."*

"Oh, right," I said. I was not comforted.

We'd taken no more than a dozen steps toward the bison and the bears when my head, or maybe it was Issa's head, I couldn't tell, felt like it was about to explode. A searing pain started above my eyes and shot over the top of my head and down the back of my neck.

Issa felt it, too. He shook his head hard, then sat down on his haunches and dropped the rest of his body to the ground. *"It's* the bear. She's trying to pull you away from me," he said. *"I forgot to tell you this might happen. A lot of the animals want to merge with humans. They want their stories to be heard, too. You need to keep your focus completely on me. And whatever you do, don't look her in the eyes. We'll be okay once she knows you're not interested. You're not, are you?"*

"No, of course not," I said, even though I was.

Issa's body shook slightly as he laughed. *"You can't fool me, Sage. I can sense your every thought and emotion. Of course you're interested in grizzly bears, everyone is. They're remarkable creatures, so strong and beautiful; perhaps the most fearless animals of all. But now isn't the time for you to enter their world. It would be far too dangerous. As long as you don't make eye contact with her, we should be okay. And don't look into the eyes of her cubs, either; she could pull you in through their bodies."*

Issa got back on his feet and I brought my full attention back to him and to the progress of the adult wolves. They had stopped on open grassland about fifty feet from the carcass. The bears were still eating as if nothing were amiss. The sow brought her head up periodically to chart the position of the wolves, but appeared unfazed by their presence. Lonestar consulted once again with the aunties, and then he headed straight for the carcass. Cinder and Goldie loped out to his left and right sides, keeping gaps of about fifteen feet between each of them.

When the wolves were about thirty feet from the dead bison, the mama bear's head flew up. She pulled her huge body away from the carcass and charged at Lonestar, bellowing her fury. Lonestar leaped sideways and loped away from the big bear, which then darted toward Cinder. She, too, easily evaded the bear. As the grizzly took off after Cinder, intending to send a clear message to all three wolves to back off, Goldie took the opportunity to race toward the carcass, barking and snapping her jaws as she ran. The bear cubs didn't move away from the bison. They stopped feeding and watched their mom fending off the wolves. I felt a pang of sympathy for the little bears. They had no sense of what could happen to them if their mom was hurt or killed.

"Don't go there, Sage," said Issa. *"They'll be okay."*

Goldie had almost reached the closest cub when the angry mama bear caught up with the female wolf and clubbed her hard across the hindquarters. Goldie yelped in pain and hobbled back toward Lonestar, while the sow quickly rounded up her cubs and chased them away from the bison.

At a nod from Lonestar, we ran to join the adults at the carcass. As we got closer to the dead bison, my mind recoiled. I wasn't sure I could stand the smell: a mix of rotting flesh, feces, and old blood. I felt Issa's eyes water and his stomach clench, and I realized my reactions were causing him discomfort. *"Relax into my senses, Sage, and your perspective will shift."* I focused on inhabiting Issa, and the foul odor dissipated immediately, replaced by an aroma that made my mouth water.

After all that work, we were dismayed to discover the bears had eaten most of the meat, but we spent the next half hour scavenging the remaining morsels. Although there wasn't much left, this was the puppies' first taste of bison, and everyone managed to get a few bites. Once we got what we could, we left the remnants to the ravens and magpies and took off at a trot, heading south. I took a good look around for the first time since Issa and I had merged. We were on the west side of a wide river valley, and the sun was about to drop down behind a tall range of snow-capped mountains.

"This is the Yellow Stone River, Sage," said Issa. "We aren't in the national park yet. We have to travel through a place called Gardiner first, but I think we're pretty close."

We stopped to rest near a dense patch of sagebrush not far from the river's edge. All the pups were exhausted from the adventure, and were content to lie down for a snooze. Before anyone could drift off, though, Lonestar took the opportunity to further our education.

"I suspect those bears had been eating off that bison for a while, or the mama wouldn't have given up so easily," he said. "Grizzlies usually beat out wolves when it comes to a challenge over food. They're extremely strong, fast, and willful. They're nearly fearless, except when it comes to humans, of course. If they're surprised or provoked, though, they will take on a human. Just like all the rest of us four-leggeds, a bear can't win a fight against guns or big traps, but an unarmed human is another story. From what I understand, the bears hold no malice toward humans, and won't go looking for a fight. Wolves are the same. In fact, most of us go to great lengths to avoid humans, partly because for such a long time so many of them have wanted all of us dead. Sadly, many of them still do."

"Why do they want us dead?" asked Rusty.

"Sometimes it's because we occasionally kill and eat their cows and sheep, like you saw with your brothers. They didn't kill that sheep, but the sheep owner didn't know that." Lonestar stopped for a moment. I was sure he hoped the terrifying memory would keep these pups away from livestock forever.

"They also don't like it when we kill and eat deer and elk and other animals that wolves have eaten forever. They're angry because they want to kill the deer and elk, even though they really don't need them to survive like we do. And sometimes they kill us just because they hate us."

"Why do they hate us?" asked Tish.

At this, Goldie leaped up and chimed in. *"They hate us because we're still wild and free, still strong and beautiful, and they aren't. They can't control us, and that terrifies them. The stories of how humans have treated wolves are truly horrific."*

"Goldie," said Lonestar. *"Do you think this is necessary? I mean—"*

"Yes, I do," Goldie continued. *"These pups need to know how humans have treated wolves. We mustn't forget. One day I hope for reconciliation, but we can't ever forget. In the past, humans would catch a wolf with ropes and then pull it apart, limb by limb. They'd wire wolves' jaws shut, so they'd starve to death slowly. They'd throw gasoline on a wolf and then set it on fire. And the very worst part of all this is, these things are still happening."*

"The humans could kill us all if they wanted to, with their guns, traps, poisons, and helicopters," Lonestar concluded. *"But we belong here as much as the elk and the deer and the wild rose. We belong here as much as the humans do, maybe more. After all, we were here first."*

Everyone settled down for the night with Lonestar and Goldie's words running through their heads. Despite being exhausted, none of the puppies got much sleep.

Chapter Sixteen
2016

"Early the next morning, on the 4th of July, two trucks pulled into the ranch with two sheriffs and three state game wardens. They arrested Keene and Bobby. They even used handcuffs." Blue took a swig of his Coke and waited for a response from his Uncle Scott, who was seated across the table.

It was three days before Christmas. Blue, Sunny, Lois, and Marshal had driven up from Jackson the day before to spend the holiday on the Double M Ranch with Marshal's mom and stepdad. Marshal's brothers, Scott and Grey, as well as Grey's wife, Abby, and their ten-year-old twin boys, Marc and Johnny, also had shown up for the festivities.

Blue's Uncle Scott was Marshal's younger step-brother. Growing up, Scott had split his time between the Double M and his mother's home in Helena, Montana. He'd set out on his own the day he turned eighteen. Scott's independent streak elevated his uncle in Blue's opinion, but even before they'd entered the bar,

Blue had been a little embarrassed. His uncle looked like he'd just stepped off a New York subway train, dressed in brown chinos, a wrinkle-free, long-sleeved white shirt, and dark brown loafers that held no trace of snow, mud, or manure. And his round glasses reminded Blue of a poster of John Lennon he'd seen on eBay. His uncle could not have provided a more stark contrast to Blue's garb of Wrangler jeans, red plaid shirt, and Justin boots.

Blue had not spent much time with this uncle, who lived near Boise, and hadn't seen him at all since the move to Jackson more than five years earlier. The two men were catching up on each other's lives. They'd chosen to occupy a small corner table at Buck's Tavern, a dimly lit, smoke-infused establishment. Located off the main street in downtown Salmon, Buck's was patronized largely by locals. An open doorway behind Scott led to another space that held two well-worn pool tables. A neon Budweiser sign attached to the wall above the front door flashed on and off, while Mary McCaslin crooned Wildcat Kelly's lament through the belly of a jukebox: "*Oh, give me land, lots of land, under starry skies above. Don't fence me in,*" Blue had picked this one; it was his favorite.

"Uncle Marshal about blew a gasket when he found out Sunny had ratted out Bobby and Keene to the feds," Blue continued. "He checked the search history on his computer and saw that I had looked up the penalties for killing a wolf. He started to rip into me, until Sunny admitted it was her idea. Then Uncle Marshal told Bobby the whole story, and almost got fired."

"Sounds about right," said Scott. "What happened after they got arrested?"

"At first they were told they'd be fined a thousand dollars each, and their hunting privileges would be suspended for a year, and they were supposed to do thirty days in jail. But, in the end, all they had to do was pay two hundred and fifty dollars each."

"That's so wrong!" said Scott. "They would've been in a lot more trouble for poaching a single elk. What's wrong with these enforcement people?"

"A lot of them hate wolves. That's what's wrong with them," Blue said. "I'm sure some of them want to protect wildlife, but others seem to be in cahoots with elk hunters and the local ranchers, who act like they have some sort of divine right to use the land however they see fit."

"Ranchers most certainly do not have a divine right to use this land," declared Scott. "No one has a divine right to use this land. If anyone has such a right, it's the wolves and the other animals that were here first."

Scott's proclamation was loud enough to stop all conversation in the bar. The locals looked around and realized the individual who had brought the room to silence was an out-of-towner. Three men, all nursing beers at separate tables, leaped to their feet.

"What? That is so full of horse crap!"

"That's one of the stupidest things I've ever heard!"

"Where you from, boy, talkin' like that?"

All three sentences erupted simultaneously. Steve Osbourne, owner of the Daylight Five Ranch, took several steps toward Scott and Blue. Another patron, Mac Johnston, who had been silent up to that point, stood up to intercept Steve.

"Take it easy, buddy," said Mac. "It's not worth jail time."

"Are you one of those panty-waist eco-terrorist woof lovers or what? One of those wolf-a-boo trolls? I bet you're one of those lawyery types from New York, or LA, right? You don't know a thing about real wolves." Steve kept talking as he tried to push past Mac, but Mac was the larger of the two men, and he had no trouble keeping Steve in check.

"Nice name-calling. Does it matter where I'm from, if I'm right?" Scott answered. He remained seated and sipped his beer.

"Um, Scott," said Blue. "This probably isn't a good place to go into all of this. Can we talk about it when we get home?"

"No, Blue. This is exactly the right place to go into it." Scott waved to Leroy, the bartender, and said, "A round of drinks on me, please."

Scott's gesture calmed the mood. Everyone returned to their tables and sat down. The low hum of conversation resumed, until a few minutes later, when Scott stood up and made his way to the center of the room and sat down at an unoccupied table. Blue took a deep breath, picked up his glass, and followed his uncle to the new location.

"I have a few questions for you gentlemen, but first I want to introduce myself," Scott said to the crowd. "My name is Scott Allen, step-brother to Marshal and Grey Morrison, both of whom I believe you all know. And I think you know Blue here, as well. It seems to me my nephew and brothers have helped most of you at one time or another in the past—Blue plowing or shoveling snow to spare your backs, and Marshal and Grey trying to keep you honest."

Scott's last words triggered a few grumbled comments that Blue couldn't hear. "And contrary to what you might think," said Scott. "I live just down the road in Boise." As he spoke, Shirley, the cocktail waitress, scurried back and forth between the bar and occupied tables, dispensing the free drinks. She kept her eyes down and said nothing.

"As I said," Scott went on, "I have a lot of questions for you all. I need your help, as I'm trying to learn a thing or two about real wolves." He stared at Steve as he spoke.

The creak of the front door pulled attention away from Scott. A cold blast of air and a swirl of large, fluffy snowflakes spun inside as Marshal stepped through the door. He removed his tan Stetson, shook a layer of snow from the hat, and stamped his boots on the entry mat.

"Evening, everybody. Why's it so quiet in here? Did somebody die and I don't know about it yet? Dang, it's cold out there." As Marshal scanned the bar, he spotted Scott and Blue, and walked over to take a seat at their table, mumbling his hellos as he passed old friends and former neighbors.

"Blue, what are you doing in here?" said Marshal as he sat down. "I thought I told you to stay away from this place." Blue was only eighteen, and Marshal was pretty sure he hadn't started drinking yet. Buck's was rough. The only reason Marshal had stepped inside was because he'd seen Scott's white Toyota Prius outside and was afraid his brother was there to stir up trouble.

"Scott came by the house after you and Aunt Lois left to go shopping, and said he wanted company. Leroy said it was okay. I'm just drinking a Coke." Blue held up his glass. "Did you guys finish the Christmas shopping?"

"It's my fault," said Scott. "I figure if the boy is going to carry on the family tradition of ranching, he might as well learn now that not everybody in these parts sees eye to eye on the subjects of sacred cows and wolves," said Scott with a shrug. "I mean, even you and I don't agree on a lot of what goes on out here."

"I'm not going to carry on the family tradition—" Blue started to clarify things, but was cut short.

"Hey, Marshal, how come we never met this fancy brother of yours?" Steve Osbourne broke the silence with a loud, slightly slurred voice. "Did you know he hates ranchers, and sleeps with wolves?"

"Ease up, Steve," said Mac.

"Actually, Steve," said Scott, "some of my best friends are ranchers. And I do let my dogs sleep on the bed, but so far, no wolves. Tell me, how many animals have you lost to wolves this year?"

"Too many, that's how many. We lost thirteen cows and eight calves, but that new Wildlife Services guy could only verify one of the cows, because the coyotes and what all made such a mess of the rest before anybody could get out there to look at them. And one or two of them may have been hit by lightning." Steve finished his Budweiser and wiped his mouth on his shirtsleeve before waving down Shirley. "But, I know it was wolves that took all those other ones. We hear 'em howling all the time, and see their tracks. It's gotten so the kids can't even play outside and be safe anymore."

"Oh, please, cut the drama," said Scott. "How about you, Mac? How many animals?"

"We only lost one, and that wasn't for sure because the cow may have died before the wolves got to her," said Mac. "But we don't have near as many animals as Steve."

"Have you plugged any of them woofs down in Jackson yet, Marshal?" Steve had switched to Jim Beam on the rocks, and his voice increased in volume again. "We took out half a dozen that was hanging around too close to our place, and we're hoping for lots more. Time to get rid of them all."

Marshal glanced at Blue before he said, "No, Steve, we haven't had any problems at all down south, not since we hired on extra help, and pulled the stock off the pastures that were too far up the mountain. And we started using those big dogs, and they seem to help. There was a colt that was killed, but they weren't sure how it died."

"Well," said Steve. "Don't say I didn't warn you when those four-legged Canadian terrorists take out a few head, and they'll take those dogs and your horses, too, you know. They're nothin' but blood-thirsty killers."

"Oh, give it a rest, you inbred parasite." Too late, Scott realized he'd given voice to his thoughts. Steve was out of his seat like a shot, pitching his chair over backwards. Marshal stood up to block Steve, but he was no match for the red-faced rancher. Blue ducked under the table when he saw Steve grab the front of Scott's shirt. Steve pulled Scott up out of his chair and landed a fist right in the middle of Scott's face.

Scott crumpled and dropped to the floor. Blue looked over at his uncle's face, and then quickly looked away so he wouldn't throw up. Blood streamed from Scott's mouth and nose, staining his crisp, white shirt. His eyes were closed.

"Dammit, Steve," shouted Leroy as he leaned over to check on Scott. "I think you killed him."

Chapter Seventeen
2018

A set of golden sleigh bells attached to a two-inch-wide cracked leather strap jingled as Adam Westin pushed open the door of Carl's Antiques. The shop occupied the bottom floor of an old Victorian, not far from the downtown plaza in the damp college town of Arcata, California. The shop's front window sported a painting of Santa's sleigh, and when he stepped inside, Adam was greeted by Alvin and the Chipmunks' version of *Frosty the Snowman*.

The mingled odors of burnt coffee, mold, and some form of fried pork assailed Adam's nose. Beams cast by the low winter sun slanted through the shop's front window and illuminated a thick coat of dust on every surface. In the far corner of the room, a tan and white Bassett hound sprawled over most of a well-worn, green plaid sofa. The dog lifted his head a few inches to observe the new arrival through rheumy eyes, stood up on the couch, circled twice and then lay back down.

Adam closed the door behind him and stepped farther into the shop, which comprised several connected rooms, all crammed full of a jumble of unorganized goods: rusted animal traps, old branding irons, what looked like a buffalo skull, stacks of books, cases of jewelry, hundreds of dolls of all sizes and shapes, a model train set, at least half a dozen wooden ironing boards, and multiple shelves covered with china, crystal, sterling silver, and a collection of glasses Adam recognized from childhood. His grandmother had been thrilled to get a similar set after collecting the right number of Blue Chip stamps.

During the past three months Adam had walked past this shop dozens of times without ever stopping to check out the wares. That Christmas Eve morning, though, he was on a mission to find a unique gift for Sage's 35th birthday, which fell on Christmas Day. She was flying up to visit Adam early the next morning, and planned to stay until New Year's Day. Sage preferred to fly on the holidays, as flights tended to be less crowded. Adam, on the other hand, hated traveling on Christmas; he felt both Christmas Eve and Christmas Day were sacred and should be spent at home with family.

As he wandered through the shop, Adam realized he was anxious about Sage's visit. They hadn't seen each other for almost two months, not since the funerals for Sage's mom and grandmother. And the last time they'd been together, Adam had told Sage he'd forgiven her, still loved her, and wanted more than anything to be with her. Her reaction to the declaration had been mixed. He was afraid he'd gotten ahead of himself again; she may not have been ready to hear all that. Adam had put the whole thing with Marlowe behind him, but he wasn't sure if the same was true for Sage.

"She's a big one, ain't she?"

Adam jumped as though he'd been shot. Lost in reverie over Sage, he hadn't seen the old man step into the room. Clearly, the proprietor was not talking about Sage, so Adam looked up to determine the identity of the "big one." His eyes widened. The pelt of a gray wolf—at least six feet long from the nose to the tip of the tail—hung by its jowls from a large brass hook affixed to the ceiling.

"Ah, yeah, big," Adam stammered.

"Got her from a guy from Idaho, said he took her up there in the Rockies somewhere. Course I don't know anything about wolves, just kinda liked the skin. It's just got one little flaw—the tip of the left ear, the one that's half white, looks like it got bit off or something, but I think that makes it more interesting."

The man was skeleton-thin, clad in a red and white plaid flannel shirt tucked into tightly belted blue jeans. He reminded Adam of the Loony Tunes character Yosemite Sam, complete with drooping handlebar moustache.

"It's been here too long. I'm asking four hundred. Make me an offer?" The man reached for a pack of Marlboros that sat on the cluttered desk at the center of the room's far wall.

"Um, I don't think so, but thanks." Adam turned and walked out of the shop, stunned by what he'd just experienced. While he'd pretended to be attentive to the shop owner, Adam had the strangest feeling that the spirit of the wolf that once occupied the pelt was speaking to him. It was as if she were pleading with him to get her out of that dreadful place.

He walked a short distance down the block and ducked into a café called Lucy's. He sat down at an unoccupied booth with a red vinyl seat laced with numerous cracks. A young waitress with small gold rings at the outermost reaches of each eyebrow walked over and handed him a menu. "I'll be right back," she said.

"I just want coffee, please," Adam said to her retreating back.

While he sipped the acidic, slightly burned brew, Adam kept hearing the wolf's voice: *"Please take me away. I can't take this place a moment longer. Take me away so my soul can fly free."*

He drank the last sip from his cup, put two dollars on the table, and left. Retracing his steps, Adam found himself at the door of Carl's shop once again. When he left the building this time, he was carrying a heavy wolf pelt over his left shoulder.

The red light on his answering machine was flashing when Adam stepped into the small rental house that served as home. He carefully laid the wolf on an overstuffed blue recliner and pushed the play button.

"Hey, Adam. It's me. I'm really sorry, but I'm not going to be able to come visit you after all. Something's come up." Adam's heart sank into his boots. Based on the succession of his past failed relationships with women, Sage's words couldn't be a good omen.

"I can't really talk about it on the phone," Sage's message continued. "I'm fine. Everything's okay. But can you come here instead? I'll call you later. Bye."

Adam's sigh of relief could be heard in the next county. Flying to Sage's posed no problem. One of the best parts of his year-long sabbatical was the luxury of a flexible schedule. It would be expensive, but, hey it was Christmas. He was so curious about Sage's cryptic message, though, that he couldn't wait for her to call. He picked up the phone and dialed.

"Hi, this is Sage," said the recorded message. "I can't come to the phone right now, leave me your number and I'll call you back." Adam left a message telling Sage to call as soon as possible. He slipped his feet out of his boots and into a pair of slippers, and walked back to the bedroom, to his computer and the Internet.

"Are you checking any bags?" The line to check in at the Eureka airport was short, which was good, because Adam arrived at the counter with little time to spare before his mid-afternoon flight.

"No, thanks," he said to the young woman as she processed his ticket. "Just carry-ons. But I do have a question." A small duffel bag and a larger sleeping bag stuff sack sat near Adam's feet. He lifted the bulging sack so the woman could see it and said, "There's a wolf pelt in here. Will that be a problem going through security?"

"I don't think so. There are rules about transporting endangered animal parts, but I'm not sure what they are. I guess you'll find out," she laughed as she handed Adam his boarding pass and looked for the next person in line.

The wolf didn't set off any alarms, but one of the security workers hand searched the bag, and gave Adam a strange look as she handed the sack back to him. He sat down in the small waiting area and took a deep breath, his first since leaving the house an hour earlier. Now that he'd stopped moving, he had time to worry about his decision to surprise Sage and arrive unannounced at her cabin. He had to fly through San Francisco, with a layover before his connecting flight left for Fresno. By the time he got to the cabin, it would be almost midnight. He hoped she'd take it in stride.

It was raining when he boarded the small puddle-jumper to San Francisco. Before he sat down in his aisle seat, he placed his duffel under the seat in front of him. As he reached up to push the heavy stuff sack into the overhead bin, the drawstring came loose, and a furry paw with big black claws flopped out of the sack. The woman in the seat across the aisle paled and turned away to look out the window. Adam shrugged, pushed the paw back into the sack, pulled the drawstring tight, and tied it in a sturdy knot before he put the wolf back in the bin. He closed the compartment door firmly and sat down. The flight departed on schedule.

Adam wandered through the airport bookstore during his layover in San Francisco and bought a book on the future of the world once humans were gone. He found a restaurant and ordered a large bowl of steaming clam chowder and a sourdough roll. Sated by his warm meal, he boarded the plane bound for Fresno and immediately fell into a deep sleep.

He awoke with a start when the flight attendant jostled his elbow as she passed by carrying a tray filled with beverages. When he tried to move, he realized his body ached all over. He was shivering, and it felt like someone had stuck a dagger under his right shoulder blade. He'd been deep in a dream. He'd been running downhill, next to a small creek in a snow-covered landscape he didn't recognize. Just before he woke up, he'd heard a soft voice saying, *"Thank you, Adam. I'm almost free now."*

Adam pulled out his cell phone and dialed Sage's number as soon as the plane hit the tarmac in Fresno. He suspected showing up without any warning at all might not be the best idea.

Sage picked up after the first ring. "Hey, Adam," she said. "Did you get my message? I'm sorry, but there was no way I could come up."

"Hi, Sage. I did get your message, and I decided to come down to see you instead."

"Oh, that's great," said Sage, looking at Issa and Tish, who were watching her. "Um...when were you thinking of coming?"

"Well, that's the thing. I'm in Fresno now, and had thought about driving up tonight." Sage didn't answer. Adam was sure she had company, and was equally sure it was some other guy.

"Sage?" he said.

"Um, yeah," Sage said. "That's not the best idea, really, Adam. It's late. I mean, it's great that you're here, but would it be okay if you came up tomorrow morning instead? I've got a turkey defrosting. I was going to save it for New Year's because I thought we'd be in Arcata for Christmas, but since we'll be here, I can cook it up, make some mashed potatoes, you know, a nice Christmas dinner...."

"Okay, I'll see you tomorrow, I guess," said Adam, unable to hide his disappointment. "I'll try to get up there before noon."

Chapter Eighteen
2018

I hung up the phone feeling guilty about making Adam stay in a motel on Christmas Eve, but I wasn't ready to have him at the cabin quite yet. Tish confirmed I'd made the right decision when she said, *"That's good, Sage. Tomorrow is much better. I'm not ready to put on my malamute costume again."*

We'd been working on the book before Adam called. The wolves were telling me about their family's arrival in Yellowstone. We'd been at it for several hours and my fingers were starting to tire. Tish gave me a long look when I shook my hands to release the cramps.

"After we got past Gardiner, Lonestar left us and took off cross-country," Tish said, while Issa got up to stretch and get a drink of water. *"He was following a scent. The rest of us slowly made our way south and east, traveling upstream along the course of the river."*

I flexed my fingers a few more times and resumed typing. Before I could get three words done, though, I felt cold drops of water run down the back of my neck as Issa gently took hold of me again.

We made the transition to Wolf Time in record speed. Once again I saw the small hole and the purple gate. I sensed that I passed through them, but couldn't be sure. For the first time, I wasn't dizzy or disoriented when we landed on a plateau above the river Tish had just mentioned. I recognized the setting immediately. We were near the Yellowstone River, just inside the northern boundary of Yellowstone National Park.

Issa and I were behind the other wolves, but no one was walking single file this time. Cinder and Goldie were side by side in the lead, and the four puppies ambled along behind them in a loose-knit group, taking time to follow enticing smells or look for good sticks to chew. Lonestar was nowhere in sight, apparently still tracking whatever odor had drawn him away from the pack.

A quick flash of movement on the ridge above caused everyone to stop and look up. A large black wolf stood silhouetted on the rocky crest. We stayed still and watched him for several moments.

"It looks like he's alone," Issa said to me. *"But this is a little unusual. He's not running away from us. All the other solo wolves we've run into have taken off immediately."*

Several more seconds passed, and then the black wolf let out three short, sharp barks, and launched himself like a rocket off the ridge and directly down the scree-covered slope. He made a beeline toward Cinder and Goldie.

"Pups!" hissed Cinder. *"Stay back. Leave this to us."*

With tails high in the air, Cinder and Goldie trotted forward in a stiff-legged gait to meet the stranger. Issa's muscles felt tense and he was holding his breath.

"What's the matter?" I asked. "Is this going to be bad?"

"Meeting new wolves is always risky," said Issa. *"In wolf groups, someone is always the leader, the boss, or alpha. Our dad, Redtail, and our mom, Tierra, were the alphas of our group, but since they were both killed, we haven't had a leader. Uncle Lonestar has played the role, but he's not really alpha material. He tends to be quiet, contemplative, and not all that self-confident. He likes to do his own thing. Like when we lost Marley and Harley—if our parents had still been with us, maybe that wouldn't have happened. And now Lonestar's gone when we most need his leadership."*

Cinder and Goldie stopped to face the black wolf when it was about fifteen feet away. We could see now that it was a huge male. His coat was coal black, except for two narrow racing stripes of white that started behind his ears and ran back along both sides of his spine to his tail.

"Oh, my," said Tish. *"He's gorgeous."*

"Shh..." said Issa, giving her a sharp look.

The new wolf took a few more steps toward the aunties, then stopped, dropped his shoulders, and splayed his front feet out to each side. With a furiously wagging tail, he barked again and then ran in big circles around Cinder and Goldie. Issa and the rest of the pups relaxed when they recognized the black wolf's invitation to play.

Within seconds, though, the mood changed. The black wolf focused on Goldie, and lunged in to nip at her shoulders and flanks. She leaped and spun to stay out of range of his sharp teeth, but eventually she was driven to run from him. She ran downhill, toward the river, with the black wolf close on her heels. He was faster. When he caught up to her, Goldie spun around to face him. She held her ground when he sidled up to her and growled. And then it was back to the circle game. The agile male danced around Goldie three more times. With each turn, he nipped

165

lightly at the tip of her tail, touched her muzzle with his nose, and then leaped quickly out of the way when Goldie snarled and snapped. After the third round, he loped back up to the ridgeline where he'd first appeared. He stopped at the crest, turned around, and stared hard at Goldie for several seconds. Then he tipped his muzzle up and serenaded her with a long howl. When he dropped his head, the howl faded to silence, and he turned his back to us and disappeared.

We were all focused on the spot where the black wolf's tail had vanished over the ridge top when Lonestar came running toward us at full speed.

"I saw him," he panted when he pulled up next to Goldie. *"Sorry I wasn't here to help. Are you okay?"* Goldie looked at Lonestar without saying anything, and then turned her head to look back up at the ridge.

"We're fine," answered Cinder. *"His name is Sly."*

Everyone was silent. I sensed all the wolves knew something had changed, but were unsure what that change meant. Goldie glanced at the huddle of pups, and then trotted over to where Cinder was sitting. Goldie rubbed noses with Cinder and licked her face. Cinder stood and the two aunties gave Lonestar and the puppies a long look. After a moment, they turned away and loped up the slope to the top of the ridge, and then they too disappeared.

Chapter Nineteen
2017

"I can't stand it anymore," said Blue. "I have to move away from here as soon as possible."

The morning sun shone through the café window where Blue and Sunny were waiting to be seated for brunch. Sunlight shot through three faceted crystals suspended on the driftwood arms of a mobile, casting rainbows across Sunny's face. It was a Tuesday, the spring equinox. It also was spring break, and the restaurant was busy with Jackson locals as well as late season skiers from out of town.

"I understand," said Sunny, as she pulled out a chair and sat down. "It hurts so much to watch. Summers here are great, but the other seasons, not so much. Can you believe we've been here almost six years?"

"Yes, and this season is my last," said Blue, as he picked at the tines on his fork. "I have to get away."

For as long as he lived, Blue knew he would never forget the shock he and Sunny had experienced right after Labor Day, at the start of their first fall season at the Lazy G. One week after the last dudes had departed, the ugliness began. The place was transformed from a happy, relatively serene dude ranch to a killing field. Blue and Sunny were mortified to learn that the ranch they were learning to call home survived the winter by hosting outfitters and hunting parties, a detail Marshal had failed to share with them ahead of time.

"I can't stay and watch the hunting anymore," said Blue. "I just don't understand people who love to kill things. If they aren't shooting deer and elk, they're killing bears and mountain lions. And the baiting thing really makes me sick. Laying out doughnuts covered with kitchen grease to lure bears in is not hunting. It's pure unethical slaughter. And then there's the trapping, even worse because of how much the animals suffer.

"You know what I read the other day?" Blue went on. "I was doing some research on pronghorn, because it seems like they shoot an awful lot in this state. Last year, hunters killed about forty thousand pronghorn, and that included about seventeen hundred fawns. And they issued licenses to kill even more—over fifty thousand. It's all too depressing, Sunny."

"I know," said Sunny. "I overheard Aunt Lois on the phone yesterday. She told Aunt Abby that when they aren't shooting anything that moves, they're trapping anything with fur. She said maybe there should be a season to trap people who wear fur. And Aunt Lois isn't really against hunting. I think what she hates are the huge numbers of animals that are killed, and the trophy hunting, which is just stupid."

"Hi, Blue. Hi, Sunny." The waitress approached their table with a steaming pot of coffee. "It's great to see you. Did y'all have a good weekend?"

Annie Wilson, tall, blonde, blue-eyed, and in Sunny's opinion, the most beautiful woman in the world, was in Blue's class at school. Sunny knew the two classmates adored each other, but they were both too shy and too afraid of rejection to be the first to admit it.

"We didn't do anything special," answered Sunny. "Just hung out at the ranch. How about you?" Blue stared at his lap and chewed the corner of his lower lip.

"Oh, I had a great time. My whole family got together in Colorado," said Annie. "We rented a big cabin at Breckenridge and did a lot of skiing. Do you want coffee?" She held the pot up and moved it toward Blue's mug.

"Yes, please," said Blue.

"Tea for me, please. Earl Grey," said Sunny.

"You got it." Annie poured the coffee and went off to get Sunny's tea.

Sunny stared silently at Blue for a few moments, and then said, "When are you going to ask her out on a date?"

"What?" said Blue. "Oh, probably never. Why would she want to go out with me? She's beautiful, super smart, and her family has lots of money. I can't match that."

"Yes, you can, Blue. You're—"

"Shh..." muttered Blue, as Annie swept up to their table and set down Sunny's teapot, along with a small plate of lemon slices and a jar of honey. Annie took their brunch orders—huevos rancheros for Sunny and salmon benedict for Blue—and headed back to the kitchen.

"For a long time, maybe even as far back as that first fall here, I've been hoping to leave right after graduation. Go get a job somewhere," said Blue. "And that bar fight with Uncle Scott that Christmas clinched it. When I saw him lying unconscious on the floor, I knew I had to get as far away as possible from both ranching and hunting. I don't think I ever told you, but the bartender thought Uncle Scott was dead. He was lucky to end up with just a broken nose."

"What started the fight, Blue? You never told me the details."

"Well, Uncle Scott basically said ranchers don't have a right to use land however they want to, and then the conversation went right to wolves. Some of the ranchers were calling Uncle Scott names. Then Uncle Scott called one of the ranchers a parasite, and the guy hit him."

"Do you think the argument was really about wolves?" Sunny asked.

"Yes and no. I think it's about wolves because ranchers get mad at wolves for killing their cows and sheep. But other animals, like mountain lions and bears, kill livestock, too, so it's not just about that. I think the wolves are a target for people's anger about a lot of other things. You've heard Uncle Marshal talk about how some of the ranchers complain about government regulations and invasion of private property rights. Because people can't do much to change those other things, I'm pretty sure they take it out on the wolves."

"But that's not fair," said Sunny.

"No, it's not," said Blue.

"So, Blue, when you leave, where do you want to go?"

"Yellowstone," Blue answered immediately. "I want to go to Yellowstone. Maybe get a job in the park and live up in Gardiner. Don't tell Aunt Lois or Uncle Marshal, but I found a job application on the Internet and I've applied to work at Mammoth Hot Springs. Hopefully they'll hire me at one of the restaurants or the gift shop. I like the idea because there's no hunting in the park, and there are wolves."

"Can I come with you?" asked Sunny.

Blue knew Sunny would ask this question. Although he often thought about how great it would be to live all alone, on his own for once, he'd always known it was likely he would be Sunny's lifelong companion, and that was okay. She'd become more socially adept over time, but was still very naïve, which was a constant source of concern for Blue.

"Of course you can," said Blue. "But you'll have to finish school first. Uncle Marshal would never let you drop out, and neither would I."

"Hmm…" said Sunny. "Yes, I know. That's okay. School's easy. I don't mind the classes or the work. But being at school is hard."

Blue's shoulders tightened as he flashed back to afternoons when Sunny would come running down the ranch road from the bus stop, flinging herself into his arms for a hug, telling him how the girls at school wouldn't let her play with them, how they'd called her names. Sunny was the kindest person Blue had ever known, but her peers rarely saw past her unusual inclination to talk to animals, plants, rocks, and herself. And even the girls who could accept this were put off by what Blue called Sunny's lightness of being—her quiet voice, her gentle manner, and her extended periods of silent daydreaming.

Sunny was a freshman, and Blue thought school was getting a little easier for her. Unfortunately, most of her female peers focused almost exclusively on their looks and the opposite sex, while Sunny was still absorbed by the natural world and spent most of her time riding, or wandering around the ranch and up into the mountains. The good news this year, though, was that Sunny had a best friend. Ginger Beatty lived up in Grand Teton National Park, which was quite a few miles from the Lazy G, so the two girls spent most of their time together at school, but this made being on campus easier for Sunny.

Annie came with their meals and they ate mostly in silence. When she returned with their check, Annie asked, "So, Blue, what are you doing this summer? After graduation?"

"Oh, ah, um..." Blue stammered. "I'm going to try to get a job in Yellowstone. But please don't tell anyone yet."

"He wants it to be a surprise," Sunny interjected. "Don't you, Blue?"

"What? Oh, right. A surprise," said Blue.

"Don't worry. I won't breathe a word of it to anyone," Annie winked at Sunny and turned to take care of patrons at an adjacent table.

"Hey! I got the job!" Blue jumped up from the kitchen table, waving his offer letter over Sunny's head. "I'm going to Yellowstone! This is perfect!" He bounced around the table to stand next to Marshal. He must be really happy, thought Sunny. She'd never seen Blue bounce before.

"I graduate in June," Blue went on. "And then I get to move up north to start my new job. Uncle Marshal, check this out!" Blue handed the letter to his uncle, who removed his hat and sat down to read.

"This is great, Blue," said Marshal, handing the letter back to Blue. "When do they want you to start? Not before school's done, I hope."

"Let's see," said Blue, scanning the letter for details. "I don't have to be there until June thirteenth. Graduation's on the third, so I'll have a few days to get ready."

Ten weeks later, under a bright, warm sun, Uncle Marshal was the first to shake Blue's hand after the small graduation ceremony ended. Lois gave him a hug, and Sunny stood up on tiptoes and kissed him on both cheeks.

"Yay, Blue! We did it!" Annie came running toward them, mortar board in one hand and diploma in the other, her shimmering veil of blonde hair trailing behind her. She grabbed Blue up in a big hug and kissed him right on the mouth. A jolt of electricity shot through Blue. When Annie rocked back on her heels and looked at him, he sputtered, "Ah, yeah, we did it."

"Hey," Annie said. "Did you get a job in Yellowstone?"

"I did," said Blue. "I'm going to work at the gift shop in Mammoth."

"Awesome!" said Annie. "And you won't believe this, Blue, but after we talked that day at the café, I decided to apply for a job at Mammoth, too. And I was hired! I'll be waiting tables! We'll be at the same place, Blue. Isn't that great? I also heard that Cori Martin and Rachel Overton, you know, from Chem class, are going to try to get jobs up there, too. How much fun is that?"

Blue's head was in a whirl. He liked Annie a lot, but wondered if he'd be able to focus on the wolves during his free time if Annie was there. He nodded and congratulated her. Sunny, standing between Lois and Marshal, couldn't contain her smile; it spread across her face like a perfect sunrise.

"Well, I gotta run. We're off to the Fairview for lunch. See you soon." Annie hugged Blue again and trotted off across the lawn, weaving her way through clusters of people and rows of white plastic chairs, many of which had been tipped over in the post-ceremony excitement.

"Well," said Lois with a grin. "Won't that be nice for you, Blue? To have someone you know in the park?"

A little over a week later, Blue was selling key chains and postcards at the gift shop in the Mammoth Hot Springs Lodge. By the end of his third day, he began to wonder if he'd made a terrible mistake. He liked interacting with the tourists well enough, and the store had been recently redesigned to promote environmentally sound products, which was great, but Blue was already bored. The visitors asked a lot of questions about the park, many of which Blue could not yet answer, so he was reading and studying in the evenings to learn as much as he could about Yellowstone, and that was good, too. Sadly, though, the question visitors asked most frequently was, "Where are the restrooms?" The important thing, though, was that he was in a place where most of the people were interested in wolves.

On his first day off, Blue rose about two hours before dawn, splashed cold water on his face, and drove up into the park to Mammoth. For at least the hundredth time, he silently thanked Uncle Marshal and Aunt Lois for his graduation present: a 2002 blue Honda Civic. The car was slow on the hills, but he knew what a stretch it had been for his aunt and uncle to buy it for him.

After slowing to a crawl to avoid a herd of twelve elk cows near the campground, Blue entered the developed area at Mammoth and turned east toward the Lamar Valley, where visitors had been reporting frequent wolf sightings. The sun was still well below the horizon. Low, rolling plateaus and the varied shapes of scattered trees and sagebrush were just emerging from the cover of night. As he drove a long straight section of road on the approach to the

Slough Creek Campground turn off, Blue's headlights revealed a line of more than a dozen cars and trucks parked along the south side of the road. He'd found the wolf watchers, the people Sunny called wolfies.

Blue pulled over and parked on the road shoulder, slipped into a light jacket, and grabbed his binoculars. The pre-dawn air was windless, cool, and quiet, except for the murmur of hushed voices and the occasional car door closing. Clusters of people, most standing, but some sitting on folding chairs, were gathered in a short pullout area. Blue made his way to the edge of the group. Everyone was facing southeast, and a row of large spotting scopes and long-lensed cameras on big tripods were aimed in the same direction. Blue noticed a few large ice chests, and saw people drinking hot beverages and snacking on unidentifiable munchies. Every once in a while, someone would walk over to the line of scopes and peer through a viewfinder, and then return to their place in the group to converse in low tones.

Feeling shy and out of place, Blue considered turning around and going home. It was still pretty dark, it was crowded, and these people were strangers. Just as he turned to go back to his car, though, someone said in a quiet, but excited voice, "There they are!"

In unison, the group moved toward the row of scopes and started fiddling with their aim and focus. Scope-less watchers lifted binoculars and panned until they found what they were looking for. "The black is coming down from that ledge to the left of the carcass," whispered a woman wearing a fluffy blue fleece jacket not far from where Blue stood.

"And there are two grays behind him," said someone farther down the line.

Blue moved closer to the outer edge of the pullout to get a better view. He held up his binoculars, strained to identify something in the low light, and saw nothing. He looked again to see where everyone else was focused and tried once more; still nothing. He felt a gentle tap on his shoulder and looked around to see the woman in the blue fleece jacket. "Do you want to look through my scope?" she asked. Flooded with gratitude, Blue nodded and followed her to one of the tripods. "It's trained on the carcass," the woman said quietly. "They'll be there soon."

Blue couldn't identify the almost flat, dark brown spot he was looking at, but he heard someone else in the crowd say "dead bison." And then, suddenly, three wolves came into his view, all moving around and pulling at different parts of the carcass. Blue held his breath so he wouldn't jiggle the spotting scope as he watched the wolves rip flesh from bone. And then there were five wolves, two black and three gray, and someone whispered, "I think it's them—the Antelope Creek Pack."

Blue spent every one of his days off searching for wolves, primarily in the Slough Creek and Lamar Valley areas. He felt lucky to see at least one wolf on each of his forays, but four weeks passed before he saw the Antelope Creek Pack again. That particular day, he was riding along with Robin Winters, a biological technician who worked for the park service. Two days earlier, Robin had offered to take him out, and Blue had been vibrating with excitement ever since. Robin had a radio telemetry antenna and receiver that would allow them to pick up signals emitted from the collars worn by many of the park's wolves. In some ways, Blue felt like using the equipment was cheating, but he knew he'd be much more likely to see wolves this way.

"Last time I saw the Antelope Creek Pack," Blue said, "about a month ago, they were up at the end of a drainage south of the road near the Slough Creek turn off." Blue twisted the lid off of his stainless steel travel mug and held the container under his chin, letting the steam warm his face.

"This group is a bit unusual," said Robin. "We'd really like to know where they came from. They showed up here last fall, and they've stayed together the whole time they've been in the park. We think four of them were sub-adults when they got here. And the larger black male may be a little older than the others. There were two other females with the group when we first spotted them, but they left the pack and hooked up with a solo black male early on. We haven't been able to catch any of them to get more data and fit them with radio collars." Robin took a sip from her coffee cup. Blue had frowned when he'd gotten into Robin's truck and seen her drinking from a disposable cup. Sunny had trained him well; she'd given Blue his travel mug at Christmas the year before.

"The Antelope Creek Pack seems to be everyone's favorite these days," said Robin. "Let's go over to the hill above Slough Creek and check for signals."

By the time they drove back to Mammoth four hours later, Robin and Blue had spotted eight wolves in two different groups, one on Blacktail Plateau and one on the far side of the river in Lamar Valley, but there was no sign of the Antelope Creek Pack.

The next day, Blue was scheduled to work a late shift that started at 11 a.m., so he decided to head out early in the morning one more time to try to find the Antelope Creek Pack. He'd overslept and gotten a later start than the day before. In a hurry to get to Slough Creek, Blue came around a curve too fast and had to slam on the brakes to avoid hitting four huge bison standing in the middle of the road. Blue was shaken by the near miss, but was impatient to get to his destination. He had no choice, though, but to sit and wait for the bison to move. A full ten minutes later the animals wandered off to the north and Blue continued on his way.

Only one other car was parked in the small dirt lot when he finally arrived at Slough Creek. An almost full moon was setting behind the hills to the west, while the sun prepared to climb into the sky. Blue walked up the low hill adjacent to the parking lot to join a lone man seated on a lawn chair next to a tripod and spotting scope.

"You're just in time," said the man. "About five minutes ago, I heard a big round of howling. It sounded like it was coming from that drainage." The man pointed to a sizable gorge that cut into the mountains to the northwest. "Hopefully they'll come down. I'm Rich."

"Hi, Rich. I'm Blue." He reached out to shake the man's large hand.

"There they are," Rich said a few minutes later. He stepped up to the scope and trained it on a spot where the drainage widened as it met the lower valley.

Blue looked through his binoculars, and realized he would be reliant on this man's generosity with the scope to get a good view. The wolves were very far away.

"There's two grays running from right to left along that low ridge," said Rich. "Can you see them?"

"Um, no," said Blue.

"Oh." Rich glanced at Blue and said, "Wait just a minute until they stop. Oh, there's two more, both black. Here, look quick."

"Thanks," said Blue. He stepped up to the scope just in time to see the two black wolves run out of the field of view. He moved back to let Rich readjust the scope.

"It looks like they're coming this way," said Rich. "We may get lucky. No, they're stopping to look at something." He panned the scope to the south. "It's a bison. I wonder if that's the cow that was here day before yesterday. She was lame and looked really old."

Blue was ready to burst. He strained to see something, anything, through his binoculars, to no avail.

"They're going over to check out the bison. No, now they've turned. Yup, here they come!" announced Rich.

Blue finally caught sight of the wolves through his binoculars. He spotted all four and followed them as they came closer, running up and over two small, tree-studded ridges, and then splashing across the narrow arms of the slough. He felt tingly all over when he heard the faint splash of water thrown up by their feet.

"Oops," said Rich. "There goes one of the black ones. It's split from the group and is heading up toward the campground."

Blue kept his focus on the three wolves running toward him. It looked as if they would pass very close to the base of the hill where the men stood. Blue struggled to keep the wolves in view. They were moving fast. As they came close and then loped past him, Blue focused on the black wolf in the lead. Although he would later admit to Sunny that his view was a bit blurry, Blue thought he saw a white patch on the black wolf's right side—in the shape of a six-pointed star.

Chapter Twenty
2018

"Ho, ho, ho and Merry Christmas, Issa and Tish!" The wolves stared at me as if I'd just dropped to Earth from another planet when I paraded out of the bedroom in my white robe, fuzzy slippers, and a furry red-and-white Santa hat.

"Okay," said Tish. *"Whatever."*

"What's Christmas?" asked Issa. *"You were planning to travel a long distance to be with Adam, and now he's coming here to be with you, so it must be something special."*

"It is special to a lot of people." I wondered how I was going to explain the whole messy history of organized religion, Christianity, the birth of Christ, and the co-opting of ancient ceremonies to Issa and Tish when I wasn't sure I really understood a lot of it myself.

"Hmm," I said. "Let me make some tea first, and then I'll explain as best I can." Once fortified with my mug of Earl Grey, I gave Issa and Tish the short version. "Many people believe that an entity called God created the Earth, and that he had a son named Jesus. We celebrate the day Jesus was born, his birthday, every year on Christmas Day, December twenty-fifth."

"*Well,*" said Tish, "*that seems simple enough. Wolves don't celebrate birthdays.*" She was quiet for a moment, and then, catching the subtleties as was her wont, she said, "*You said many people believe in this story, but not everyone does?*"

"No, not everyone," I said. "And, as strange as it may sound, that's one of the biggest reasons humans fight with and kill each other, arguing over who created the earth and how people should live in accordance with that creator's wishes."

"*Wow,*" said Tish. "*Like I said before, humans are way too complicated. Wolves sometimes kill each other if we encroach on each other's territory, but that's mostly about protecting our food and families.*"

"It is complicated," I said. "And pretty stupid. Anyway, back to Christmas. The day means different things to different people. For some, it's an excuse to buy things for themselves and each other, and a chance for people who sell things to make lots of money. For people who are having hard times in their lives, or who have sad memories, Christmas can be depressing. For me, it's a time I like to be with my friends, eat good food together, and listen to music that's particular to Christmas. I often think about the past during Christmas, remembering people I've loved who have died, and the Christmases we spent together when they were alive. And that leads me to feeling grateful for my life." The worst Christmas of my life suddenly flashed into my head, the year of the accident. I felt my eyes glisten and hoped the wolves wouldn't notice.

"*It's important to you,*" said Issa.

"Yes," I said. "It is."

"Merry Christmas, Sage," said Issa.

"Yes," said Tish. *"Merry Christmas. Now, Issa, can we go for a run, please?"*

I watched them depart into a gray, cloud-covered dawn. Another four inches of snow had fallen overnight. The wolves' sedate trot quickly turned into a high speed chase across the snowy meadow, which sent the light, fresh snow flying. Issa had the lead. When Tish caught him halfway across the meadow, he turned to face her and they both reared up on hind legs, batting furiously at one another with their front paws. The mock battle ended with no clear winner, and the two wolves then took turns gently biting at each other's neck ruffs and cheeks, tails held high in gently wagging upturned curls. A moment later, they were trotting side by side toward the road and the forested slopes beyond.

After they disappeared, I looked around at the gravel driveway and dirt road covered in snow and wondered if the roads were open, and if Adam would be able to get through. As if he'd tapped into my thoughts, the phone rang.

"Hi, Sage. Merry Christmas! I wish I were there to give you a hug, but that's going to have to wait. The roads into the park are closed, but the plows are out. They're saying they should have everything opened up by noon. So, I'm guessing it will be about 2:00 or 2:30 before I can get there."

"Merry Christmas, Adam. That's okay, there's no hurry," I said with some relief, still worried about Adam's upcoming meeting with the wolves. We chatted for a few minutes about his flights and the motel he'd found in Oakhurst, and then I said, "Be safe. See you soon."

After I hung up, I took a good long look around the cabin. Muddy paw prints covered most of the wood floor, and a surprising amount of wolf hair had accumulated along the baseboards. I'd been afraid to run the vacuum in the presence of the wolves, so I took advantage of their absence to clean up.

Issa and Tish returned about an hour later, and they were hungry. I told them about Adam's delay while we shared a meal of onion bagels and cream cheese with smoked turkey. After the meal, I put a piece of aluminum foil over the Christmas turkey and set it in the oven to roast.

As I was drying the few plates we had used, Issa said, *"Sage, would you like to try another merge into Wolf Time before Adam gets here? Maybe we could try to do it without the biting part this time. I haven't tried this before, but I was told it's possible."*

"Okay," I said. "I just need to have the energy to make dinner when we're done."

At Issa's direction, I sat cross-legged on the floor. He sat facing me, about eighteen inches away. Our eyes were at almost the same height. *"All you have to do is stare into my eyes and relax,"* Issa said. I did as instructed. After a few seconds, I felt as if I were being pulled right into his eyes. A mild wave of nausea washed over me and then passed, then I was spinning and falling again, as I had during previous merges. Unlike my earlier experiences, though, this time I sensed myself when I landed, and was conscious of squeezing through the hole and approaching the purple gate. I tried to see what was beyond the gate, but the view was concealed by a misty fog.

The scene became clear once I stepped through the gate. It was almost dawn, and Issa and I were loping along a low ridge, west of a series of shallow ponds and connected waterways. There was no snow on the ground. The temperature was probably in the fifties, so I guessed it was summer. Two humans stood on a low hill southeast of our route. Issa ignored them.

I knew right away where we were, but to confirm my bearings, I looked east in search of a large rock outcrop. The formation had caught my attention the first time I'd visited this part of Yellowstone. On subsequent visits I made it a point to pay my respects to this particular place and to the rock, which looked like a large, intricately carved bison. Yes, this was the place.

Two gray wolves and a larger black wolf stood near the hindquarters of the stone bison. I recognized Lonestar and Tish, and thought the smaller gray must be Rusty. When we approached them, they stepped forward to greet us. After the usual exchange of face licks, nips, and growls, Issa asked, *"Hey, where's Seeker?"*

"He's gone up that drainage to the north to check on an elk carcass that may still have a little meat left on it," said Lonestar. At that moment, Seeker came bounding down the hill toward them. He crossed one arm of the slough and flushed a pair of sandhill cranes, who lifted their heavy bodies slowly into the air and chastised Seeker with a series of disgruntled honks.

Seeker joined us near the bison rock and we all greeted each other again. It was as if we hadn't seen one another in months with all the yipping, dancing, and face-licking. *"There nothing left on that elk, but the ravens told me about another kill south of the road,"* said Seeker, once the reunion had been completed.

"Let's go!" said Rusty.

Lonestar and Seeker took the lead as we dropped downhill to a gravel road and turned left. Issa and I brought up the rear. We all broke into a trot on the road, and I noticed one of the humans, a blonde young man, had descended from the hill and was walking along the side of the road. Of the four wolves ahead of us, Lonestar was the only one to take a few seconds to glance at the man. When Issa and I jogged past, I felt the man's eyes on us, and I said, *"Issa, wait. Stop."*

Issa stopped and looked back, and when we made eye contact with the man I felt a small jolt of recognition, but I didn't know if it came from the man, from Issa, or from me. Issa turned back toward the pack and we trotted on, hurrying to catch up.

After we crossed the paved road, Rusty caught up with Seeker and trotted along in tandem with him. Their steps were perfectly synchronized. They looked oddly similar, even though the gray-coated Rusty was a few inches shorter and had a leaner frame than his black brother.

"Issa," I said as we jogged along behind the pair. "I see a strong similarity between Seeker and Rusty. Even though their outward appearance is different, they almost seem like they're the same wolf." I knew my comment sounded weird, but I sensed there was something about the two brothers that was not readily apparent.

"They also seem able to read one another's thoughts," I added.

Despite my speaking in a whisper, and Tish's earlier assurance that others couldn't hear me during a merge, Seeker must have overheard my question. He stopped and turned back to join us. The rest of the group stopped as well and circled around us.

"Hi, Sage," he said. "I know you're with us and I'm glad to finally be able to speak to you directly. I think you're picking up on a few different things. Wolves communicate in a multitude of ways, including telepathically. But beyond that, Rusty and I have spent time together in many different lifetimes. And, although this may not make sense to you yet, we share parts of each other's spirits, or as humans refer to them, souls."

At his words, a rapid succession of memories and visions of my own past lives flooded through my head: exploring the Black Hills, riding a paint horse down into the canyon of the Little Bighorn River, witnessing a massacre in South Dakota. During my shamanic training, we'd done several journeys to explore past lives. Up to this point, though, I hadn't given them much credence. Now I was hearing that animals had past lives, too, which was an even greater stretch for me, due to my training as a scientist.

"I think Sage understands you quite well, Seeker," Issa said, as he saw the mini-dramas unfold in my head as clearly as I did.

"Wow," I said. "I had no idea animals were so similar to humans in that respect. This might take me a while to process."

"Why wouldn't we be the same? We're all part of the same creation. We all came from the same energy source," Rusty joined the conversation, and then brought his left hind leg up to slowly scratch a spot behind his ear.

The sharp squawk of a raven pulled our focus toward a swale to the west. As if summoned by the raven, a large coyote popped its head up above the rim of the swale, no more than a hundred feet from where we stood. As soon as the coyote saw us, it spun away and loped down the draw and back across the paved road. Seconds later, the coyote emerged near the edge of a shallow pond. Without hesitation, it jumped into the water with a huge splash and paddled across the pond, flushing four mallards and a great blue heron. The coyote continued running once it reached the far side of the water.

"Coyote! Let's get him!" cried Rusty as he took off after the smaller canid.

"Leave him be, Rusty." Lonestar called him back. *"We won't be seeing him again anytime soon. And you may want to save your energy. I haven't had a chance to tell you this yet, but we need to move again. The local wolves who claim this territory told me our time is up."*

"What does he mean?" I asked Issa.

"Ever since we left our first home," said Issa, *"we've been traveling near, and sometimes through, territories where other wolf*

packs have already established dominance. In ordinary times this can be dangerous, as wolves vigorously defend their territories from intruders. But all of the wolves understand that we, as a species, are literally under fire, so there has been less territorial aggression. Apparently, though, we are being asked to move on, out of this area."

"We're planning to head south," said Lonestar. *"To a place called Pelican. We'll be leaving tomorrow."*

For the next two days, Issa and I traveled with the pack. The weather was mild, and the pace set by Lonestar was reasonable. On the second day, the young wolves had their first experience with a new type of prey. Lonestar, in the lead, was the first to smell the animal. He stopped and stood stock still. *"Freeze,"* he whispered.

We all stopped, waiting for more information.

"Prey," said Lonestar. *"Moose."*

As soon as he said it, Issa and I spotted the moose calf standing in the shallows at the edge of a wide, slow-moving creek, nibbling on a clump of bright green willows. The dark chocolate-brown animal was about fifty yards away, on the far side of the creek.

Lonestar crept forward a few paces and stepped up onto a large boulder for a better view. He stood completely still and watched the moose for several minutes. He told us later that we had the advantage because the wind was in our favor, carrying our scent away from the calf. As we all watched, the moose moved forward, splashing water around her tan legs, and reached up to browse on a cluster of yellow leaves that hung from a low growing alder branch.

"She's young and hungry, pups," Lonestar finally said. *"See how hollow she looks in the flank? She's probably weak, too. Does anyone hear or smell any other moose? I think she might have lost her mom."*

"No other moose around here," reported Tish, who had the strongest scenting abilities in the group. *"Should we take her down?"*

"It's worth a try," said Lonestar. *"Issa and Tish, I want you two to take the lead."*

"I was afraid you were going to say that," said Tish, who was not overly fond of cold water. In addition to having a great nose, Tish was fast, but not quite as fast as Issa.

"Issa," said Lonestar. *"You'll need to get out in front of her, to head her off and prevent her escape."*

"Let me make eye contact with her first to see what she has to say," said Issa. He crept along the creek bank toward the moose. He hadn't progressed more than ten feet when the moose lifted her head and looked at him. Issa noted her dull, almost lifeless eyes.

"This should be easy," said Issa. *"I think she's ready. Hold on, Sage, this will be fun."*

Issa wasted no time. We trotted out across the creek directly toward the moose, Issa's wide feet slipping on the rocks and cobbles of the riverbed. The water felt numbingly cold to me, but Issa didn't seem to notice. The moose watched us for a moment, then pulled her shoulders up and lurched toward the creek bank. Issa jumped over a small downed log and increased his speed, leaping out of the water in pursuit. At the same time, I saw Tish had crossed the creek, but she'd headed straight across and up the bank, planning to circle around the moose and push her back toward Issa and me.

The moose grunted as she topped out above the creek on a small plateau. She stopped and turned to look back. Too late, the moose realized that Issa and I were right there. Before I could process what was happening, we were attached to the moose's broad velvety muzzle. With a deep squeal of pain, the animal swung her head around. Issa and I were lifted off our feet in a great curving arc, but we managed to hold on while the moose tossed her head up and down and from side to side. I was terrified, and couldn't believe this was a normal and necessary occurrence in the life of a wolf.

"I really hope we get some help here soon," Issa said as he tried to strengthen his grip on the moose's muzzle. And then the moose stumbled and dropped to her knees. From the corner of my eye, I saw Tish had grabbed the moose's left flank. Somehow, though, the moose managed to get back up on her feet, and she kicked out hard to dislodge Tish. Both wolves held on, and we were soon joined by Lonestar, Seeker, and Rusty. After two more strong kicks, one of which barely missed Tish's head, the moose gave up and dropped to the ground. Lonestar quickly moved to her belly to finish the kill.

I was quite relieved when Issa decided to spare me the experience of biting into still warm flesh, and we snapped back to my cabin. Tish was sitting by the fire, just as she had been when we'd left.

Once I had come back to myself and secured a large glass of water, Tish said, *"Pelican Valley was wonderful. Of course, there were already other wolves there, but we managed to stay out of their way. Right after we got there, though, we started hearing stories of wolves being shot as soon as they left the national park. We're just not good at detecting invisible boundaries imposed by humans, such as where park land begins and ends. And this injustice is what convinced Issa and me to make this journey to find you."*

Chapter Twenty-One
2017

It couldn't be him, thought Blue. No way. As he continued to watch, the three wolves stopped near the base of a rock that Blue had noticed the first time he'd visited Slough Creek. The rock looked like a carved statue of a bison. The resemblance was uncanny, and Blue wondered if the bison spirits had put it there to honor their species.

The three wolves milled around the stone bison for a few minutes, and then, simultaneously, they all turned their attention to the west. Another gray wolf was trotting toward them.

"Do you think this is the Antelope Creek Pack, Rich?" asked Blue, even though he was pretty sure it was.

Before Rich could answer, the second black wolf reappeared in the drainage to the north, returning to the group. All five wolves acted as though they hadn't seen each other in months, running together around the bison rock and touching noses, licking faces and smelling rumps, their tails up and wagging furiously all the while.

"This is amazing," said Rich. "Do you know how lucky we are to see all this? Five wolves! And nobody else is here yet. They'll be mad when we tell them about it. I don't know which pack this is. This is my first visit to the park."

At that point, with reluctance, Blue took a desperately needed break and headed for the restroom, which was just south of the car. He descended the hill and turned to walk down the dirt road, which put the wolves behind him. He wasn't worried. He didn't think they'd harm him, but he kept glancing back over his shoulder, just in case.

After their greeting session, the wolves started moving downslope to the south. They, too, decided to use the dirt road. As soon as Blue realized they were coming up behind him, he stepped to the side of the road and turned to face them. They picked up a trot, and, with relief, Blue saw they weren't paying any attention to him at all. The two black wolves were in the lead, followed by the three grays. They passed so close to Blue that he could hear their panting breaths.

When the first black wolf, the one Blue thought might be Lonestar, trotted past, he stared hard at Blue for a few seconds, but did not break stride. The next three wolves acted as though Blue wasn't even there. But the last wolf in line, the gray that had joined the group last, trotted two paces past Blue, then stopped and turned back to look at him. The wolf's amber eyes carried a message, but Blue wasn't sure what it was. There was one thing he was sure of, though—he'd seen those eyes before.

The gray wolf turned away and loped a few easy strides to catch up with the rest of the group.

Just before 8 p.m. that night, right after Blue got home, the phone rang. "Hi, Blue, it's me, Sunny."

"What's wrong?" asked Blue. This was the first time Sunny had called him in the five weeks he'd been in Yellowstone. Something had to be wrong.

"Nothing's wrong, Blue. Everything is right. Did you go wolf watching today?"

"I did. And yesterday, too."

"Did you see any wolves you recognized?" asked Sunny.

"How did you know?" Blue was irked. He'd wanted to tell Sunny he thought he'd seen Lonestar, but she beat him to it.

"Lonestar has a message for you that he asked me to deliver," said Sunny. "About the other wolves he's traveling with."

"I thought it was him!" said Blue. "And a funny thing happened with another one of the wolves, too. It was a gray, and I'm pretty sure it was a male, but its eyes had a look that felt female. He or she looked at me like they knew me. There was something very familiar about this wolf, but I can't pinpoint what it was," said Blue. "What's the message?"

"Well," said Sunny, "part of it is happy, but part of it is sad. Which do you want to hear first, the happy part or the sad part?"

"Oh, come on, Sunny," Blue said. "Just tell me. Okay, tell me the happy part first."

"Those four wolves Lonestar is traveling with are Tierra's puppies!" Sunny sounded gleeful. "They're three years old. There's a big, black one named Seeker, and three grays: Rusty, Issa, and Tish. They were born up near the Frank Church Wilderness, but they had to move south because there was too much hunting and trapping, and they heard Yellowstone was safer. But, Blue, the sad news is Tierra was shot and killed by a hunter when the puppies were very young. The puppies' dad was a big gray named Redtail, but he was shot, too, even before Tierra had the babies. Lonestar, Cinder, and Goldie all took care of the puppies, but now Cinder and Goldie have gone off to form a new pack." Sunny was out of breath by the time she finished her tale.

Blue knew better than to express any doubts about Sunny's otherworldly knowledge, but he struggled to believe everything she was saying. On the other hand, if she wasn't getting her information directly from Lonestar, how could she know how many wolves Blue had seen, or their colors?

"That's amazing, Sunny," he said, deciding, as usual, that most likely everything Sunny said was true. "Somehow I think I knew Tierra was dead. Do you remember that dream I told you about? When was it? About three years ago? I saw her with Aspen and Sister in a high mountain meadow with deep grass and flowers like larkspur and columbine. They were next to a big lake with a cascading waterfall feeding into it. It was the most beautiful place I'd ever seen. I didn't think much about it at the time, but now I guess maybe that was some sort of wolf heaven."

"Thank you for reminding me of that dream," said Sunny. "I will imagine them in that place."

"Now that I think about it, though," said Blue, "there was something odd about the dream. Sister and Aspen were in full color, and very visible, but Tierra was kind of pale, and fuzzy around the edges. What do you think that means?"

"I don't know, Blue," said Sunny. "Maybe she wasn't all there yet."

"Maybe not," said Blue. "Hey, I have some other news. I'll be working here at least until October fifteenth, and maybe longer if they move me over to the general store."

Sunny was silent.

"Sunny, are you still there?"

"Yes, Blue. I'm here. I'm happy for you, but I was hoping you would come back and stay here for a while."

"Are you okay?"

"I'm okay. I just miss you. Well, I gotta go. Aunt Lois needs help with dishes. Love you."

"Love you, too, Sunny," said Blue, wishing with his whole heart that he could be in two places at once. "Bye."

Blue stayed on at the gift shop until mid-October, and gave up the room he'd rented in Gardiner at the end of the month. He returned to the Lazy G, but planned to stay only until he could find another position in one of the parks.

"I want to get back to Yellowstone as soon as I can," he told Sunny as he shuffled the cards for their next hand of gin rummy. Heavy snow had begun to fall around midnight the night before, and now all they could see outside the window was a gauzy curtain of white.

"For the short term, though, I'm thinking about Grand Teton," Blue continued. "I just haven't had time yet to apply."

"That would be good. You'd be closer," said Sunny. "You could even come back here on your days off."

"Honestly, Sunny," said Blue, "I don't think so. But you could come up to see me."

"That would be good. And when you go back to Yellowstone, I would love to visit the park wolves," said Sunny. "I've been thinking a lot about them."

"Well, you need to know, Sunny," said Blue, "the last time I saw the Antelope Creek Pack, about three weeks ago, Issa and Tish weren't with them. I asked Robin about them, and she said they hadn't been seen for several weeks. She hoped they hadn't wandered outside the park and gotten shot."

"I knew they were gone, Blue," said Sunny. "They told me they were leaving. They said they were going to California. I think they will be fine."

"Of course they told you," said Blue with a sigh.

By noon the snow had stopped falling. Late in the afternoon, Sunny and Blue put chains on Blue's car and drove into town in search of a present for Aunt Lois, who would be celebrating her birthday on the tenth of November.

Blue drove, and Sunny talked his ear off. "Blue, I have to tell you, it's just awful what's been happening here. These so-called wildlife managers have really messed things up for the wolves—even worse than for other species that they hunt. Get this: In the northwest part of the state, they're calling wolves Trophy Game Animals. Licenses cost eighteen dollars for residents. A wolf is worth eighteen dollars, Blue, doesn't that make you sick? In most of the rest of the state, about eighty percent of it, wolves are considered Predatory Animals. No license is required, there are no closed seasons, and there's no limit to how many can be killed. And then, this is the dumbest part of all: There's a zone where wolves are Trophy Game Animals from October 15th through the end of February, and Predatory Animals the rest of the year; like somehow they become different animals. This makes no sense."

"That's a great example of why I had to leave," said Blue. "Gardiner isn't perfect, not by a long shot. There are conflicts between ranchers and bison and wolves there, too, but at least I can escape into the park easily."

"You should have seen Keene at breakfast this morning," Sunny went on. "He made me want to throw up." As an assistant cook, Sunny was now an official part of the ranch staff, and she often ate meals in the mess hall with the rest of the employees.

"His exact words were: 'Yee haw and yippee shit! Pretty soon, and then we get to kill as many wolves as we want.' He was almost beside himself with joy, the creep."

Blue was taken aback by this new, more gregarious version of his little sister. Aunt Lois had taken him aside the day after he'd returned from Yellowstone and told him Sunny seemed to be coming out of her shell. Now he'd seen it firsthand. He grinned as he watched her animated face, how she grimaced when she talked about Keene, easily said words like shit, and actually called Keene a creep.

"Oh, I almost forgot to tell you, I wrote a story for you, Blue." Sunny leaned over and pulled several pages of paper out of her fanny pack. "Do you want me to read it to you?"

"Sure," said Blue.

"Okay. It's a revision of Little Red Riding Hood called Large Redneck Camo Ballcap. I wrote it for a class, but no one else thought it was as funny as I did."

Sunny read: *Once upon a time in the middle of a run-down subdivision stood an unremarkable tract home, the residence of an average-looking, middle-aged, overweight man known as Large Redneck Camo Ballcap. One morning, Ballcap's pain-in-the-butt mother shoved him out the front door, saying, "Your Uncle Bob's going hunting tomorrow. Take him this rifle. And be quick about it, I need you to take me to the beauty parlor when you get back."*

As Ballcap walked down the driveway, he said to himself, "Don't worry. I'll gun this quadrunner all the way to Bob's and back without stopping."

Hung over from the party he'd attended the night before, Ballcap made his way through the streets of town, but soon forgot his promise to his mom. I think I'll just pop into Reggie's for a beer, he thought, maybe it will quell this nasty headache.

Ballcap parked the quad and stumbled into the smoky bar. "Bring me a Michelob, Reg. I'm a hurtin' puppy." The beer came in a tall mug, cool, just the way Ballcap liked it. Yummy! Delicious! The beer went down so smoothly, Ballcap decided to have just one more, then be on his way. But a second led to a third. Mmmm.

Suddenly Ballcap remembered his mother, his promise, and the rifle. She was going to be pissed. He stumbled out of the bar to his quad. But, when he turned the ignition key, the vehicle wouldn't start. He looked around the parking lot, scratched his crotch, belched, and with a sigh, returned to the bar for another beer.

Meanwhile, two large amber eyes were spying on the bar from behind an adjacent fence.

Ballcap emerged from the bar twenty minutes later.

"Where are you going, Ballcap, all alone in town?" The voice came out of nowhere.

"I was taking Uncle Bob a rifle, but my rig won't schtart," slurred Ballcap.

When he heard this, the wolf (who was big and black) politely asked, "Does Uncle Bob hunt carnivores?"

"Oh, yesh. Anything that moves." Ballcap climbed into the driver's seat once more and tried to start the quad again. The engine roared to life.

"And Bob is friends with the governor, isn't he?" asked the wolf.

"Sure is," said Ballcap as he pulled away. "Good friends. They're hunting together tomorrow."

"Goodbye, then. Perhaps we'll meet again," said the black wolf without revealing himself. He loped away and thought, I know where Bob lives. I'll get there before Ballcap, eat Bob first, and then lie in wait. After trotting a long distance, the big black wolf spotted Uncle Bob's trailer.

Knock! Knock! The wolf rapped on the door.

"Who's there?" asked Uncle Bob.

"It's me, Large Redneck Camo Ballcap. I've brought you a rifle so you can shoot wolves tomorrow." The wolf was proud of how well he'd disguised his voice.

"Come on in," said Uncle Bob, unaware anything was amiss until the wolf emitted a deep growl. Poor Uncle Bob! The wolf leaped across the room and swallowed Uncle Bob in a single large mouthful, and then put on Uncle Bob's cowboy hat and slipped into the bed. Soon afterward, Large Redneck Camo Ballcap rapped on the door.

"Hey Bob, you awake?" Ballcap called.

Imitating Bob's voice, the big black wolf replied, "Yup, come on in."

Ballcap walked in, but couldn't see anything in the darkness. Once his eyes adjusted to the low light, he said, "Hey Bob, you got any beer?"

"Yeah, in the fridge," said the big black wolf. "Get me one too, would ya?"

"Bud Light!" Ballcap exclaimed as he opened the fridge. "Is this all you've got?"

"Yup, that's it."

"Can I eat this leftover pizza, too?" asked Ballcap.

"If you bring me a piece."

"Okay," said Ballcap as he walked over to the bed. "Stuff your big mouth with…Hey, what's with the Halloween teeth?"

"Payback's a bitch, Ballcap," growled the wolf. He jumped up from the bed and swallowed Ballcap. Then, with a full, fat tummy, he dismantled and destroyed all the guns in the trailer. He sang as he worked, "Loves to eat those fat old hunters, hunters is what I loves to eat. First you bite their swollen heads off, and then you nibble at their stinky feet."

A few minutes later, the governor stopped by the trailer to see Bob. After he'd worked so hard to get wolves removed from the endangered species list, the governor had sworn he'd shoot the first wolf in the state. He and Bob had to plan their strategy for the next day's hunt.

As he approached Bob's trailer, the governor heard someone singing. It seemed to be coming from inside. He peered through the window and saw the big black wolf.

"Holy cow!" cried the governor with glee. "Maybe I don't even have to leave town to bag the first wolf."

Without making a sound, he carefully loaded his gun and opened the door, only to find himself staring down the barrel of a rifle. BANG! The governor was dead.

On a whim, the big black wolf walked out to the governor's truck and opened the camper shell on the back. To his amazement, out popped two gray wolves, safe and unharmed.

"You got here just in time," murmured one of the dazed animals. "We hopped in here when the governor wasn't looking, and planned to leap out and jump on him, but the inside latch to open the camper shell door is broken!"

"It's safe to come out now. We can all go home," the big black wolf said with a huge smile. "The big bad governor is dead and gone, and Wild Earth Justice has filed suit on our behalf, with the support of a whole bunch of other groups."

The two gray wolves yipped with joy and leaped about. And they all lived happily ever after.

"Wow," said Blue, as he pulled into a parking space on the town square. "That's terrific. I love it. Can I share it with Annie?"

"Of course, Blue. I knew you'd like it. Now, I'm thinking we should look for some kitchen things for Aunt Lois. There's a good store about a block from here."

They left the square and spent twenty minutes debating whether Aunt Lois needed a new stainless steel frying pan or a Christmas-themed set of placemats and napkins covered with snowflakes and reindeer. Sunny won out, and the cashier carefully wrapped the table settings. They paid and made their way to the door.

Blue spotted the black wolf as soon as he stepped out of the shop, while he held the door open for Sunny. The animal was tied fast to the roof of a white Ford Explorer, spread-eagle on its stomach, with each paw lashed to a corner of the vehicle's roof rack. Bloody flesh hung down from a gaping wound in the side of the dead animal's neck. A swelling crowd had gathered around the vehicle, which was parked on the west side of the square. Two men stood on the sidewalk and high-fived each other, as if to celebrate this gruesome death. A young woman, holding the hands of two small blond children, leaned over and said something to the boy and girl, and then hurried them past the spectacle.

Blue grabbed Sunny's arm to turn her away from the sight, but she stopped, turned toward the town square, and said, "Isn't our car this way?"

"Oh, Blue," Sunny said when she caught sight of the wolf. "This is wrong. Very wrong." She started to cross the street to get closer, but Blue pulled her back. "C'mon, Sunny. Let's just go home."

Sunny pulled out of his grasp and continued across the street. She pushed through the crowd of about thirty people and made her way to the wolf's head, which hung down over the windshield. Standing on her tiptoes, Sunny reached up to stroke the animal's forehead, while the crowd looked on.

"Hey, girlie girl," said a short, stocky man wearing a Budweiser cap. "You leave him alone, now. He's mine."

It was as if Sunny hadn't heard the man. She took a few steps toward the rear of the Explorer and ran her hands through the hair on the wolf's right side. Blue came to stand next to her and she turned to him, her face hardened into a mask of anger and pain.

"I knew it," she said. "Look."

Blue glanced at the patch of fur between Sunny's two small hands and saw the distinctive white patch—a star with six points.

The silence in the car was as thick as the earth's crust when Blue drove back to the Lazy G. He'd been relieved that Sunny offered no resistance when he took her arm and led her back to the car, half afraid she would do something terrible to the man in the Budweiser cap, the man who'd shot Lonestar. Blue was surprised the black wolf had traveled so far south from Yellowstone.

Picking up his train of thought, Sunny said, "I wonder where Seeker and Rusty are."

The sun set that evening in a blaze of orange and red, which matched Sunny's mood perfectly. She leaned over the kitchen sink to scrub sticky macaroni and cheese residue off Lois' favorite pot, and asked her aunt, "Would it be okay if I borrowed your car for a little while? I'd like to go visit Ginger. Her dog just had puppies."

"No, Sunny," said Lois. "Remember, you just have your learner's permit, so you need to have someone with you when you drive. If you can get Blue to take you over, that's fine, but not alone."

"Okay," said Sunny, "Maybe I'll wait and go another time."

"I'm sure Blue would take you if you asked," said Lois.

"No, that's okay," said Sunny. "I have to get my Civil War paper done anyway. It's due at the end of the week."

"What did you decide to write about?"

"The war horses. The whole thing was awful for them, too."

Sunny dried her hands and wandered upstairs to look for Blue. She found him in his room, sitting behind his small desk.

"What are you doing?" she asked.

"Reading about the wolf reintroduction in Idaho and Yellowstone," said Blue, without looking up.

"Um, Blue," Sunny said. "I need to run an errand in town. Could you possibly drive me?"

"We were just there," said Blue. "What do you need? Can't it wait until tomorrow?"

"Please? I can't drive myself yet; otherwise I wouldn't ask."

"Tell me what for," said Blue, finally turning around to look at Sunny.

Sunny remained quiet, as she tried to decide how to explain. "It's about Lonestar..."

"No, Sunny. We can't. We just can't. That's crazy."

Sunny climbed out of Blue's car and walked toward the large arch made of elk antlers that stood at the corner of the plaza. There was no one in sight; all the saloon patrons were inside. She trotted over to the Ford Explorer, which had not moved since the afternoon.

"Hi, Lonestar," she whispered. "I am so sorry."

She reached up with a large Buck knife and quickly sliced through the rope that held one of the wolf's front paws. She did the same with the three other lashings, and then, with great effort, she pulled the dead wolf off the vehicle and laid him on the ground.

She looked around to be sure no one was watching, and then she tried to stuff the wolf into a large plastic lawn bag. The body had begun to stiffen. Sunny gagged several times, but forced herself to stay with her task. When she'd pushed as much of

Lonestar into the bag as she could, she waved her arms in the air to signal to Blue, who drove up and stopped behind the Explorer. The two of them loaded Lonestar into the back of the Civic and drove off into the night.

Chapter Twenty-Two
2018

The crunch of vehicle tires on snow pulled me out of a deep sleep. After the merge with Issa, I'd stoked the fire, checked the turkey, and then reclined on the futon to wait for Adam. Issa and Tish were out foraging.

I shook my head to dispel the images left over from my dream, in which two very large crocodiles were stretched out on my front porch, trying their best to get inside. It was a great relief to know this time it really was just a dream. A car door slammed outside, and I heard Adam approach the cabin. He knocked, pushed open the front door, and said, "Hello, the house!"

I sat up and caught my breath. My pupils dilated and my heart rate increased. Adam had affected me this way the first time I saw him, and my reaction hadn't changed over time. He stood about six feet tall, had wavy dark brown hair and turquoise blue eyes, and was blessed with a body that was admired by everyone who saw it—male and female alike.

"Hey," I said, stifling a yawn. "You made it. Merry Christmas!"

"Merry Christmas and Happy Birthday, Sage." He leaned over to plant a kiss on my cheek and then turned back to retrieve his two bags from the front deck. "I made it, but it wasn't fun on the roads. Luckily there wasn't much traffic. But boy, is it beautiful up here."

"Nothing better than Yosemite in fresh snow," I said. "The forecast says it's going to snow on and off for at least the next week."

Closing the door behind him, Adam looked around the cabin and sniffed a few times. "Why does it smell like dog in here? Did you bring one of Maggie's pups up from Davis?"

"Um, no," I said, "I'm dog-sitting for a friend. There are two. He said they're Alaskan malamutes. But they kind of look like wolves."

"Really?" said Adam. "That's an interesting coincidence, because guess what's inside this stuff sack?" He picked up the sack, put it on the futon, and worked to untie the drawstring. As he pulled the wolf's head free of the sack and held it up, he said, "It was the weirdest thing, Sage. I..."

"Adam," I cut him off. "We need to take this back to the bedroom. I don't know how the, um, dogs will react to seeing it." I reached around Adam to push the wolf pelt back into the sack.

"Oh, okay," said Adam. "Where are the dogs?"

"They're out," I said, and immediately realized my mistake.

"Loose? In the park?"

"Yeah. I'll explain. Let's get this sack out of sight first."

I picked up the stuff sack and carried it into the bedroom with Adam trailing behind me. I glanced around to find the best hiding place and decided to shove it toward the back of the upper shelf in the closet, well out of reach of the wolves.

"So do you want something to drink?" I asked when we returned to the front room. "Coffee? Tea? A beer?"

"I'd love a beer. Do you have a Guinness? If not, there's a sixer out in the rental car."

"Of course I have Guinness," I said, heading for the kitchen.

As I searched for a church key to open the bottle, the dog door popped open and Tish and Issa walked in, leaving large clumps of wet snow near the door where the opening scraped the slush from their bodies.

Both wolves stopped just inside the door and put their noses in the air, pulling in the new smells of Adam, and, I realized with dismay, the pelt. They sniffed for several seconds, and then Tish walked right up to Adam and looked him in the eye. She didn't say a word.

That morning, I'd told the wolves how important it was that they not talk to Adam unless they wanted him to know the whole story. None of us thought that was a good idea, and we decided to keep the secret for now. So Tish didn't say a word, but she didn't have to. Her eyes roiled with suppressed fury.

Adam stepped backward and held out his hand in a gesture of calm greeting. Tish ignored the hand and walked past Adam into the bedroom, to the closet door, where her nose continued its investigation. She pushed at the door with her right paw, until Issa walked up beside her and pushed her away with his body. The two wolves exchanged looks, and returned to the living room.

"Adam," I said, "this is Issa and Tish."

"Hi, dogs," said Adam. Tish rolled her eyes up to the ceiling in a most dramatic fashion. Adam looked at me, knowing something was different about these dogs, but not quite able to put his finger on what that difference was.

"I'm sorry, Sage," Tish's message to me was clear. *"I don't think I can do this."* She turned away from me and went back outside. Issa gave me an apologetic look, and followed Tish outside.

"I don't like him," said Tish after they'd put some distance between themselves and Sage's cabin. Tish was feeling hot all over; the crisp outside air helped cool her temper.

"Why not?" asked Issa. *"He seems okay to me."*

"Because he smells like a dead wolf, that's why not," said Tish. *"There's only one reason why a human would smell like a dead wolf. Don't be dense. And the scent he was carrying seemed familiar to me, besides the fact that it's wolfish. And it's in that closet."*

"Tish, your imagination is off and running again. I smelled the canine scent on him, and, yes, it was wolfish. But try not to jump to conclusions. Try to be nice to him. If you want this book written, it wouldn't be good to get on the wrong side of Sage's beau."

"Beau?" said Tish. *"What's a beau?"*

"A mate," said Issa.

"Do you think they're mates? Really?" asked Tish, momentarily distracted by the curious concept of human pair bonding. *"He's so tall, and not very appealing."*

"Not to you, maybe," said Issa. *"But Sage must like him well enough. And that's why you need to be nice to him."*

The subtle snap of a branch breaking caused both wolves to come to attention. Standing still as stones, with their noses in the air and all senses on alert, they waited. A slight breeze soon brought the scent that explained the noise.

"Deer," whispered Tish.

"And it's young," said Issa, as he caught sight of the animal about fifty yards ahead of them on the trail. *"Do you see or smell a mama?"*

"Nope, not close by, anyway. What do you think?" Tish's voice carried an electric current of excitement as she looked at Issa.

"I think it's a go." Issa dropped his body into a crouch and began to inch forward.

As soon as the wolves left the cabin, Adam said, "That was weird. I got the distinct feeling the smaller one didn't like me."

"That's Tish," I said.

"She looks ferocious. Are you sure they're dogs?"

"Okay, here it is, Adam. I wasn't going to tell you this yet, but no, they're not dogs. They're wolves. And they communicate with me. They came here from Yellowstone to ask me to write a book, to tell their story."

Adam's eyes and face went through a series of emotions: first surprise, followed by confusion, and then concern. It took him a while to find his tongue. "That's a good one, Sage," he finally said. "Is this like an Advanced Animal Communications self-study program? Or have you gone completely off your rocker? I know some people keep wolves as pets. Who do these guys belong to?"

Adam wasn't ready to accept my words at face value, and who could blame him? I decided to stop trying to control the situation and let things play out in whatever fashion they were meant to. But I wasn't going to lie anymore.

"They don't belong to anyone. They just showed up at the door a few nights ago."

"Oh, then maybe they're strays? Did they have collars?" Adam was still trying to put the wolves into a context he could understand.

"No, no collars," I said, remembering Tish's opinion of such trappings.

"Hmm. Maybe after the holiday you should run them down to the humane society. See if they can find their owners."

"Yeah, we'll see how it goes. Are you hungry?"

"Starving."

We snacked on cheese and crackers and drank a few beers while we caught up on the trajectories of each other's lives. Adam had come down to Davis when Mom and Grandma died, and supported me through that horrible time. We hadn't seen each other since then, but usually talked on the phone several times a week. Our last in-person conversation, when he declared his love for me, still hung heavy on me. I loved Adam, but wasn't sure that we were meant to be life mates. When we'd first gotten together three years earlier I was smitten, and thought we'd eventually get married, but then last year Marlowe came along, and I'd been in a world of doubt ever since.

"I like Humboldt a lot," Adam was saying. "It's pretty rainy, but because it's so close to the coast, the storms are dynamic, and they move through. And, you were right, the redwood forests are amazing. When do you think you might come up for a visit?"

"I'm not sure. I haven't been back there in twelve years, not since I graduated."

"It would be great if—"

Adam's sentence was cut off as Tish crashed through the dog door. She marched up to Adam's chair and demanded, *Do you shoot animals for fun?*

I watched Adam's mouth open, then close, and then open again, with no words coming out. So he could hear them, too. The wolves must have decided they could trust him, or else Tish was so worked up she wasn't thinking clearly. I knew she'd continue to pressure Adam until he told her the truth about the pelt.

When he was finally able to form words, Adam croaked, "Me? No."

"Then why do you smell like a dead wolf?"

"Tish," said Issa, who had just come through the door. *"Lighten up. Maybe he just smells like a dog."*

Tish stared at Adam for a few more tense moments, glanced at Issa with a derisive snort, and then turned and walked away. She made her way to the fireplace and lay down, without looking at any of us.

"Sage," said Adam quietly. "Can we talk outside?" His face had lost most of its color, and his breathing was shallow and quick. I hoped he wasn't going to pass out.

"I tried to tell you, Adam, but you didn't want to believe me," I said as we cleared snow off the deck and sat down on the top step. I stared at him as his breathing slowly returned to normal. "I couldn't believe it, either," I said. "But it's happening. And the fact that they can communicate with us telepathically in a language we understand is only the half of it." I bit my tongue as soon as the words escaped my lips.

"What do you mean?"

"Oh, well, just the stories they've told me, about their travels and all." Issa and Tish were right, Adam was not ready to be told about Wolf Time and Links and the Council. Honestly, I wasn't sure if anyone I knew was ready to hear about this other realm.

"In a nutshell, they want me to document their lives, and, by doing so, help them get the word out that humans need to stop persecuting wolves. Their parents, and two of their brothers were shot, they had a sister who was trapped, and—"

"You're not kidding, are you? This is really happening. It's not induced by drugs, or alcohol, or—"

"No, Adam," I said, rubbing his shoulder. "It's real. They've been here for about a week. Now, do you want to tell me about the pelt?"

After Adam finished telling me the story of his visit to Carl's antique store, we stood to go back inside. I opened the door and Tish pushed past us to get outside and took off at a trot through the snow. Issa was right behind her. He nodded to me and then loped after Tish.

At 5:30 p.m., the thermometer told me the turkey was ready. I pulled it out of the oven, and Adam and I whipped up a large bowl of mashed potatoes, a pan of gravy, and a salad to round out the meal. Adam had brought a bottle of Mumm's Napa Brut, knowing my weakness for champagne. We sat down at the table, and as I was laying my napkin across my lap, Adam held up his champagne flute and said, "Here's to us, Sage. Merry Christmas and Happy Birthday."

"Thank you, Adam. And a Merry Christmas to you, too." I lifted my glass to clink against his and took a sip. "I forgot to mention it with all the wolf stuff, but later this evening, if you want, Chris and Emily invited us to their place for dessert, I think Emily said pumpkin and apple pie. You remember Chris? He's the park's wildlife biologist? Their cabin is just a short walk from here, so we don't have to worry about driving."

"I do remember them," said Adam. "That sounds great."

After cleaning up the kitchen, we searched the cabin for two functioning flashlights and stepped outside. It was snowing again. "Hold on a minute," I said. "Let me grab a coat." My everyday fleece jacket was drying by the fireplace, but I decided to wear something a little nicer for our evening with friends. I scanned the bedroom closet and selected a thigh-length, white down coat.

The wrap did not come easily off the hanger when I tugged at it, so I gave it a solid jerk and it cooperated. I closed the closet door and went to join Adam.

Chris and Emily and their kids, two-year-old Robbie and three-year-old Eliza, welcomed us at the door with big hugs and offers of coffee or tea. The conversation over dessert turned, as it always did with Chris, to wildlife and its management. I told my story about my dismal experience working for the U.S. Fish and Wildlife Service, Chris lamented the short-comings associated with working for the National Park Service, and we all agreed that most of the roadblocks preventing true protection of wildlife and habitat were political.

"What about the agency called Wildlife Services?" Adam asked the group. "I've been seeing a lot of criticism aimed at them on social media."

"Oh, those guys," said Chris. "They used to be called Animal Damage Control. They started as part of the U.S. Fish and Wildlife Service back in the early 1930s. They say their goal is to allow people and wildlife to coexist, but almost whenever there's a conflict, or even a perceived conflict, they kill the wildlife—not exactly co-existence."

"In the late 1990s," I added, "they figured out their name was no longer politically correct, and they changed it to Wildlife Services. Now it's part of the U.S. Department of Agriculture. When you think about it, though, Wildlife Services is a gross misnomer. A better name would be Wildlife Dispatchers. It seems like all they do is kill animals."

"Initially, the program was supposed to help ranchers." Chris continued. "And they called their targets vermin and varmints. I saw a handwritten sign outside a store up in Idaho not too many years ago that said 'Varmint Guns on Sale.' Can you even believe anyone alive in the 21st Century could use the word varmint and keep a straight face?"

"Ah, Idaho," I said. "Not a big surprise. And now that the wolves are back, they're getting hit hard, too. I read that in 2011, Wildlife Services killed 365 wolves. I remember the number because it's equal to one wolf every single day of the year. That same year, they killed about 83,000 coyotes, which amounts to 228 coyotes killed every day of the year. That's just outright brutal slaughter."

Chris got up to fill his coffee cup, and then returned to the living room. "For a long time," he said, "pretty much any animal that bothered ranchers in any way became a target. Coyotes were the primary offenders, but those guys would kill anything that moved—gophers, prairie dogs, raccoons, foxes, mountain lions, bears—"

"Bears?" I interrupted.

"Yup, sometimes grizzlies were killed for taking lambs. And black bears were killed—get this—because they'd steal honey from beehives. In Montana, bees were considered livestock. And those maniacs didn't just shoot animals. They used any means at their disposal: traps, snares, poison, whatever it took. They even shot animals from low-flying airplanes and helicopters."

"Would anyone care for more pie?" Emily squeezed into the conversation. "And, Chris, maybe we could talk about something else."

"More pie sounds great," said Chris. "But, really, Em, we need to shout this from the rooftops until enough people get mad and are provoked to take action to stop it. No more burying our heads in the sand. Have you ever heard of an M-44? It's a device that shoots cyanide into the mouths of unsuspecting coyotes and foxes who are simply doing what they need to do to survive. It's got to stop."

Twenty minutes after Adam and Sage had departed from Sage's cabin, Tish pushed her head through the dog door. *"Okay,"* she said. *"They're gone. Let's do it."*

"Tish," said Issa, right on her heels. *"I don't think this is a good idea."*

Ignoring him, Tish walked into the bedroom and stood in front of the closet, studying the door. She pushed at it with her paw, but the door didn't move.

"I think you have to turn that knob. But I still don't think..." Issa stood behind her, shaking his head.

"How am I supposed to do that? I don't have thumbs. Maybe I can bite it." Tish reached up and took hold of the brass-colored doorknob and twisted her head to the right. The knob turned, but the door didn't open.

"Turn and pull at the same time," said Issa. Even though he felt they were violating Sage's privacy by doing this, he was also curious about the smell. On the next try, the door swung open toward them and both wolves jumped backwards. A wolf pelt hung from the closet shelf, half in and half out of a blue sack. Wolf and sack appeared to be caught on something, which kept them from falling to the floor. The pelt's head hung at eye level with Issa and Tish, with empty eye sockets gazing at the floor. When Tish noticed a white-tipped ear with a small, ragged tear in it, the hackles on her back stood up and she turned to Issa in a white hot rage.

"Issa, that's it. I'm going to kill him."

Chapter Twenty-Three
2018

"Good morning, ladies. It's so nice to see you all!" The tall, clean-cut man shook hands with the three women at the corner table before he sat down to join them. "Thank you for inviting me to meet with you. Now, before we get started, please let me introduce myself."

The Early Bird Café, reputed to serve the biggest breakfasts in Salmon, Idaho was bustling with patrons, each one taking a few moments to stare at the stranger, whose chocolate brown felt derby stood in sharp contrast to the more common ball caps and Stetsons.

"Oh, I don't think that's necessary." With a smile, Annie cut him off before the man could go on endlessly about his past accomplishments as circus performer, flautist, novelist, and now, alternative energy guru. She'd heard it all before. She knew her two female companions didn't care about Gordon Wilson's past either; they just hoped to gain access to some of his money and influence. "They know who you are," she gave her uncle a smile. "Your reputation precedes you."

"But—"

"I think we should get right to the reason we're here. Before we start, though, please excuse me for just a moment." Annie stood, smoothed down the front of her royal blue wool skirt, and walked to the far end of the cafe to the door marked "Ladies." She stepped into the poorly lit restroom's single stall and reached for the cell phone in her jacket pocket. As she closed the stall door, Annie sent up a prayer of thanks for keeping the ladies room empty while she made the call.

She punched a number into the phone, and grimaced when she heard her significant other's recorded voice. "Hey, it's Blue. You know what to do. Long live the wolves." His message was followed by a long, low howl.

"Blue, it's me. We're here. He doesn't know why we've asked him to meet with us, except to talk about our opposition to the wolf and coyote derby. It's perfect. Come down now." Annie spoke quietly while perched on the toilet seat lid.

When she exited the restroom and walked back toward the group, Annie could hear her uncle waxing eloquent about his past. She'd known he would start as soon as she left. This was good. He'd feel as if he'd won the first round.

"...and at the awards banquet, I was the only person to be honored twice in the same year. Oh, Annie, you're back already. I was just, well..." he trailed off.

"So," Annie said, sitting down next to Gordon. "How are we going to proceed? It's clear this idiocy must stop. The delisting of wolves in Idaho, Wyoming, and Montana has been a total disaster, and this derby is a perfect illustration. It's completely unacceptable." She pushed her long bangs away from her eyes and looked across the table at her female companions. Annie knew Cori Martin and Rachel Overton from school, and they'd bumped into one another occasionally when they'd all worked in Yellowstone, but Annie hadn't really gotten to know them until they all became serious about advocating for wolves. Cori was tall and lean, had long, black wavy hair, and was as tough as nails. Raised on a ranch south of Bellevue, Idaho, she'd never been one to back down from a challenge. Rachel, on the other hand, was slight of stature, with long reddish-brown hair that fell in cascading ringlets down her back. Despite her small size, though, Rachel, too, was tough. You had to be, if you were going to play in the wolf arena.

"Are you all ready to order?" The waitress, whose name tag read Patty Sue, towered over them, her note pad and freshly sharpened pencil held firmly in the air in anticipation. Deep creases lined the woman's forehead, and her bun of coarse gray hair slumped hard to the right, on the verge of falling apart completely. Patty Sue glanced around the table at her customers with a tired smile. When she looked at Annie, though, the smile disappeared. The waitress lost her grip on the pencil and fumbled to keep from dropping it. Annie winced; she'd hoped no one would recognize her.

"I think so," said Gordon, oblivious to the tension. "I'll have the vegetarian omelet and coffee, please." Annie and Cori ordered waffles, and Rachel asked for sides of fruit and potatoes. After she finished writing the orders, Patty Sue looked at Annie and hissed, "We don't want you here." Before Annie could respond, the waitress stalked off to the kitchen.

"What was that all about?" asked Gordon.

"Not sure," said Annie with a shrug. "Maybe she's mistaking me for someone else."

"Have you already become a pariah in this town?" asked Gordon.

"I can't imagine how that could have happened," said Cori, covering her mouth to hide her grin.

"Wouldn't it be a good idea to befriend the people here, and not make them your enemies?" Gordon asked.

Annie chose to ignore the question, but a surge of anxiety ran through her when she thought about Blue and Sunny's planned endeavor. Had this been a mistake? How would Gordon react?

"So, Annie," said Gordon, after adding a slug of creamer and three packets of sugar to his coffee. "What do you want from me? If it's just money, that's easy. I can't offer much of my time, though, as this latest acquisition is close to fruition." Annie recalled Gordon telling her about the series of dreams he'd had about ten years earlier. Vivid and in full color, he'd said his subconscious had clearly shown him the future of energy production in the world, and it was all based on ecologically friendly, renewable sources. He'd taken the dreams seriously, and shifted his lucrative fossil fuel-based investments to research and development of efficient, low cost solar technologies. His new venture, SunLife, had grown by leaps and bounds, and he was about to take on a dozen small solar installation companies.

"You know, Gordon, I'm not sure exactly what we want," said Annie. "Stopping the derby would be great, but the problem is so much bigger than that. If I had the money, I'd buy up a huge piece of land somewhere in the Rockies and start a non-profit that focused on wolves. In my dreams, I see a sanctuary or preserve with all native species fully protected. The place would have a retreat center and a large educational program, especially for kids, because it's the kids who will save what's left of the planet. I'd also set up an endangered species education center in every state."

Annie stopped talking as the image of the preserve took hold in her mind's eye, as it had almost every day for the last three years: a wide valley surrounded by mountain ranges, a big meandering river with tributaries feeding lowland meadows, the smells of sagebrush and wood smoke on the air, and herds of bison, elk, and pronghorn grazing, watched from above by grizzly, wolves, and the occasional cougar.

She was a bit embarrassed when she described her dream to others, because it sounded so romantic, not based in reality. But, she thought, why not think big? Why not imagine a place where a full complement of wildlife could live without harassment from hunters, ranchers, and recreationists? If no one held such a dream, it was guaranteed to never happen. If enough people held the dream, Annie had convinced herself, it would happen. It had to happen.

"We also need to figure out how to have more influence in the political games," said Rachel, who was Executive Director for the non-profit Predators Forever. "These backwater states like Idaho…" She broke off as Patty Sue approached the table with their meals.

The plates were deposited without a word, and everyone at the table was busy for a few minutes with salt, pepper, and Tabasco sauce as well as lots more cream and sugar.

"So, Rachel, tell me more about the politics," said Gordon after everyone had taken the edge off of their hunger. "What needs to change?"

"Besides everything?" Rachel couldn't help herself. She was so tired of the state-sponsored torture and killing.

"Well," said Annie. "Where should we begin?"

"The derby," said Cori. "That's the most pressing issue."

"Right, the derby," said Annie. "This weekend, tomorrow and Sunday, there's a wolf- and coyote-derby based right here in Salmon. The idea is to get hunters to kill as many wolves and coyotes as possible. A thousand dollars go to the hunter who kills the largest wolf. Even kids are being encouraged to participate in the slaughter. It's outrageous, criminal even, the product of sick and fearful minds."

Annie noticed that conversation at nearby tables had ceased, so she lowered her voice. "I don't think we'll be able to stop the derby, but we can all send messages to the canids to steer clear of this area for a while. On another note, the state of Idaho recently paid people to go into remote wilderness areas to kill entire wolf packs, sometimes blasting them from helicopters. Their rationale is that wolves are killing off the elk. This is so far from the truth. Elk numbers are up in some areas, and in other areas, humans have been mismanaging elk habitat for decades. Destructive logging practices, fire suppression, and too much hunting have a much greater impact on elk than wolves. As goes habitat quality, so go the animals that depend on it. It's not rocket science. But what's most ironic about this criticism of wolves is that poachers kill far more elk than wolves do every year." Annie twisted a lock of her hair around her finger as she spoke, and felt her heart rate increase. Gordon had to help. The wolves' situation was growing steadily worse under state management.

"It's also fair to say that now that wolves are back, hunters may have a harder time bagging their elk," said Rachel. "The presence of wolves seems to have made prey species more attentive and smarter. Hunters have to work harder, big boo-hoo."

"Shh...," Annie said, when she noticed the patrons in the booth directly behind Rachel—three burly men in Carhartt jackets with red-faces and clenched jaws—staring at the young woman's back. The three men rose and made their way out of the restaurant. Before they stepped outside, the last man in line looked back over his shoulder and sent energetic daggers toward the wolf advocates' table.

"We need to keep our voices down, or go somewhere else," said Annie in a whisper. "I think some of these people are capable of getting very nasty."

"Just let 'em try," said Cori, and then she picked up the conversation where Rachel had left off. "There's more, Gordon. The Idaho Fish and Game Commission is a bunch of self-proclaimed avid hunters appointed by the governor, some of whom would be happy to see all the wolves in Idaho disappear. Supposedly, no more than four of the seven commissioners can be of the same political party. Right now, four are Republicans, and three are Independents. I wonder how many of the Independents will show their true red colors once their positions expire. The stated goal of the Commission is to get the wolf population in Idaho down to one hundred and fifty animals, and then keep it there. That's the number the feds have said is the minimum required to keep wolves off the endangered species list in Idaho. That means killing around five hundred wolves right away and ensures a perpetual slaughter every year forever. Does that make any sense at all?"

"If we're going to have wild wolves, and we are, by God we are," said Rachel, slamming her fist on the table hard enough to make Annie jump, "we have to allow them to establish natural population numbers and fluctuations. That means no more hunting or trapping of wolves, and it might mean no more hunting of wolf prey by humans. It means ranchers have to change their grazing practices, and it sure would help if the state and feds put money into aggressive habitat restoration."

"Speaking of money, you'll love this," Annie's voice rose as she was pulled into the energy of her friends' outrage. "Idaho's governor has pumped millions of dollars into a state Wolf Control Board, basically to coordinate the killing of wolves. Idaho is ranked 49th of all 50 states in the quality of its public education, yet the governor has used millions to kill wolves. Idaho desperately needs a new set of leaders."

"Well," said Gordon, after taking a long swallow of coffee, "at this point Idaho is completely red. You have a Republican governor, and a supermajority of Republicans in the state and federal legislatures. To turn things around, you'd need to replace them with people who truly care about wilderness and wolves. That's a tall order. And if you're hoping to buy politicians, and that's pretty much what you have to do these days, you're competing with mega-rich fossil fuel barons with endlessly deep pockets. I'm not saying that's a bad strategy, but I'd suggest buying up land and grazing leases first."

"And that's just Idaho," said Annie. "Don't forget Montana, Wyoming, Wisconsin, Minnesota, Michigan, and even the reputedly green state of Washington. Everywhere the wolves have been de-listed, the states are condoning, and even promoting, wolf hunting and trapping."

The group went silent for a few moments, and Gordon looked around for their waitress, wondering if she'd ever return to refill his coffee. He waved to catch Patty Sue's attention, but the woman turned her back as if she hadn't seen him.

"In addition to the political problems," Rachel resumed, "we need to transcend the divisiveness that crops up among pro-wolf groups. Just because leaders of these groups have differences of opinion, like whether or not humans should eat meat, or whether or not any wolves at all should be killed, doesn't mean they can't work together. I would hope they could bridge those differences, for the sake of the wolves."

"It's no different than any other advocacy group. If the strongest people in these groups don't see eye to eye on everything, the groups splinter," said Cori. "In some cases, that can be good, like when Dave Brower left The Sierra Club to start Friends of the Earth, and then left Friends to start Earth Island Institute. He created new groups when the old ones departed from his primary philosophy. His new groups appealed to different kinds of people, so the environmental movement probably benefited."

"I think it's different with the wolves," Rachel responded. "We're talking about long-term survival of a species known to be critical to the health of its habitat. If we want wolves to survive in the United States, where people with a lot of money and clout want them gone, we have to build a very strong united front."

"The first issue that needs to be addressed is this state-by-state de-listing," said Gordon. "It sets a bad precedent. The next thing they'll try to do is remove wolves nation-wide from the endangered species list."

"That's already been proposed. It will be up to the administration, specifically the Secretary of the Interior, to decide," said Annie. "And now even some of the feds are actively trying to undermine the entire Endangered Species Act. What a disaster."

Patty Sue approached their table and filled Gordon's coffee cup. Instead of stopping before the cup overflowed, the waitress allowed the brown liquid to flow over the cup's rim and onto the table. "Oh, excuse me," she said, before she turned to walk away. "What a disaster."

"Nice," said Gordon, as he grabbed all the napkins on the table to mop up the spilled coffee before it dripped onto his lap.

"Anyway," he said, "you probably already know this, but the oil and gas industry giants are working hard to undermine all restrictions on energy development on public lands. Believe it or not, they're also paying off the National Rifle Association to gain their support. Throw the livestock industry into that mix, and it becomes a very strong front opposed to endangered species or any other environmental legislation. You're right, Annie, it's a recipe for disaster."

The conversation stopped for several minutes, as everyone pondered a future world with greatly diminished wild lands and the extinction of ever-increasing numbers of species. Cori broke the silence. "Do you remember that scene from *Crocodile Dundee*, where the kangaroo came to life and began hunting the hunters? I so loved that scene. Would it be possible to do something similar without getting shot?"

Annie smiled at the image, and then glanced out the café window. She gasped when she saw two patrol cars bearing a cadre of county sheriffs pull into the parking lot. Of course, she thought, this is a small town, and it's 10 a.m. on a Saturday—coffee and donut time.

"Sorry, excuse me again for a minute." Annie jumped up and hurried back to the ladies room. When she pushed open the door, it bumped into an elderly woman about to make her exit.

"Oh," Annie said. "I'm so sorry. Are you okay?"

"Hmph. Yes, I guess so. But you might want to take more care," the woman said as she rubbed a deeply wrinkled elbow. She looked up at Annie, glared at her for a moment, and said, "You know, you're not welcome here. You're just begging for trouble showing up in this town. We all know who you are and what you're up to."

Annie looked at the little woman. She was dressed in a powder blue knit twinset, and her hair was piled high on her head like an icy blue ocean wave. Who is she? Annie wondered. And who does she think I am?

"Do I know you?" Annie asked.

"That story you posted on the Internet about a guy named Ballcap. It's gone viral up here. We've all seen it. In fact, someone printed a bunch of copies and mailed them out to everyone who lives here, with your photo, and that young man Blue, too. We've all seen your Facebook page. No, there's no mistaking you. We were told to watch out for you radical enviro wolf-lovers. You should go home, and never come back, if you know what's good for you." The woman glared at Annie a moment longer, and then pushed past her to exit the restroom.

Annie couldn't take time to worry about the old lady, she had to reach Blue. She got his voice mailbox again. It's probably too late, she thought as she waited for the howl to end. "Blue," she said to the machine. "Don't come. It's a really bad time."

Annie heard the rising volume of voices in the café before she even opened the door to leave the restroom. She stepped out and pulled up short at the view out the window fronting Main Street. A large cardboard sign borne by Blue was bobbing along toward the café's entrance. It read: "The Governor of Idaho wants to kill ALL the wolves! Impeach Him Now!" A second placard, carried by Sunny, followed the first. Her sign said: "Confucius Say He Who Shoots Wolves Has Tiny Man-Parts."

Before the two protesters could walk the full length of the block, the county sheriffs swarmed out of the Early Bird. Two officers approached Blue with their arms at their sides, hands poised and ready to grab gun or baton if things got out of hand.

"Put the sign down, buddy," said the taller of the two officers. Blue, fearing arrest, quickly complied.

At the same time, another sheriff strode up to Sunny and grabbed her right arm. She dropped her sign and cried out as he twisted her arm behind her back. Annie was already out of the café and heading toward Sunny. Hearing the pain in Sunny's cry, Annie lunged at the sheriff and grabbed for his hand. He let go of Sunny, turned toward Annie and swung his arm, catching Annie in the jaw. Annie dropped to the ground, while Sunny picked up her sign and prepared to hit the sheriff over the head from behind.

"No! Sunny stop!" Blue yelled as another patrol car raced up and parked behind the melee. Two men jumped out of the car and immediately took down Annie and Sunny. The women ended up sprawled on their bellies on the icy gravel parking lot, hands in cuffs behind their backs.

Gordon, Cori, and Rachel stood on the sidewalk in front of the café, helplessly watching as the law enforcement officers loaded their friends into the back seats of two vehicles and drove away.

Chapter Twenty-Four
2018

When we returned to the cabin, Issa was sitting on the front deck with his rear end planted firmly against the door. A cacophony of scratching and yowling was coming from inside. *"You two need to stay out here for a while,"* said Issa. *"And explain to us about the wolf pelt. Talk loud so Tish in there can hear you."* Issa sounded calm. He didn't look as if he wanted to hurt us, but chills ran down my spine when I realized the same was probably not true for Tish.

By the time Adam finished telling his story, and explained how he sensed that the spirit of the wolf who had once inhabited the pelt had thanked him for taking her away from the shop, the noise from inside the cabin had abated.

"Can we come inside now, Tish?" asked Issa. *"Will you be nice?"*

"Maybe."

"I think we're good," said Issa. He stood up, turned around, and stepped through the dog door. Adam and I glanced at each other. I slowly opened the people door and peered into the cabin.

Tish sat in front of the fireplace with her back to us. Once we all were inside and Adam and I had removed our coats and boots, she turned her head to look at us over her shoulder. *"In case you haven't figured it out yet,"* she said, *"that wolf pelt in your bag belonged to Tierra, our mom."*

The next two days passed quickly. Tish questioned Adam in great detail about the pelt, wanting to extract every bit of information she could about where it had been, and what messages he had received from Tierra.

"Issa," she said on Saturday morning, as Adam was packing his belongings and getting ready to head for the airport. *"Can we go to this place called Arcata with Adam and talk to Mr. Carl about the pelt? I want to track the person who killed our mom. Maybe Mr. Carl can help us find him. Adam, can we come with you?"* Adam looked at me imploringly, not wanting to be the one to disappoint Tish.

"I don't think we can do that," said Issa. *"Remember what Adam said about flying in an airplane? I doubt they would let us fly. I also doubt very much that we could find the person who killed Mom. And, really, Tish, what's the point? Mom's clearly in transition to the other side, based on what she said to Adam. We need to let her go."*

"I suppose you're right." Tish hadn't been herself since Adam had arrived at the cabin. Her usual energetic, upbeat attitude had been replaced by a dispirited, forlorn mien, broken occasionally by furious outbursts of anger.

"But, Adam, could you at least leave the pelt with Sage, so we can be with her for a little while longer?"

"I'd be happy to. Is that okay with you, Sage?"

"That would be fine."

Adam left at noon to catch a 4:00 p.m. flight to San Francisco. The weather had finally cleared and the sun was resplendent in a deep blue sky. The reflection of sun on snow was blinding, and I had to shield my eyes as I tipped my head back to give Adam a farewell kiss.

"I wish I could stay for New Year's," said Adam at the conclusion of our kiss. "I'd love to spend more time with you, and get some skiing in. But I told my housemate I'd look after his cats while he was out of town. So, next time, I guess. How about spring break? That's not too far away."

"I'll be here," I said. I knew Adam was hoping for more enthusiasm on my part, but I was still on the fence about our relationship. My insistence that he sleep on the futon during his visit hadn't gone over well, but I needed more time to figure out what I wanted.

"Okay," he said. "I'll be off. Talk to you tonight if it's not too late when I get home. Love you." I felt sad that I could not say those words back to him.

After Adam left, Issa, Tish, and I took advantage of the weather and drove down to the river. The wolves had never tried fishing, and Issa expressed an interest, so I parked the truck at a pullout a few miles downstream from El Portal and the Foresta Bridge. The light dusting of snow that had fallen at this lower elevation had completely melted by the time we arrived. Tish and I sat next to a copse of tired-looking willows and watched Issa as he bounded across the cobbles to the water's edge.

"I don't think wolves catch fish too often," said Tish. *"I guess if you lived where there wasn't much else to eat, though, you'd get pretty good at it. What does fish taste like?"*

I was at a loss. How could I describe the taste of fish if I couldn't use fish as a reference point? "Well," I said. "if it's really fresh, it doesn't have much flavor, at least not a strong taste. I would say it tastes like the river, or like the sea, if it's an ocean fish."

I thought the chances of catching anything were slim at this time of year, but Issa was insistent. He was slowly working his way downstream on the south bank, staring intently at the water. As we watched, he stopped and then stood as if frozen. Seconds later, he leaped straight up in the air and came down muzzle first in a small pool, splashing water in all directions. When he brought his head up, he was soaking wet and his mouth was empty. Undaunted, he continued his hunt.

"I hardly think it's worthwhile to try to catch something you might not even want to eat," said Tish.

"Oh, I'm pretty sure you'll like fish, Tish," I said.

"Okay, then," she said. *"Why not?"*

Instead of stalking her prey along the south bank like Issa, Tish strode directly into the river. The water was deep enough to pull her off her feet into a dog-paddle. She swam to the far bank, stepped out of the water, and shook herself hard. She then proceeded to mimic Issa, strolling west along the north bank. I was impressed by the unspoken cooperation between the two wolves.

Much to my surprise, the fishing trip was successful. Issa caught four good-sized rainbow trout, which he tossed up on the bank for me to retrieve. Tish managed to catch three trout, but she ate each one as soon as she caught it, unwilling to wait for the cooked version. She swam back to Issa and me and used her paw to wipe water and fish blood from her muzzle before she voiced her opinion: "*Not bad, not bad at all.*"

Back at the cabin, we dined on fried trout and Belgian waffles with frozen blueberries, which Tish said was the best meal of her entire life. After we ate, the two wolves stretched out in front of the fire, flat on their sides. I was learning that naps usually followed meals in the life of a wolf. I sat down in the recliner and opened up a book titled *Wolves and Humans: A History*, part of my self-imposed crash course on all things wolf.

Half an hour later, I looked up from my reading and silently gazed at Issa and Tish for several minutes, feeling peaceful and warm as I took in the sound of Issa's soft snores. Seconds later, I was jolted from my happy place by the sound of three gentle knocks on the door.

At the first tap, both wolves' heads snapped up and they looked at one another, and then looked up at me. I put my book down, and went to the door. Very few people came to visit without calling ahead, especially in winter. I ran through the possibilities: old Mr. McKenna from the cabin up the road, a friend from town, Jehovah's Witnesses. But I hadn't heard a vehicle.

Before I opened the door, I realized that no matter who it was, I didn't want them to see the wolves. "Issa and Tish," I said. "Can you please go wait in the bedroom while I see who this is?"

"*Um,*" said Tish. "*I don't think that's necessary.*" It took me a moment to understand: It was another wolf.

Sure enough, when I opened the door and peered out, there was a white wolf sitting on the doormat looking at me with very round, luminous, golden-green eyes.

"*It's okay, Sage. You can let her in.*" Issa stood up and padded over to stand behind me. I glanced down at him and could swear he was grinning.

I looked again at the new visitor. She was smaller than Issa and Tish, more petite, and softer. The edges of her coat appeared fuzzy, slightly out of focus. The most unusual thing, though, was that I could see her aura, a ring of soft, pale light that surrounded her like a loose-fitting sweater. I'd seen auras around a few people before, but never around an animal, and never one this color. The light was a clean white, with faint traces of violet and gold, almost like tiny specks of glitter.

"*Hi Sage,*" said the white wolf in a voice that matched the airiness of her form. "*Remember me? I'm Snow.*"

My thoughts came so rapid-fire I thought my head was going to explode. Without a word, I opened the door. Snow walked in and greeted Issa and Tish with the usual energetic face and muzzle licking. All three wolves then walked to the fireplace, turned around and sat down. Lined up in a row, they all looked at me.

"What?" I asked, unable to quell the turmoil in my head. "Oh, sorry." I'd forgotten that Issa and Tish had been famished when they first arrived at the cabin. "Can I get you something to eat, Snow?"

Tish and Snow exchanged a quick glance. Issa stared down at his paws.

"*Ah,*" said Tish. "*Um… No. Snow doesn't need food. You do know—*"

"Of course I know," I snapped, immediately ashamed of my outburst. "But how…no, wait, maybe I don't want to know." I walked over and collapsed into the recliner, brought my knees up to my chest, and wrapped my arms around my legs, striving to get as close to the fetal position as possible.

"*Wolves are just like humans, Sage,*" said Issa. "*And, like all other living beings, we have eternal souls that come and go in bodies that live and die on the earth. Sometimes, when an incarnation, or life-time, ends, the soul stays in a kind of intermediate place. It doesn't immediately cross over, back to the other side of the veil. It becomes what you would call a ghost, or a spirit.*" He stopped for a moment, but I could find no words to respond.

"*Sorry to throw all this at you so quickly, but there really is no time to waste.*" Issa stepped over to the side of the recliner, sat down next to me, and gently licked my hand. "*I know it's a lot to take in.*"

"Yes, it is. I know about human spirits not always crossing over, but I thought it was because they were too attached to something or someone on Earth to let go, or that they didn't know they were dead because they'd died suddenly, in a traumatic accident or something like that." Before I even finished my sentence an image of a small white wolf caught in a heavy metal trap flashed before my eyes. "Oh, I'm sorry, Snow."

"*It's okay. You're right. But in my case it was none of those reasons. I stayed on this side for something quite different.*" Snow lifted her right paw and licked at a wad of ice that was stuck between her pads. Then she stood up, walked toward me, and came around to sit on the side of the recliner opposite from Issa. When she got close to me, her energy felt different from that of the other two wolves. The air around her seemed warmed by her presence. Silly me, I'd always thought ghosts were accompanied by chilling winds. Before I could process this new information, Snow reared back slightly, leaned toward me, and grabbed the back of my neck with her teeth.

"No!" I cried as I tried to twist away. "You can't do this. You're dead! I can't go with you!" Too late; I was already falling.

Merging with Snow was different. I was more aware of the passage of time. The transition state of suspended animation lasted longer than it had with either Tish or Issa, and it felt as if we were tumbling straight backwards, head over heels, as we fell, instead of falling back and spinning.

As with the first journeys I'd taken, I awoke feeling groggy and disoriented. This time, for the first time, I had a mild headache. My eyes focused slowly. Once my vision cleared, I found myself on the inside of a snow globe—one of those clear glass orbs that, when turned upside down and righted again, provide the viewer with a glimpse of a beautiful snowy scene in miniature. It was as if the entire world consisted of this one small clearing in the midst of a towering coniferous forest. Although there was little light, I could see clearly. Large flakes of snow fell, but the ground was free of snow. There was no wind. I looked up, puzzled to see a thin slice of a crescent moon and a vast array of stars overhead. The falling snow had led me to expect a thick layer of clouds.

Snow was lying on her belly, and we were just outside a circle of bright orange light cast by a small, but vigorously burning campfire. I counted nine people gathered around the fire. A woman with long, dark hair sat on a flat rock and gently jiggled her knee to pacify a baby wrapped in a white piece of fur. Two younger women sat on the ground next to her, working with a large, dark animal skin. Three men, all of them lean and muscular, stood back from the fire, deep in discussion. A boy who looked maybe four or five years old chased a smaller, younger girl around rocks and trees near the forest's edge. A large piece of meat cooked on a crude spit over the fire, sending up a delicious aroma, and sizzling when small drops of fat landed on the hot coals.

"I'm confused," I said to Snow. "I thought I was going to experience your death at the hands of those trappers. I'm glad I was wrong, but where are we? What's happening?"

"We've stepped way back into the past, much further than you went with Issa or Tish. Merging with ghosts is different. We have a lot more options available to us. And those of us designated as Teachers, Sages, or Guides have been granted the highest degree of freedom and flexibility. We can go back to any time in history, or forward to any point in the future. We can go anywhere on the earth, and sometimes, beyond."

"Okay," I said slowly, not really sure any of this was okay. "But where are we now? And when?"

"Let's just be quiet and watch," said Snow.

I tried to relax, but failed. "Please tell me, Snow. I don't like this."

"You're fine, Sage. Time to cowboy up, you've been chosen. Think of it as an opportunity to learn about trust."

"But—"

"Shhh. Just watch."

Just when Snow succeeded in getting me to be quiet, the older woman lifted her head and called out to the running children. They paid her no mind, and continued to race around the fire. The girl held tight to a rock the size of a coconut, and she seemed determined to keep it away from the boy. Their game brought them closer to the rest of the group. As they passed between me and Snow and the fire, the little girl stumbled on an exposed tree root. Off balance, she swayed toward the fire and screamed.

"No!" The older woman gasped and stood to help the girl, but was hampered by the babe in her arms. The men were too far away to help.

"*That's our cue,*" said Snow. She leaped up and loped three strides to the girl. By approaching her at an angle, Snow managed to push the child gently away from the fire. The girl fell to her knees, sobbing, while the family rushed to gather around her, fussing and speaking in a language I didn't understand. Snow quietly slipped away, back into the forest.

When we turned around to face the group again, the young boy was pointing toward us and talking in an excited voice. Everyone turned our way. We sat very still and waited. Without hesitating, the tall woman handed the baby to one of the younger women and stepped up to the fire. She carefully pulled several strips from the roasting piece of meat, blew on them to cool them, and walked toward us. Two of the men reached out to restrain her, but she brushed them off and continued. She stopped about ten feet away from us and put the meat on the ground. She put her hands together and bowed to us, and then turned away and went back to the fire. Snow rose and stepped forward to consume the offering. And then we were falling backwards again.

Once again, when we landed, I could see a fire and a small group of people. Snow and I sat at the edge of a large pond lined with cattails and sedges. We were fifty or so yards from the group, hidden in the vegetation. It was morning, and a serenade of birdsong graced our ears from all directions. Fresh green leaves on broad-leaved trees indicated it was spring.

A fury of noise erupted as I was getting my bearings. The chorus of high-pitched snarls, growls, and grunts came from behind a large rock to the right of where Snow and I were sitting. It sounded like dogs. Snow stood and we walked slowly in a big arc around the noise-makers to gain a better view. Behind the rock, three gangly-looking wolves were sparring over a large, bloody piece of meat that looked like the haunch of an elk.

In yet another guttural language I couldn't understand, one of the humans yelled at the wolves and heaved a baseball-sized rock at the trio. I didn't understand his words, but his meaning was clear. The fight over the meat stopped, but the three wolves were not frightened and they continued to argue quietly over the last few stringy scraps of meat remaining on the bones.

"*Those wolves, they are still young, only about a year old,*" Snow said to me.

"What are they doing here, so close to these people?" I asked. "They don't seem too friendly."

"*These humans heard the puppies yipping in their den just after they were born. One day the parents were away from the den, probably out hunting, and the humans took the five pups. The women chewed up meat and fed it to the pups, like she'd seen the adult wolves do for the puppies. The babies were probably at least six or seven weeks old, or they might not have survived. As it was, two of them died soon after they were taken. The mother of these babies still comes around, but she lurks at the edges of the camp. She's afraid of the humans. She tells her puppies to not get too friendly with them.*"

Snow stood and stretched. "*How are you feeling, Sage? Are you up for one more time and place?*"

"I guess so," I said, although my headache had become more noticeable.

It was early evening when I opened my eyes the third time. We were on the move, trotting on the frozen surface of a river or creek. When I looked down and saw we were moving on ice, my heart lurched. You know the feeling: When you start to feel your feet slide out from under you, and you know the landing will be painful? With every step, I expected we'd lose our balance and slide freestyle into a tree or large rock. But Snow was sure-footed, her four legs providing a degree of stability I was not accustomed to.

Once I realized I could trust Snow with the travel details, I looked up and saw we were following someone. A lone, naked human moved at a quick jog along the edge of the creek, where sparse patches of cottonwoods and willows occasionally required the person to change course. Broad shoulders coupled with a narrow waist led me to believe we were tracking a man. Unlike Snow, he was doing his best to stay clear of the ice.

We followed the gently sloping creek uphill for about twenty minutes, and reached a point where the creek split into two arms. The human stopped and looked back at us. The curved outline of breasts told me I'd been wrong about gender. The woman had dark skin, and dark hair woven into a long braid. She carried a heavy tree limb with a stone affixed to one end.

Snow trotted up next to the woman and sat down. The woman scratched the wolf's head briefly and spoke to her in a foreign tongue that Snow seemed to understand. Snow stood and we took the lead up the right fork of the creek. Five minutes later we were pulling dead leaves and branches off of a freshly killed animal that looked like a small, spotted deer. I didn't recognize the species. Snow ate right from the kill, while the woman scraped pieces of meat from the carcass. When Snow had eaten her fill, we all continued up the creek until it meandered close to a large rock wall. Snow leaped up to a wide ledge in the wall about five feet above the creek, while the woman climbed up a narrow crack to reach the ledge.

A small, ash-filled fire pit ringed by rocks sat on one end of the ledge. The woman set to building a fire, using a stash of branches and bark stacked next to the pit. After cooking and eating her meat, she crawled into a shallow natural cave in the wall that was lined with a dense mat of pine needles and leaves. She pulled a skin of some sort up around her shoulders, and Snow and I moved in to lie down behind her. When Snow laid her head gently on the woman's hip, she reached up to stroke Snow behind the ears.

After witnessing this third vignette of wolves and humans from the distant past, we awoke back in the cabin. I was still in the recliner, and I leaned back to consider what I had just experienced. The merge with Snow had left me with more questions than answers about the mechanics of the merge as well as its purpose.

"Snow, why was it sometimes we seemed to be inside another wolf from the past, like when you rescued the child from the fire, or accompanied the woman, and the other time, with the young wolves, we just observed from the sidelines?"

"*It has to do with the ways of Wolf Time,*" she answered. "*When we were inside another wolf in the past, when we were fully merged, that wolf was one of my direct blood ancestors, or it was me from one of my past lives. If we were to fully merge with a wolf in the future, it would have to be with one of my direct descendants. Since I died young, I will have no descendants from this lifetime. We could, however, merge with one of my descendants from a past life. When we're just watching, it means I'm not related by blood to any of the wolves present.*"

"I know we were witnessing some of the relationships between early humans and wolves, but why?" I asked.

"*A couple of reasons,*" said Snow. "*One is so you could see humans and the wolf ancestors came together in relationships at many times and many places in history, as well as what you call prehistory, for various reasons. Second, there are about one billion domestic dogs on*

Earth right now, and every one of them is related to the wolf ancestors. Dogs are man's best friend. They guard their human's homes and families, help with hunting, find people who are lost, provide aid to people who are blind or otherwise unable to cope with life alone, keep people warm, and provide an unsurpassed quality of companionship. Every one of these dogs has wolf inside. Genetically speaking, 98.8 percent of the DNA in wolves and dogs is identical. Despite this close kinship, however, wolves continue to be persecuted and defiled in the worst ways. This makes no sense to us, Sage. No sense at all."

Chapter Twenty-Five
2018

"Oh, Aunt Sage, thanks for getting here so quickly. I don't know how we could have spent another night in this town." A young man with close-cropped blond hair clad in Levis and a dark blue fleece jacket stepped out of Room 17 of Big Pine Motel onto a small, deeply cracked cement porch. He walked the few steps between us and embraced me in a big bear hug. Light snow fell from an iron-gray sky, dusting his bare head and the shoulders of his jacket.

I took a small step back and held my nephew at arm's length. I hadn't seen either Blue or Sunny in about fourteen years. Blue had been six, and Sunny only two and a half. I never expected to see them again, but when Blue called and told me they were stuck in Salmon with no money and were afraid to call Marshal and Lois, or any of their local family members, there was no way I could refuse to help.

"I'm glad I was able to come," I said. "But you might not have a choice about staying here another night. I'm exhausted, and this storm is packing a big punch."

"Hi, Sunny." I turned to greet the petite redhead who stood a bit behind Blue. "How are you? You probably don't remember me."

"Oh, I know all about you, Auntie Sage," said Sunny.

That's what I was afraid of, I thought.

"Happy Holidays," Sunny said as she stepped forward with a big smile and gave me a hug that carried so much energy it sent shivers down my spine.

The call from Blue had come late in the afternoon on Saturday, the same day Adam had left the cabin to return to Arcata. Blue carefully explained that he and Sunny hadn't been arrested, exactly, but that they'd been told to get out of Salmon as soon as possible and never come back. He refused to tell me what had led to the confrontation with the police.

I'd made the drive from California in two days. The timing of the trip turned out to be good. We hadn't run into any particularly bad weather and had arrived in Salmon just ahead of a major storm. The forecasters were calling for a foot of snow by the next morning.

Although the drive was easy, I felt like I had a bad hangover by the time I arrived in Salmon. I never liked to rush when packing for a trip, but in this case I'd had no choice. Then I had Issa and Tish to think about. They'd wanted very much to come with me to pick up Blue and Sunny, but I had deep reservations about letting them join me. How would I explain the wolves to a niece and nephew I didn't even know? For all I knew, they could be rabid anti-wolf people. On the other hand, I worried about leaving the wolves behind in California; there was no end to the trouble they could get into. Tish wore me down in the end, and I let them join me. We decided there would be no talk of Wolf Time with Sunny and Blue. Just before we left the house, Tish asked me to bring Tierra's pelt along for the ride.

In reality, though, my concern over the wolves was only a small part of my stress. The surprise call from Blue, and the drive to Salmon, had forced me to revisit an event from my past that I thought I'd laid to rest. I was wrong.

We'd left Yosemite early Sunday and drove straight through to Winnemucca, Nevada, where I got a decent night's sleep at a motel with attached smoky casino. The next morning, as we set off to the east toward Elko, the tape of the worst night of my life replayed in my head.

It was Christmas Eve. I was living in Arcata, working on my undergraduate degree at Humboldt State, and I'd flown to Idaho to spend the holidays with my family. My older sister, Marta, her husband, Greg Robinson, and Sunny, their young daughter, had met me at the Boise airport, and we were all headed back to the ranch near Salmon. Greg had said he was tired, so I'd offered to drive their F-150 pickup on the return trip. At my stomach's urging, we'd stopped in the small town of Stanley for an early supper of hamburgers and pumpkin pie, and we'd just merged back onto the highway. The last leg of our journey home was about sixty miles long.

Marta occupied the middle of the front seat, and held Sunny in her lap. Sunny was fast asleep, clutching a small stuffed bear. On Marta's other side, Greg also was fast asleep, with his head wedged up next to the window. Marta had pushed a tape into the player and Bing Crosby crooned songs of the season to us at low volume.

"The last forecast I heard for tomorrow was partly cloudy with a slight chance of snow," I said. "Maybe we'll have a white Christmas after all. That would be wonderful."

"I hope so, and I hope it keeps snowing and stays cold," Marta responded. "This pattern of mixed rain and snow is a nightmare. It freezes overnight and turns everything into an ice field, and then melts into a muddy quagmire. It makes it so hard to take care of the horses, slipping and sliding down to the barn every morning in the dark to feed, and breaking up the ice on the water tanks with a sledge hammer. It's a wonder I haven't broken my neck."

"I have to admit I don't miss that," I said. "And, hey, thank you guys so much for coming down to get me."

"I'm glad you were able to come, Sage," said Marta. "Do you realize we've never missed a Christmas together? As of tomorrow, it will be twenty-one years. Happy early birthday! Now you can have a glass of champagne for the holiday toast, and be legal!"

"And this was the year I almost didn't make it, with all the stuff happening with John and his family," I answered. "I don't really understand what's going on, but he's been a mess over it." I flipped on the windshield wipers and pulled the lever to eject a spray of washer fluid over the dirty surface. It was dusk and every passing car splashed water and mud on us as it passed, making it hard to see the road.

"What's the issue? You said something about his sister?"

"Yeah. It's complicated. They don't get along too well. He's never told me why, except to say she's too controlling. They haven't spoken to each other in a while, and their brother is trying to get them to patch things up, because their sister has been ill, but it's not working. I don't see John as a stubborn person, but he won't budge on this one."

"Are you two going to get married?" asked Marta.

"I have no idea. Not anytime soon, that's for sure. I'm nowhere near ready."

"Oh, you'd be surprised. I didn't think I was ready either, but then I got pregnant before Greg and I had even talked about getting married. The babies decided for us, and look how good it's all turned out." Six-year-old Blue had stayed back at the ranch with our mom and grandma, as well as our other sister, Lois, and her husband, Marshal, while the rest of the family made the trek to pick me up.

We rode in silence for several miles, watching the sagebrush landscape fade into shades of gray and silver as daylight disappeared. Marta leaned her head back and closed her eyes. My thoughts returned to Marta's question about marriage, and I wondered if I'd ever be ready. I loved John, but I still felt so young and so excited about my life. I'd just finished my first quarter of college, and I couldn't have been happier. Marriage and children just weren't a high priority. Besides, I had Blue and Sunny to provide me with kid fixes when I needed them. I was so lost in thought I didn't see the white wolf step out onto the road until it was almost too late.

"No!" I screamed and turned the steering wheel hard as I hit the brakes. The road was icy. The truck went into a skid, and we careened off the pavement, dropped into a ditch, and rolled.

I woke up in a hospital about six hours later to learn that Marta and Greg were dead. But, cradled in Marta's arms as they flew through the windshield, Sunny had survived.

I shook my head when I realized Sunny had been speaking to me. "I'm sorry, Sunny. What?"

"Oh, I was just thanking you for coming to help us," said Sunny. "It wasn't that bad here, though. They treated us okay. The policemen took us to the jail for disturbing the peace, and threatened to arrest us. But they ended up just letting us go, because no one got hurt." I marveled at how beautiful she was and berated myself for losing so many years with my niece and nephew.

"And they suggested we stay out of Salmon," added Blue. "They said if we were caught doing anything the slightest bit wrong here in the future, full charges would be pressed." As Blue was talking, a tall, willowy woman emerged from the motel room. She was bundled up in a long, tan coat, a rainbow patterned silk scarf, and dark brown, fuzzy boots. A gust of wind swept her long, straight blond hair across her eyes as she walked the few steps between us and offered her hand for a shake.

"Hi," she said. "I'm Annie."

"Oh, um," Blue stammered. "Aunt Sage, this is Annie, my girlfriend."

"Nice to meet you, Annie," I said, shaking her gloved hand.

"You too, Sage," she replied. "Thanks for coming to our rescue."

"No problem. I'm glad I was able to get up here. I'm looking forward to hearing the whole story. Right now, though, I'm famished. Do you guys have any suggestions?"

"There aren't a lot of choices," said Blue. We settled on a Subway, which was just a few blocks away, ordered sandwiches, and sat down at a table.

"How did you get up here?" I asked, after I polished off half of my turkey on sourdough.

"We hitch-hiked up from Gardiner," Blue said. "We thought about going home the same way, but with this weather, and without any money, we figured that might not be the smartest choice. We couldn't call Aunt Lois and Uncle Marshal because Lois has been sick. She got the flu just before Christmas, and then it went into pneumonia. She's getting better, but we couldn't see bothering them. Uncle Scott is still in Tanzania. And as for our relatives here in Salmon, well, we didn't think they'd understand what we are trying to do."

Blue was quiet for a few moments, and then continued. "And I'm not sure if it's connected or not, but all of a sudden, out of nowhere, about two weeks ago Sunny started talking about you. About how much she wanted to meet you, and how much you two had in common, which I thought was strange, considering we haven't seen you for such a long time. And we never really knew you. Anyway, after we rejected all our other options, Sunny suggested we call you."

"I'm glad you did," I said. "But what's the plan now? Where am I taking you? I assume you want to go back to Gardiner?"

"Yes, could you take us home? We could all spend New Year's together. That would be fun. Our place isn't huge, but we have a guest room with an air bed. Annie and I don't have to be back to work until Saturday the fourth," said Blue.

"That works," I said. "You're lucky I'm flexible right now, between jobs and all."

"Yes, we are lucky," said Sunny. "In so many ways." I looked at her and wondered why she seemed different, and then I remembered a few fragments of long ago conversations with Lois that I'd tried hard to forget.

"...didn't make a single noise for months..."

"...never asked about the accident or her parents..."

"...became very attached to the animals..."

"But what are we going to do about tonight?" Annie broke through my memories. "It's getting late, and it's supposed to get pretty stormy."

"I think we should just go," Blue cut in. "Now, I mean. At least get out of Salmon. The snow's not sticking yet. Under the best conditions, it takes about five hours to get to Gardiner from here, but it's only a little over two hours to Dillon. We can stop there for the night. I can drive. Here, Annie, can you look at road conditions and the updated weather forecast?" Blue bent down and pulled an iPad from his backpack and handed it to Annie.

"She's faster at it than me." He shrugged and gave me a small grin.

A few minutes later, Annie looked up and said, "It looks like most of the storm is tracking farther north, and it's coming in slower than they thought. Roads are open. We should be okay." I gave in with little protest. The truth was I didn't want to be in Salmon, either. The place held too many painful memories.

"There's just one thing I need to do first," I said. "I'll meet you all back at the motel in about twenty minutes. Does that work?"

We parted company and I got in the truck and turned back down the road I'd come in on. When we'd driven toward Salmon earlier that evening, the wolves had started to get very excited about ten miles outside of town. Tish had pushed her nose up against the camper shell window, and swore she could smell her natal den. She begged me to let them go out and stalk something. I agreed to drop them off, suggested they not roam too far away, and told them to listen for my whistle when I came back through to pick them up.

I drove back to the place where I'd let them out and pulled off on the road shoulder. I rolled down the window, stuck my thumb and index finger in my mouth and let out a long, sharp whistle. The two wolves came loping across a small drainage right away. I opened the camper shell, dropped the tailgate, and they jumped in.

"Okay, here's the deal. My niece and nephew, Sunny and Blue, and Blue's girlfriend, Annie, are just up the road. I haven't yet told them you're here, and I have no idea what they think about wolves."

"*Oh, it's all good, Sage,*" said Tish. "*In fact, if I understand correctly, and I think I do, Network members communicate with Sunny all the time.*"

Of course they do, I thought.

Everyone was packed and ready when we got back to the motel. I met them when they emerged from Blue's room. "I didn't tell you guys earlier, but I have two dogs with me. They're malamutes, pretty big. But they're friendly. I was babysitting them for a friend when you called, and I couldn't leave them alone." Blue and Sunny looked at each other, but said nothing.

"Oh, fun," said Annie. "Malamutes are the best."

I walked to the back of the truck and let Issa and Tish out to greet their fellow travelers. Tish and Sunny locked eyes for several seconds, after which Sunny smiled and nodded her head. After hands were licked and heads were stroked, we loaded gear and wolves into the back of the truck. Blue took the driver's seat, I sat shotgun, and Sunny and Annie crawled into the cramped jump seat. As soon as we left the yellow glow of Salmon's lights behind, I turned around in my seat and said, "So Blue and Sunny, tell me about yourselves. I want to know everything. I'm so sorry we've never spent any time together, but—"

"It's okay, Sage," Sunny broke in. "We're together now."

Silence filled the cab of the truck, and then I couldn't stand it any longer. "I know you're living in Gardiner, and you're both working in Yellowstone, but fill me in. How did you end up doing that? And what was this altercation with the cops all about?"

"We're mostly working at Yellowstone because of the wolves," said Sunny. "They, um, well..." Her voice trailed off.

"Wolves," I said. "Okay. It begins to make sense. I'm guessing you were up here because of this wolf and coyote shooting derby thing that happened this weekend?"

"Yes," said Sunny. "The derby's over now. They didn't kill any wolves. A lot of people told the wolves to clear out of the area, and it worked. But twenty-one coyotes got shot for no reason at all. I guess they didn't get the message."

"How did you two get so interested in wolves?" I asked, trying to figure out how much of my own experience I could share.

And then the story rolled out. I heard about Blue's first sighting of Aspen, and Sister's puppies, and her death in the trap.

"And, after Sister was killed," Sunny continued, "the pack left the den site, but one of the puppies was very sick. They had to leave her behind. So Blue and I took her home and nursed her back to health, then she rejoined her pack before we moved to Jackson."

"It was so much fun having her with us," said Blue. "I remember one morning when our dog, Angus, was playing with her. They got a little too rambunctious, and Angus took a bite out of the puppy's ear. It was chaos. There was blood everywhere and lots of yipping and growling, but it all turned out okay."

I caught my breath and turned around to look directly at Sunny.

"Did this wolf puppy have a name?" I asked, studying her face in the pale glow of the dashboard lights.

"Yes. Her name was Tierra."

Chapter Twenty-Six
2018

I stared out the window at the pitch black night. A new moon was due on New Year's, just two days away. The only features visible on the landscape were scattered clumps of snow-covered sagebrush and rabbitbrush grazed lightly by our passing headlights. I considered the wolf puppy named Tierra. Could it be the same wolf whose pelt was in the back of the truck with Issa and Tish?

"After he graduated," Sunny continued. "Blue started working in the park, at Mammoth. He was out looking for wolves one day, and he saw Tierra's puppies. They weren't really puppies at that point; they were mostly grown up. Lonestar was with them—"

"Wait, did you say Lonestar?" I asked. There was a slim chance there could be two wolves named Tierra, but Lonestar? This was too much to be mere coincidence. I looked back at Sunny for the third time. Behind her, I saw the outlines of two dark wolf faces pushed up against the pass-through window between the truck bed and the cab. Four golden eyes sparkled, reflecting a glimmer of light from the dashboard. Tish's mouth curved up slightly at the edges as she watched the facts line up like dominoes in my mind. I was flooded with images of running with Issa while we were merged in Yellowstone, seeing the large stone bison near Slough Creek, and meeting the eyes of a young blond man watching us as we ran past him. I shook my head, rejecting the idea, yet knowing it was true.

"Yes," said Sunny. "Lonestar was a full brother to Tierra, only he was a year older. He and Tierra's two sisters, Cinder and Goldie, took care of the family after Tierra was killed. But then someone shot Lonestar and tied his body on top of an SUV. So Blue and I went and took him. We skinned him and tanned his hide in secret, which was pretty hard. We learned how to do it on the Internet. The ground was frozen, so we couldn't just give him a good burial." My head spun as I imagined the scene with Lonestar's body, and I bit my tongue to keep from spilling the entire story of Issa and Tish, and their visit to my cabin. I knew, though, that I had to wait and consult with the wolves, to be sure they were okay with bringing Blue, Sunny, and Annie into their confidence.

"That's quite the story," I said. "You two are very brave. But, tell me, how did you come up with names for these wolves?"

"They told me their names," said Sunny.

"Blue and Annie," I said. "Did you hear them, too?"

"Not me," said Blue. "Sometimes I'd get a sense of what they were saying, but I was never as good at it as Sunny."

"I never knew any of those wolves," said Annie. "I do get messages from animals, but they don't come in words."

The remainder of the ride to Dillon passed quickly. Sunny and Annie fell asleep, while Blue and I chatted about wolf ecology. He was particularly interested in the cascading effects of the reintroduction of wolves on the Yellowstone ecosystem. Recent research indicated the presence of wolves was affecting everything from elk behavior to the survival of young willows and cottonwoods. And most of these effects were beneficial to ecosystem health.

Once we got to town, we found an inexpensive motel and registered for two rooms. While my three human companions hauled their gear inside, I let the wolves out to do their business, and then put them back in the truck.

"*Maybe we should have stayed in California,*" Tish moaned. "*This is killer boring.*"

"I'll let you out again for the night as soon as everyone goes to bed." I said. "But promise me you'll stay far away from humans or anything related to them. It's not safe for wolves around here."

"*We promise,*" said Tish.

We were almost too tired to eat, but we found a diner not far from the motel. Conversation flagged while we ate tuna sandwiches and salads with iceberg lettuce topped with a trace of dried-up, grated carrot. We returned to the motel and said our goodnights. I closed and locked our door, changed into a long red nightgown, and crawled under the covers of the single bed. Sunny was already tucked in, staring at the pages of a tattered paperback: Farley Mowat's *Never Cry Wolf.* She looked over at me as soon as I was settled. "Aunt Sage, the wolves in your truck, they are Tierra's children."

"Yes, they are," I said. "How much have they told you?"

"Oh, that Tish is a real talker. She told me all about their visit to Yosemite and the book you're writing."

"Well, that saves me a lot of explaining," I said. "But I don't think we can share this with Blue or Annie quite yet."

"No, but soon," said Sunny. "Oh, they're here." Sunny pushed back her blankets and climbed out of bed. She padded to the door, slid the chain out of its keeper, and opened the door to a very cold night. Tish and Issa marched in and looked up at me. "*Hi, Sage,*" said Tish. "*You were right. It's not safe out there. In fact, we got shot at twice in the space of about twenty minutes. Is it okay if we sleep in here? Do you have any food?*"

I rooted around in my duffel bag and presented Tish with three individually wrapped pieces of string cheese, half a bag of dried apricots, and eight Fig Newman's cookies. She looked up at me and said, "*Okay, I guess. If that's the best you can do. Can you...?*"

"Oh, sorry," I said, realizing at that moment just how tired I was. I pulled the wrappers off the cheese sticks and dumped the apricots out on the floor, while Sunny sat on her bed in silence, beaming at the wolves.

We departed for Gardiner early the next day. Intermittent snow flurries and icy roads slowed us down in a few places, but we arrived at our destination well before noon. The weather gods had spared us from a true blizzard during the drive, but now that we were home safe, Blue and Sunny were hoping for a huge New Year's storm. From the dark, brooding look of the sky, I thought it likely their wish would be granted.

Blue and Annie lived in a rented home on the southeast end of town, not far from the Yellowstone River, and just a short walk to the Roosevelt Arch and park entrance. The two-bedroom, single-story house was an off-white color, trimmed in sky blue, and it perched on a slope that afforded a wide view of the town.

"I think I need a nap," I said, after we'd unpacked the truck and I'd moved myself into the small guest bedroom. I offered no argument when Sunny insisted that she would be the one to sleep on the sofa.

"Do you have plans for tonight?" I asked Blue.

"Nothing set. Probably the usual: a bottle of cheap champagne and watching the ball drop in New York," he said with a grin.

"Sounds pretty wild to me," I said, relieved that I wouldn't be expected to go bar-hopping until the wee hours. I retreated to the bedroom, leaving the door slightly ajar in case Issa or Tish also needed a quiet place to crash. I was drifting off when I heard the door squeak slightly. I looked up to see Tish nose her way inside. She walked over and lay down next to the bed. I rolled over and closed my eyes. And then she bit me.

We landed in a complete whiteout. A bitterly cold, hard wind whipped the snow sideways, and frigid fingers of air and ice penetrated the layers of Tish's dense coat. We stood belly deep in soft snow on a rocky slope that supported scattered, dense patches of pine and spruce. The rushing roar of water and the low-pitched rumble of rocks tumbling over one another told me we were close to a creek or river.

"*Brr,*" Tish said with a full body shiver. "*I'd almost forgotten how cold it gets here. Luckily, we don't have far to go. And I think they're expecting us.*"

"Who is 'they'?"

"*You'll see.*"

"Tish, are we in the past? What year is this? What's the date?"

"*No, this isn't the past,*" Tish said. "*We're in real time. Based on your calendar, it's still December 31st. And we haven't traveled very far. We're in northern Yellowstone.*"

As we plowed our way through the snow, I prayed Tish knew this terrain. It was impossible to see the contours of the land, but

I could tell by the varying shades of white and gray, and the way Tish's body canted slightly to the right, that we were on a steep slope. One wrong step on an icy patch could be disastrous. After we'd progressed about thirty feet, the outline of a wolf lying on the snow gradually materialized out of the white backdrop.

"*Hey, Seeker,*" said Tish. "*It's us.*"

Seeker stood up, shook a heavy layer of snow from his coat, and walked out to meet us. After the customary nose sniffs and face licks, Seeker said, "*Everyone else is inside. We holed up in this cave until the storm passes. Milla has been looking forward to this visit, but she wasn't sure exactly which day you'd be here.*"

The cave entrance was right behind the spot where Seeker had been waiting for us. The opening was just large enough for us to squeeze through. Once inside, though, the passageway widened to about three feet, and extended at least twenty-five feet into the mountain. The air inside was warm and still, and carried the distinct smell of wet wolf. We followed Seeker to the far end of the cave, where an expansive space held his growing family. A large, snow-white wolf stood to greet us, her fluffy tail wagging. "*Tish and Sage, it's so good to have you here at last.*"

"*Sage, this is Milla,*" said Tish. "*Seeker's mate. And these are their pups. From left to right, we have Whisper, the only girl, and the three brothers, Flat Ears, Sniffer, and Scout. The boys are kind of hard to tell apart. Flat Ears is completely black and has, well, flat ears. Sniffer is the black with the white ear tips, and he's quite a bit larger than Scout, who is solid black.*"

Whisper was a beautiful cream-colored wolf, a sharp contrast to her brothers. The puppies were almost as big as the adults, but they looked leaner, rangier, and their legs seemed long relative to their bodies. I also noticed a quality of lightness, probably due to the carefree existence of puppyhood, and an eager brightness in their eyes that was missing in the adults. While I was admiring Seeker's family, another wolf stepped into the cave.

"*Rusty!*" Tish bounded over to the newcomer and almost knocked him down in her enthusiasm. She nipped and licked his face, which I thought was pretty disgusting, as his muzzle was covered with fresh blood and some bits of unidentifiable flesh.

"*There's a big chunk of deer outside for you pups,*" Rusty announced once he was able to escape Tish's affections. The puppies jumped up and dashed outside, smacking into one another and growling as they all tried to be the first to reach the food.

"*You three can go back to the remains of the deer and eat if you want to. I'll stay here with the puppies,*" said Rusty. "*Drop down to the creek and go west. It's not far, but you might want to go soon. I smelled coyote out there.*"

"*I'm good,*" said Tish. "*But Seeker and Milla, you go. We'll stay here and visit with Rusty.*"

Seeker and Milla left right away, and Rusty brought us up to speed on the family's recent activities. The puppies were remarkably quiet and well-behaved as they shared the deer meat outside the cave. I must admit, though, that despite all my travels in Wolf Time, I still cringed when I heard the snapping of bones as the wolves feasted.

"*These past few months have been hard,*" Rusty said. "*In the fall, there was plenty to eat with the elk and deer who wandered through, and we scavenged bison carcasses that some of the other packs killed. This has been a good place for us, with the big creek to the south. We head up an old trail to the northeast for most of our hunting. But we've had trouble since winter set in. There are a lot of wolf packs in this area. At first, they were patient with newcomers, but now that we've become more established, and have started to have pups, the locals are getting testier, more likely to challenge us.*"

"*Is there somewhere else you can go?*" asked Tish.

"*Seeker wants to go back down to the southeast corner of the park. We were doing okay down there when you and Issa left, but when Lonestar disappeared, we decided to return to this area.*" said Rusty. "*We'll probably move south again come spring.*"

The puppies finished their meal and came back inside. All four of them walked past us to the back of the cave to lie down. Milla and Seeker returned about twenty minutes later.

"*You pups stay here,*" said Seeker. "*We'll be right outside. We have some things to talk about.*" I looked back at the pups. There was no question about them staying put, they were already fast asleep. We filed outside and walked for a few minutes to a narrow flat area large enough for all of us to sit comfortably. The snow had tapered off, and I could see a few stars sparkling between cloud masses.

"*So, Sage,*" said Seeker. "*Tish told me you had a few questions about what I said when we last met at Slough Creek.*"

"Do I?" I struggled to figure out to what he was referring.

"*Yes, Sage,*" said Tish. "*Remember when you were asking about soul development? You may not have actually asked me outright, but I've been seeing your thoughts. I figured since Seeker was the first to bring it up with you, he'd be a good one to explain more about it.*"

"Oh, right," I said. "Seeker, you mentioned past lives that day. I have a friend, Mary Beth, who practices shamanism. She believes humans have eternal souls that reincarnate over and over, and for each lifetime, we come in with a master plan, a script, about how that life is going to go. Basically, before we're even born we choose our parents, our life path, the various challenges we're going to face, and the lessons we want to learn. What I'm wondering is, does it work the same way for wolves?"

"*It does,*" said Seeker. "*Just like humans, each wolf has an eternal soul that reincarnates in different bodies at different times and places, with the ultimate goal being refinement or evolution of the individual soul. As with humans, before we are born into a lifetime, we decide how that life is going to play out. We pick the lessons we want to learn, which aspects of soul development we want to work on.*"

I was quiet for a minute, and then said, "I'm still not sure how to think about all this, even in terms of human lives, and this is the first time I've ever thought about it with respect to animals."

"*There's another aspect to the concept of soul as it relates to animals that you need to know,*" said Seeker. "*This also applies to the humans, but most of you aren't aware of it. It has to do with what we call Wolf Clan Soul. Each wolf has an individual soul, but all wolves are part of a collective wolf soul as well, which has a specific mission on Earth, and a similar desire to refine and develop itself.*"

"So what's the mission of the Wolf Clan Soul?" I asked. "Based on the history of your species, at least the part that involves humans, it seems like it must have to do with creating a super high level of controversy."

Seeker laughed. "*You could say that, yes. Part of the mission of the wolves is to bring the deepest, ugliest aspects of the human psyche to the surface, to expose the potential for humans to experience deep hatred and loathing, so these destructive emotions can be recognized and transmuted. As far as we understand it, the ultimate goal of the evolution of all souls is to live in and act from a place of compassion and love, in harmony with all living and non-living beings. To attain that goal, all the human qualities that don't reflect compassion and love have to be brought up, worked through, and left behind. We help humans recognize and transmute their hatred, and the fear that underlies it. For some people, these ugly emotions surface and are inflicted on other people. For others, it's not directed at people, but*" at other species, which is where we come in. The controversy occurs because, thankfully, many humans already are living in that place of love and compassion, but many are still learning."

"Wow," I said. "That makes sense, but what an awful job you have."

"*It does seem that way sometimes, but somebody has to do it,*" Seeker said, grinning. "*If you have more questions, Issa can probably answer them, but he wanted you to be in Wolf Time for this introduction. Additionally, Milla wanted to meet you, and have you meet our family. Thank you.*"

"I'm happy to be here," I said. "It strikes me that Issa is very wise, and he always maintains his composure. Is he a really old soul?"

"*Issa is a Master Teacher,*" said Tish. "*He's the one who initiated our journey to California to meet you. And, yes, he's a really old soul.*"

"*If it's okay with everyone,*" Milla interjected, "*I think it's time to get some rest.*"

"*Sounds good to me,*" said Seeker. He stood and led us all back to the cave. Tish and I curled up just inside the mouth of the cave, leaving the rest of the space to the family.

"*We'll be leaving at first light,*" Tish said to Seeker before everyone found their resting places. "*So this is goodbye for now.*"

"*Okay, safe travels,*" said Seeker. "*Thanks for coming to visit, and Sage, thank you for speaking on our behalf.*"

We awoke just before the sun came up. The cave entrance faced southeast, so we were greeted by dawn's first pale glow. We lay quiet and watched the sky lighten. When the sun crested the eastern ridge, we could see the storm had passed and the sky was a deep blue, with a few leftover pearly-white cumulus clouds scurrying off to the northeast.

"*Okay, Sage, time to go,*" Tish whispered.

We crept out of the den, and Tish glanced briefly to the northeast, searching for the faint game trail that we'd used the night before. At this point it appeared as just a narrow trough in the deep snow. When Tish looked up, I spotted an old wooden sign affixed to a metal t-post south of the trail. I squinted to read the sign, and barely made out the words "Entering Gallatin National Forest."

The reality of what I was seeing, and what it meant, hit me like a lightning bolt. Milla, Seeker, Rusty, and the puppies were traveling back and forth over the park boundary to hunt. I wracked my brain to remember the dates for the wolf hunting season in Montana. I'd looked it up after the first merge with Issa in Yellowstone. Was it the first of October through the end of December? No, that was Wyoming. And Montana had a longer season, something like mid-September through mid-March.

"Tish," I cried. "We can't go yet. We have to..."

But I was too late.

Chapter Twenty-Seven
2018

"We have to go back right now!" I sat up in bed, wide awake as soon as we returned to Blue's house. "Seeker's family is in danger. From what I've been reading, the wolf haters wait for Yellowstone wolves to leave the park and then shoot them. As soon as a wolf steps across the park boundary, into a national forest or onto private land, he or she becomes a legal target. In fact, for some sick reason, the shooters find extra pleasure in killing park wolves."

Issa had joined us in the bedroom, and, at my words, Tish shot him a concerned look. Neither spoke for several minutes. I got up from the bed and paced back and forth across the worn, dark green carpet. Outside, snow was falling heavily, just as it had been when Tish and I had arrived at the cave. This was disorienting, because when we left the cave the storm was departing. It took me a moment to remember that Tish and I had stayed overnight at the cave, but it was still New Year's Eve here in Gardiner.

"So, are we going back?" I asked. "Milla and Seeker's den is very close to the park boundary. Just as we were leaving, I saw a sign marking where the national park ends and the national forest begins. The trail Rusty said they use when they hunt leads out of the park. We have to go back to warn them."

"*We can't, Sage,*" said Issa. "*A human can't travel in Wolf Time more than once in a twelve-hour period. It takes too much energy from you, and puts a great deal of pressure on your brain. If you travel too soon, you might not come back the same.*"

"We have to go," I insisted. "I'm strong. I'm willing to take that risk."

"*Maybe we can just send a message to Milla telepathically. She's pretty good at that,*" said Issa.

"*Not that good,*" said Tish. "*I sent her at least a dozen messages about when Sage and I were coming to visit. Seeker said Milla was expecting us, but she didn't know when we were coming. I think Sage is right, someone has to go back to warn them.*"

"Could one of you go alone?" I asked.

"*Ordinarily, wolves don't do much time or space travel alone,*" said Issa. "*Chronological time has little meaning to us, and we don't navigate the same way humans do. We aren't attuned to calendars, clocks, or maps, which are all human constructs. That can make it difficult for us to return to the time and place we started from. I could probably get to Seeker and Milla's cave, but there's no guarantee I could come directly back here. I hadn't thought about it this way before, but in some ways, humans anchor us to the planet.*"

"I still think we have to go now," I said. "It was a gorgeous sunny day back there, and they'll be heading out to look for food." I walked across the room to Issa, and sat down in front of him with my legs crossed.

He sighed and said, "*Okay, I sure hope this works out.*" We stared at one another for a few seconds, I felt the pull into his eyes, and then we were off, falling backwards.

We landed in the same place Tish and I had left just a few minutes earlier. I felt as if I were in a movie, as we'd once again gone from an intense snowstorm in Gardiner to a fine clear day at the cave.

Just as I'd predicted, Seeker and his family were heading northeast, up the trail. Rusty was tailing the group, and Issa called to him quietly, "*Hey, Rust.*" Rusty stopped and turned around. His face lit up when he saw Issa. We trotted toward Rusty while he loped back to greet us.

"*What are you doing here?*" asked Rusty. "*Sage, how can you be here, too? Isn't that against the rules?*"

"*It is,*" said Issa. "*But it was urgent that we return. Sage told us you were in danger. She said you were hunting in an area where you could easily get shot. This trail leads right out of Yellowstone into a hunting zone.*"

"*We've been fine all year,*" said Rusty with a frown. "*Although lately we haven't spent much time up on the northern plateau, because there's been plenty of game congregating to the south and west. This is the first time in a few moons that we've gone north.*"

"*Go catch the family, and bring them back here so we can explain,*" said Issa. Rusty loped off at high speed, and a few minutes later, the line of wolves came trotting back toward us. The entire group exchanged greetings with Issa, and I was once again impressed with how similar they were to people in that respect. Each wolf in Seeker's pack participated in the ritual of nose sniffing and face licking with Issa. The wolves were better than most people in acknowledging one another.

"*Rusty told us briefly why you came back,*" said Seeker after the greetings were completed. "*I must admit, although I've scent-marked the post that holds that sign many times, I never considered what it might be for. Thank you for alerting us, Sage. We'll know in the future to be watchful, and to try to pay attention to these boundary markings. It's hard, though, because it's such a different way of understanding the land than the way we're accustomed to. Humans have strange rules. Can you tell me why humans can legally shoot us on one side of an invisible line, but we're safe on the other side?*"

"Oh, Seeker," I said. "It's very confusing. It depends on which agency manages the land. The rules are different for different agencies."

"*I don't know what 'agency' means. And I don't think I want to know. We'll just take your word for it and try to be careful. Issa, will you two be staying for a while?*"

"*No,*" said Issa. "*It's best if we get back. I want to keep Sage's time in Wolf Time to a minimum. This is her second trip today and the return could be stressful on her.*"

It was still snowing hard when we got back to Blue and Annie's house.

"*How does your head feel?*" asked Tish.

"Fine," I said. "It's a little fuzzy, but not too bad."

"*Well, good,*" said Tish. "*We can't afford to damage you, or we'll have to find another writer and start all over again.*"

"Gee, thanks for your concern over my well-being," I said.

"*I didn't mean it that way, Sage. I was trying to be funny,*" said Tish.

"*Come on, Tish,*" said Issa. "*Let's clear out. I'm pretty sure Sage is going to need some sleep.*"

After the wolves left, I closed the bedroom door, flopped down on the bed, and fell fast asleep.

The house was full of the mingled smells of coffee and garlic when I finally rolled out of bed at 8:00 a.m. the next morning. I walked to the bedroom window, pulled up the wooden blind, and peered outside. The storm was clearing. I dressed and wandered down the hall to the kitchen. Everyone else was already up. Annie was busy at the stove, and Blue and Sunny sat at the table nursing cups of tea. All three greeted me at once.

"Good morning!" I said. "Happy New Year! Annie, it smells amazing in here." I pulled a chrome chair with a red vinyl covered seat away from the matching kitchen table, which was topped with an enamel surface. The set dated to the 1940s, and was identical to one that had lived in my grandmother's kitchen for as long as I could remember.

"Doesn't it?" said Sunny. "My stomach is growling like crazy. Annie is an amazing cook."

"Almost ready," said Annie, who was wrapped up in a blue-and-white gingham apron. She set out plates and silver, and we served ourselves a feast of huevos rancheros and red potatoes sautéed with onions and red bell peppers, accompanied by fresh cornbread muffins.

"This is my small way of saying thank you for picking us up and getting us home safely, Sage," said Annie once we were all seated.

"No problem, Annie," I said. "It's been such a pleasure to spend time with you all. I'm not going to want to go home."

"You're welcome to stay as long as you want," said Blue.

"Well, I had kind of planned on..."

"*Ahem*," Tish cleared her throat. She and Issa had been lying near the front door, but, hearing Blue's invitation, Tish rose and walked over to the table. "*I think Sage has work waiting for her back home. Don't you, Sage?*"

I looked down at Tish, who stared up at me with her eyebrows raised.

"Yes, I guess so," I said. "And—"

"*And Issa and I talked about it last night,*" Tish interrupted. "*We decided it would be okay to tell these guys about the book project, and about Wolf Time. But it needs to stay within this group. And we need to get you home to finish the story.*"

"*Tish,*" said Issa from across the room. "*Give it a rest.*"

Tish lay down by my feet, and, between bites, I explained my experiences of the past ten days. Blue and Annie stared at me, open-mouthed, while their breakfasts got cold. Sunny continued to eat and smile. No one asked any questions.

"Then we got your call for help," I said. "And you know the rest. But, Issa, I have a question for you. The first day you and Tish were at the cabin, you explained the Network to me, and said there was a time of reckoning coming. What did you mean by that?"

Issa walked to the table and sat next to Tish. He was silent for a moment, as if gathering his thoughts. "*You probably already know this, or at least sense it,*" he said. "*Humans have reached a critical mass on Earth. There's a limit to the life-sustaining capacity of the planet, at least as humans perceive that capacity, which is in terms of the life forms humans consider important—the plants and animals they eat or use for clothing or shelter, the other species they admire, and most of all, themselves. Humans have reproduced a lot, have taken over the habitat of almost all other species, and have*" contaminated a lot of water, air, and soil. This way of being cannot continue without major consequences for most of life on Earth.

"In response to what we understand is a difficult time for humans on Earth, select members of the Animal Network as well as members of various elemental networks, like the Fire and Water networks, are becoming more vocal, and more visible, to try to show humans that there are other ways to live. It's time for humans to take a huge step forward in their evolution, and one of the first tasks at hand is to develop reverence for all the other-than-human beings on the planet—the other animals, the plants, the rocks, the rivers and lakes as well as the objects you craft from these entities in order to survive. It's time for humans to re-learn to honor all that is of the earth, to recognize you are but a part of the whole, and to live accordingly.

"We sense many humans believe they are somehow separate from the rest of creation, but when you think about it, isn't that silly? You wouldn't survive for more than minutes without the Air Network, no more than days without the Water, Plant, and Animal networks. And imagine if the Solar Network decided to alter its intensity for even seconds? Despite the obvious connectedness of all things, at some point, humans began to think they were separate from, and superior to, the entire rest of creation. We believe it happened when your thought-processes called religions came into being.

"In terms of a time of reckoning, I meant that now is the time to change what it means to be human on this Earth, before the planet is wracked by too much human-induced change that will cause immense suffering. The Networks are showing up to help accelerate the necessary lifestyle changes. The Wolf Network happened to pull one of the short straws, so we, along with a few other species, are in the vanguard."

"Are all the wolves that are alive right now working on this?" I asked.

"*To some extent, yes,*" said Issa. "*Seeker told you about past lives, reincarnation, and soul development. Some of the wolves on Earth now have been reincarnated a multitude of times, have spent many lifetimes on Earth. For other wolves, this life may be their very first. So there are young and old souls. The older their soul, the more abilities wolves have in the realm of inter-species communication, and the work of the Networks. Tish and I have been here for more than one hundred lifetimes; we're pretty old souls, so we can merge with humans and enter Wolf Time. Middle-aged souls like Seeker and Milla can communicate with humans, but they can't merge. And the young souls don't have these abilities, but they do play an important role in the evolution of both wolves and humans, and the time of reckoning, because they also accepted the task of assisting humans with transmuting hatred and anger.*"

"That's a lot to think about," I said. "Even though this is all new information for me, it somehow feels as if I've known it all along."

"You have, Sage," said Sunny. "But when you passed through the veil at birth, you had to forget it. This is a tremendous gift that Issa and Tish are giving us, to teach us this part of the grand plan for life on Earth."

On that note, we finished breakfast and cleaned up the dishes. I packed my duffel and loaded it into the truck. We said our goodbyes, which included a lot of hugs shared between wolves and humans, and promised to stay in close touch.

Before we climbed into the truck, Sunny said, "Oh, I almost forgot, I had a dream last night. With all the talk this morning, I forgot to mention it. Tierra came to me and asked if we could have a ceremony to honor her and Lonestar. She would like us to take their pelts to the Lamar Valley, and she'd like us to do it on the spring equinox."

"That's a wonderful idea, Sunny," I said. "Let's plan on it."

"I looked up the date this morning," said Sunny. "Here in Gardiner, it's at 10:57 a.m. on March 20th.

"We'll be here," I said. "Count on it."

The drive back to California took us two full days. We spent the night again in Elko, and got back to the cabin late in the afternoon the next day, right before another major storm. By the following morning, there was a foot of new snow on the ground. As usual, the wolves were away when I woke up. Before I fixed breakfast, they returned and announced they would be leaving for a while.

"*We heard from the ravens that a small wolf pack traveled down from Oregon into California while we were away,*" Issa explained. "*They want to establish territory in a place called the Modoc Plateau, but there's a lot of ranching up there. Tish and I are going to head up that way to help them find a safe place to den. We're not sure how long we'll be away.*"

And then they were gone, heading northeast at a steady trot. I missed them dearly, even before they disappeared from my sight.

Chapter Twenty-Eight
2019

After Issa and Tish left on the third of January, I knuckled down and put all of my attention on their story. I read, researched, and wrote, to the exclusion of almost everything else. On March 17th, at about 9:00 p.m., a little over ten weeks after they had left, I heard a familiar scratch at the front door. Flooded with excitement and relief, I jumped up from my chair to let them in.

Tish stood on the deck steps, looking fit and shiny. In fact, she looked as if she'd put on quite a bit of weight. Issa, on the other hand, looked terrible. His head hung low, he'd lost as much weight as Tish had gained, and his coat looked rough and matted.

"Come in, you guys," I said, opening the door wider to give them room. "Issa, what's wrong?"

Instead of answering me, and without making eye contact, Issa walked slowly to the fireplace, made one circle, and lay down with a deep sigh. He put his head on his paws and closed his eyes. I looked at Tish.

"*He's been sick for over a week,*" Tish said. "*I don't know what's wrong. I thought it was from some rotten fish we found when we raided a garbage pile, but he's not getting better. He's got a runny nose, and he complains of being too hot one minute, and too cold the next. He won't eat, and he's not drinking much. He doesn't know what's wrong, either. And he's getting weaker every day. We barely made it back here.*"

"Well, there's not much we can do tonight, but I think we need to get him to a vet first thing in the morning." I wondered how Dr. Anderson down in Mariposa would respond when I brought a wolf into her waiting room.

"*What's a vet?*" asked Tish.

"A person who takes care of sick animals."

"*He's not going to like that. He keeps saying he just want to be left alone.*"

"He might die if we don't get him help," I said. "I'm not an expert, but it could be distemper, which can be fatal." I walked over to Issa and knelt down beside him.

"Issa," I said. "Will you let me take you to someone who can help you?"

"*No,*" he said, without lifting his head. "*I'll be okay, just not there yet. Need to sleep.*"

"*Sage,*" said Tish. "*Didn't Blue say our mom had distemper, and that's why he and Sunny ended up taking her home? Maybe you should ask him what to do.*"

I went immediately to the phone and dialed Blue's number. "Blue, it's Sage."

"Hi, Sage," said Blue. "Haven't heard from you in a while. What's new? Did Issa and Tish ever come back?"

276

"They did, just a bit ago. And that's why I'm calling. Issa is really sick. We think it might be distemper."

After I described Issa's symptoms and condition, Blue said, "It could be distemper. And, if it is, there's little a vet can do to help, except provide support and administer fluids, if necessary. For the most part, they either get over it or they don't. Keep him warm, try to keep his eyes and nose clean, and be sure he drinks a lot of water. He's pretty strong. I'm guessing he'll be okay."

We chatted for a few more minutes about the upcoming memorial ceremony for Tierra and Lonestar, and Blue's new job as an assistant tour guide for wolf watchers. Then we said our goodbyes.

"Thanks, Blue. I'll keep you posted, and we'll see you in two days." After I put the phone back in its charger, I wondered if we really would make it to Gardiner with Issa so sick.

I walked over to the fireplace and sat down next to Issa. I put my hand on his head and gently stroked the spot between his eyes. "Issa," I said. "Blue told me the most important thing for you right now is to be sure to drink a lot of water. If you get dehydrated, you could die. And if I see you're not drinking enough, we will go to the vet in the morning." I knew it was an empty threat. There was no way I could get his hundred-pound body into my truck without his full cooperation.

"Tish," I said. "Distemper is very contagious. How are you feeling?"

"*I'm fine,*" she said. She curled up next to Issa by the fire and put her head across his back.

"Okay, then." I went to fill their bowl with clean water. "Drink, drink, drink, and I'll see you tomorrow."

The next morning Issa felt about the same, no worse, but no better. I looked at the water level in the bowl and saw someone had been drinking. I looked at Tish, who nodded and said, "*He's drinking, not to worry.*"

I was reluctant to broach the subject of the ceremony, so I went to the kitchen and started to heat water for tea, and dropped two slices of sourdough in the toaster.

"*You two have to go,*" said Issa.

I looked up, wondering what he meant.

"*To Gardiner,*" he continued. "*To honor and celebrate Tierra and Lonestar. You have to go. I'll stay here. I'm not quite up to traveling yet, but I'll be fine. I checked in with the wolf ancestors last night and asked them to show me just a bit of my future. What they showed me made me believe I have more work to do in this lifetime. And, if that's not the case, I'm at peace with it. Really. You two go.*"

"No, Issa," I argued. "We're staying right here with you. We couldn't possibly—"

"*Yes, we could,*" interjected Tish. "*And we will. It's important for us to be in Yellowstone for this. I'm sure Issa will be okay; otherwise, I wouldn't go either.*" I knew continuing to argue would get me nowhere, so I shrugged and said, "Okay, Tish. We have to leave by noon today. Are you ready?"

"*Not quite,*" said Tish. "*I'm going to try to track down a rabbit or a few squirrels, or maybe even a deer, for some breakfast. And I want to bring back food for Issa, too, for when he gets hungry.*"

While Tish was out, I filled a dozen large bowls and buckets with water and put them in the kitchen. When she came back, we cached four large, dead gray squirrels outside, under the cabin steps where they would be less likely to rot quickly. Issa promised he would drink and eat. I was very worried about him, but I was in the minority when I lobbied once again to stay home.

Tish and I left the cabin just before noon, and it was almost midnight by the time we pulled into Elko. We caught a few hours of sleep, ate a quick egg and English muffin breakfast and then pushed on to the Bozeman airport, where Adam was due to arrive at 1:30 p.m. He was flying in from Denver, where he'd been attending a conference. I left Tish in the back of the truck, and walked into the airport's small baggage claim area. Adam was sitting in a molded plastic chair staring at his iPad.

"Hey," I said.

"Hey, Sage. There you are."

"Sorry I'm late," I said, even though I didn't think I was.

"No, you're right on time. Our flight got here a few minutes early." Adam stood and pulled me into a big hug. Feeling a slight catch in my chest, I turned my face away from his intended kiss. He pulled back and let go of me. "How are you?" he asked. "You look great."

"I'm good. A little tired, and worried about Issa. We had to leave him back in California. I think he has distemper. He insists he's going to be fine, but I felt bad leaving him."

"How did he get distemper?"

"I don't know. He and Tish traveled up to northeastern California and back over the last few months, so I guess he could have picked it up anywhere."

"Is Tish here?"

"She's in the truck. Are you ready to go?"

"I am. I can't wait to get over to the park. I haven't been to Yellowstone in I can't remember how long."

We left the airport, made a quick stop at a health food store for groceries, and headed for Gardiner. Adam talked almost nonstop about the Denver conference, which was focused on recent anthropological work in the Great Plains.

The streets of Gardiner were quiet when we arrived and drove through to the south side. Towering piles of dirty snow were heaped up along the road shoulders and against buildings. The roads were glistening wet. Most of the ice from the night before had melted under the slight warmth of the sun and the friction of tires. It was between seasons in the park. Snowmobile season was tapering off, and the summer tourist season was still months away. Most park facilities were closed, which made it perfect for our equinox event. The only thing I could see that might be cause for concern was the layer of dark cumulus clouds that was massing to the southwest. I hoped, if it did snow, that the amount would be slight. The plan was to hold the ceremony late in the morning, and the road to Slough Creek could be impassable if the coming storm proved to be significant.

We arrived to find there was no place to park at Blue's house. Puzzling over who all the cars belonged to, we left the truck in front of a neighbor's house and walked back over a treacherous obstacle course of ice and snow. Adam knocked, and when Blue opened the door to let us in, I was so surprised I had to take a few steps back. The house was full of guests.

Unbeknownst to me, Blue and Sunny had invited a lot of people. The Morrison clan, in particular, was well represented. Blue had invited Marshal and Lois, as well as Marshal's brother Grey, his wife Abby, and their twin boys, Marc and John. Even Scott, Marshal's step-brother, had flown in the day before. Annie had invited fellow wolf-advocates Gordon, Rachael, and Cori, all of whom I was told had been present at the Salmon event. Everyone was lodging at the River View Guest House, just a short walk from Blue and Annie's house.

The bustle created by so many people was overwhelming compared to the months of silence I'd just spent cloistered in my cabin. As soon as Adam, Tish, and I stepped into the house, we were enveloped in a sea of hugs and handshakes. When the twins, who looked about twelve years old or so, saw Tish, they both backed hurriedly into a corner of the living room, almost falling down in their haste to get away.

"It's okay," said Blue. "This is Tish, and she is very friendly."

Tish sent me a look that said, "Boy, do I ever have him fooled." But she played her part well when she walked into the house, lay down on the large faux sheepskin rug in the middle of the room, and rolled over on her back. Side by side, the boys slowly walked over to Tish, dropped down on their knees, and softly stroked her belly.

After we'd all gotten inside and shed our coats, I looked across the room to the kitchen and saw Lois leaning up against the door jamb. She was much thinner than I remembered, and her hair had gone completely gray. It was the first time I'd seen her since I had run away from Salmon and my guilt over the deaths of our sister and brother-in-law. As soon as I saw her, I knew I hadn't left the guilt behind—it lived within me like a parasite. To hide my tears, I turned left and hurried down the hall to the guest bedroom. Before I could reach the door, Lois was behind me, reaching out to touch my shoulder.

"Sage," she whispered. "I can't believe you're still carrying it around. It was not your fault. It was an accident, just a terrible, terrible accident."

I pulled away from her, pushed past duffel bags and piles of clothing, and threw myself on the bed, engulfed by grief and wracked by sobs. Lois sat down next to me and put her hand on my back, waiting for me to cry myself out.

Chapter Twenty-Nine
2019

"It's so good to see you again, Sage," said Lois, after I returned from the bathroom, where I'd gone to rinse my face and dry my eyes. I sat down next to her on the bed, and she put her arm around me. "It broke my heart over and over when you stopped returning my calls, and didn't respond to the letters I sent."

"I just couldn't," I said, taking a deep breath to prevent any more tears from falling. "I hope you can forgive me. I see now how stupid I was, and how much time together we lost because I was so selfish with my guilt."

"Selfish?"

"Yes, selfish. I held onto the guilt, blaming myself even though everyone told me it wasn't my fault and to let it go. But I held on to it. I let it define me as unreliable and unstable, as some sort of failed human being. And then there was the added guilt I felt for running away from Salmon. I realized last night, while I tossed and turned in a cheap motel in Elko, that I've used the accident as an excuse for many things that haven't gone right in my life. It's been a weird sort of crutch, one I used to explain why I had so much trouble making any kind of commitment—to a place, a job, a relationship. I know I have more work to do with all of this, but I think I'm ready to let go of it now, once and for all."

"Wow," said Lois. "That seems like a lot of self-analysis. My only suggestion is be kind to yourself. Anyway, all that aside, I'm so glad the wolves brought us all together again. Marshal and I can't wait to hear the whole story. The only thing Blue and Sunny shared is that you befriended two wolves and are writing a book about them. And then, of course, there's the amazing coincidence of how Adam found Tierra's pelt at a shop in California. Truth really is stranger than fiction. We can't wait to hear more."

"Ah, yeah, well," I stammered. "Of course, I'll tell you all about it soon."

We both stood and shared a long hug before rejoining the group. As soon as we got to the kitchen, the doorbell rang, and a delivery man from Tony's Pizza handed Blue three large, garlic-infused cardboard boxes. After Annie laid out napkins, flatware, and plates, everyone served themselves and found seats at the dining table or various places in the living room. All available couches, chairs, and some floor space were occupied. Tish settled in front of the wood stove, but quickly realized it was way too hot with so many people in the house. She went to stand at the back door, and I rose to let her out. "Be careful," I whispered. "There are a lot of antis in this area."

"*Antis?*" she said.

"Yes, wolf haters."

"*Got it. I'll just catch the river and wander along the bank, for old time's sake. My biggest concern is running into other wolves. I'll be back soon.*"

The room was quiet when I returned, except for the sounds of chewing and swallowing. When I took my seat again, Marshal looked across the room at me and said, "Well, Sage. Are you ready to tell us what this reunion is all about? We were all here last night and got up to speed on Adam acquiring Tierra's pelt, and Blue and Sunny admitted that they were, in fact, responsible for the theft of that dead black wolf a while back in downtown Jackson. How they never got found out is beyond me. So now it seems you want to have some sort of ceremony for the dead wolves? Honestly, at first it sounded a little too touchy-feely for me, but Lois insisted we come. And it did seem like too much time had gone by that we hadn't been together as a family, so here we are."

"Thanks for coming all the way up here, Marshal," I said. "I know you had to do a lot of extra driving because of road closures." My eyes started to tingle again, and a few more tears spilled down my cheeks. I wiped them away with a napkin and said, "I'm sorry. I'm just so happy to see everyone again. The ceremony we have in mind is pretty simple. We want to take the pelts out to a site near the Lamar Valley where Lonestar spent part of his life, and where we believe Tierra was planning to go before she was shot, and bury them. Sunny, Blue, and I thought it would be a good way to say goodbye. As it turned out, it also seemed like an opportune time for our family to reunite. Thanks again, everyone, for coming."

"Wouldn't have missed it," said Scott.

"Hear, hear," said Gordon. "I'd like to propose a toast. Here's to Sage, Sunny, Blue, and Annie for their commitment to the wolves." Everyone raised their beverages and clinked containers. "I'm also very happy to tell you that, along with several other investors and landowners, I've been working on a project that will help wolves as well as numerous other species. I can't share details yet, but it involves the purchase of land and grazing leases in some important habitat areas around Yellowstone." Sunny and Blue jumped up and clapped at Gordon's words, and I found myself near tears once again.

The next morning, as we lingered over coffee, I told everyone about the book project. I left out a few details, including the fact that the wolves were telling me the story, and that I merged with them to travel long distances in time and space. I figured that might be too much information for the group to digest.

"I did a lot of research, and got some ideas from dreams," I explained. "One of the most profound things I've learned is that wolves are a lot like humans. They're deeply committed to their families, especially their children. They love to play. They're strong and smart. Yet we've used them as examples of the epitome of evil in the world; you know, all the big, bad wolf garbage that's foisted off on us when we're young and impressionable. And many humans have tried hard to kill all the wolves every place they occur, to completely destroy the species. Is this because people can't stand the thought of a predator that may be smarter and more effective than humans are?"

"That's part of it," Sunny chimed in. "But humans kill a lot of whales and dolphins, too, and bears and mountain lions, but none of these other animals generate the extreme animosity that wolves do. No one hates dolphins or whales. Okay, so wolves sometimes prey on livestock, but so do coyotes, and bears, and mountain lions, yet few people deeply hate any of those species. When it comes to wolves, what is it that makes people completely lose touch with their humanity?"

"Some folks have obvious reasons for their anger at wolves," said Marshal. "If they lose a cow or a sheep, or their horse or dog to wolves, it makes sense that they'd be mad. But it's completely irrational to want to annihilate an entire species, or torture animals because you're angry at one or two members of that species."

"It's bigger than that, Marshal," said Scott. "A lot of people are harboring a lot of anger. They're mad at the President. They're mad at the legislatures. They're mad at Democrats, their bosses, their neighbors, or an estranged family member. Or they're just mad in general because their lives aren't going the way they want them to. And these people are looking for a scapegoat, something to use as a target for that anger. The wolves just happen to be that target."

"I think it's time for those people to grow up," Sunny said.

It took us almost two hours to drive from Gardiner to the Slough Creek turnoff, as we had to stop three times for bison on the road. A few inches of snow had fallen overnight, but the plows had cleared the route. There were no other cars on the road. We parked in the dirt lot across from the bison stone and walked up to the top of the low hill northwest of the lot. When I first stepped out of the truck, it seemed as if we were completely alone. I saw no wildlife, not even a bird. Closer inspection revealed a pair of old bison cows slowly climbing up out of a draw south of the slough, and a pair of ravens circling above a cluster of conifers on the ridge due west of us. And then the howling started.

At first it was a solo wolf sending a message to all beings within five or six miles. Then the first was joined by another, and another, until the chorus expressed the sentiments of at least five or six individuals. We all stood silent and listened, all of us except Tish, that is. She stood up tall, tipped her head back and let out a loud howl that caused the hair on the back of my neck to stand up. I looked around at our group as Tish let out a series of eight individual howls. Marc and John were wide-eyed and slack-jawed.

Marshal seemed a bit worried, with deepening creases across his forehead, and Lois looked like a kid at Christmas, holding her hands together as if in prayer, a huge smile on her face.

As soon as Tish's last howl faded, Seeker, Milla, and their almost full-grown puppies came loping down the drainage that extended up to the north. I counted the pups as they came into view, but I only saw three, not four. Tish and I exchanged looks, and she let me know that Flat Ears had not made it through the winter. He'd been helping to pull down an elk and was killed when the elk's powerful kick connected with his head.

After Seeker's family joined us, I looked around to be sure we were still alone. It would not be good if visitors or park employees saw us cavorting with wild wolves. Blue had found a place for the ceremony a few weeks earlier and we needed to get there, and out of sight, as soon as possible.

Blue and Sunny directed everyone back down the hill, and across the dirt road to the east. We climbed up a steep, rocky, forested hill for about twenty minutes. I was impressed to see everyone was in reasonably good shape, and the climb was not a struggle. We were fortunate the snow was not deep. The hill eventually levelled off and we continued north for several more minutes. Then Blue led us down a final gentle slope and stopped at the edge of a small, flat clearing. I gasped when I saw the structure in the middle of the clearing.

"Blue..." I said. "What is this? Did you build this?"

A scaffold, about five foot square and six feet tall, stood above the snowy ground. The supporting poles were straight and set firmly into the rocky substrate. Dozens of large black feathers attached to the scaffold fluttered in the cold air, and a bison skull had been placed on the ground at the east end of the structure. Four shiny stones that looked like black tourmaline were set in a diamond pattern in front of the skull, and a large piece of rose quartz sat in the center of the black stones.

"Sunny didn't think it felt right to bury the pelts," said Blue. "So she and I and Annie came out here and built this instead. This way they'll be in the open air and can be joined by the spirits of their friends, both living and not. The corner poles are aligned with the cardinal directions."

"It's perfect," I said. I looked at Tish and the other wolves to gauge their reactions, hoping all the work that had gone into the structure had not been in vain. The wolves stared at the scaffold for a few minutes while the rest of us remained quiet. We watched as Seeker and Rusty walked to the scaffold, sniffed it, and then circled it in a counter-clockwise direction. As they circled, they both lifted a leg to pee on each of the four corner posts. I assumed this meant they accepted it. I looked at Tish; she was nodding her head.

Sunny and Blue carefully placed Tierra and Lonestar's bodies on the top of the scaffold. They arranged Lonestar over Tierra so the two formed a cross, with their heads oriented to the northeast and southeast. Their long furry tails, which still looked very much alive to me, hung down over the edges of the scaffold. Tish crawled underneath the structure and lay down, with her head to the east. Milla and Whisper lay down on either side of Tish, with their heads pointing west. Seeker, Rusty, Sniffer and Scout each went to a different corner post, sat down, and stared off into the distance, standing sentry.

At Sunny's quiet urging, the humans made a circle around the scaffold and joined hands. I stood directly across from Sunny, while Blue was across from Annie. Everyone else filled in between the four of us. As soon as we joined hands, the wolves began to howl once again. The requiem lasted several minutes, rising and falling in volume and complexity, and then rising again.

Just as the final howl, which came from Rusty, dispersed into the cool air around us, I noticed five more beings with slightly fuzzy edges to their bodies had joined the circle. Three wolves, two white and one gray, hovered just behind Sunny. The smaller of the two white wolves was Snow. I recognized her translucent soft white aura, laced with a hint of violet. I guessed the identity of the other two. My suspicions were confirmed when Sunny looked at me and mouthed the words, "Sister and Aspen."

Standing behind the spirit wolves were two humans, also with fuzzy boundaries. My mother and my grandmother, who had not even visited me in my dreams since their deaths almost six months earlier, had chosen to join us in ceremony. A shiver ran from my chest up to the top of my head, then down to my toes, and then back up again. My eyes softened and my vision cleared when this flow of energy poured out through the crown of my head to join the energy of wind and sky.

We all stood silent after the howling ceased, lost in thoughts and imaginings. The air was still and quiet. I thought of Issa, and hoped he was feeling better. A soft breeze stirred the raven feathers on the scaffold, and then, in a matter of seconds, the breeze turned to a strong, sharp wind that swirled erratically around the scaffold, the wolves, and the assembled group. Lois and Annie pulled their jackets tighter. Another chill raced through my body, but it wasn't due to the cold. When I glanced up at Tierra and Lonestar, I was shocked to see their furry pelts grow slightly larger. Their fur, which had been very flat just a moment earlier, looked fluffier. The wind stopped suddenly, and I had the strangest feeling the land itself was holding its breath. Less than a minute later, the pelts returned to their previous condition.

Marshal echoed all of our thoughts when he said, "That was just the wind, right?"

"No, Uncle Marshal," said Sunny. "I'm pretty sure the spirits of Tierra and Lonestar came to say thank you."

We said goodbye to Seeker and his family at the scaffold, assuming the parking lot would be crowded with visitors. "*I'm sorry we have to leave so soon,*" said Seeker. "*But we're on our way to rendezvous with the rest of our pack. Thank you for what you are doing for us, Sage. Our fate is in your hands, and in the hands of others who care deeply about wolves, and about all life on Earth.*"

Milla walked up to me and gently licked my hand, and then the five wolves threaded their way to the edge of the forest that surrounded the clearing. A broad plateau opened up in front of them on the far side of the trees, and they took off at a lope, heading northeast, farther into the snowy mountains.

As soon as we returned to Blue's house, Adam and I packed our things and got ready to start the long trek back to California. We made solemn promises to stay in touch and plan another reunion soon. Blue, Annie, and Sunny walked us out to the truck for final goodbyes.

"I don't think you know this yet, Tish," I said as we all stood around the truck, reluctant to part. "But for the past couple of months, while you and Issa were up in northern California, I worked like crazy on the book, and I'm happy to tell you it is finished."

"*That's great news,*" said Tish. "*But, you know, Sunny's been telling me about all the other species that are being persecuted, like bears and lions, and the ones being hunted almost to extinction, like elephants and rhinos, or losing their habitat, or finding that their sources of food and water are no longer available as the climate changes. It's not just wolves who are in big trouble. What about all those other species? Like the frogs, and the turtles, and—"*

"All in good time, Tish." I said. "All in good time."

We pulled into the parking area next to my cabin just as the sun was setting in a glorious blaze of red and orange. As soon as we stepped through the door, I knew Issa was not there. Tish and Adam searched every room, but he was nowhere to be found.

"He's probably out hunting," I said, fervently hoping I was right.

"I'm sure that's it," said Adam, looking at me with raised brows.

"*I would feel it if he were dead, wouldn't I?*" said Tish. Never had she looked so diminished. It was as if she'd suddenly gotten much smaller. She looked at me with pleading eyes, wanting me to assure her again that Issa was okay.

Chapter Thirty
2019

The next morning, I opened the front door and stepped into a morning blessed by a cloudless azure sky and a breeze that carried a slight blush of warmth. "That was a perfect way to say goodbye to them, Adam," I said, stretching my arms up and over my head while taking three slow, deep breaths.

"It was perfect. I know Tierra's spirit was set free when I took her out of that shop in Arcata, but I often sensed she was still hanging around, waiting to complete some unfinished business. I'm sure the same was true for Lonestar."

Adam stepped out of the cabin behind me, wrapped his arms around me, and gave me a solid squeeze. "And that makes me think you and I have some unfinished business of our own." He nuzzled the back of my neck, and was headed toward my right ear when, much to my relief, Tish burst out of the cabin and leaped down the steps to the snowy flat below. She landed in a crouch, then turned and leaped up into the air, swinging her paws up and around. She leaped and danced in circles, her fluffy tail swirling behind her like the robes of a dervish. To add to the show, Tish sang while she danced, in a wild refrain of snaps, yips, and low puppy-like growls. After at least half a dozen circles, she stopped at the bottom of the stairs. With shoulders dropped and rump high in the air, tail swishing deliberately, she looked up at Adam and me with a big grin.

Before anyone had a chance to speak, Issa stepped out of the cabin and stood next to me. "*Tish is a pretty happy girl this morning,*" he said. "*And it's all thanks to you, Sage.*"

"*Can you go to Fresno to meet with the publisher tomorrow, Sage?*" Tish stared up at me with wide, bright eyes. "*Please? You said the book was finished, and I'm sure it's great. There's really no time to waste, you know.*"

Adam sighed and shook his head slightly, as if he realized he would have no quiet time alone with me until Tish had her book.

Sometimes wolves can be so pushy.

Epilogue
2019

Tish came to me in a dream on April 14th, about three weeks after the ceremony in Yellowstone. She and Issa had gone back up to northern California right after our return from Gardiner, once Tish was satisfied that the book was on track to be published. In the dream, I was sitting up in bed, while Tish stood just inside the bedroom door. She looked radiant, and the extra weight she'd been carrying was gone.

"*Hi, Sage,*" she greeted me. "*No, this isn't a dream.*" True to form, I thought, she can read my mind even in my dreams.

"*I'm really here,*" Tish continued. "*It's just a different kind of time travel. Remember when we were in Gardiner, and we watched that movie called Star Trek IV? It was about whales. Remember how they beamed up the whales to save the earth? What I'm doing is kind of like that. I just asked to be beamed up and over to be with you. Just a geographic shift, that's all. And now we're going to merge.*"

I waited while she walked over to the bed, and then I turned around to expose my neck. After the bite, I felt the familiar sensations of entering the merge, falling backwards, spinning, and eventually landing.

"Where are we?" I asked, as soon as I could speak.

"*Northeastern California. This is where Issa and I came after New Year's.*" We walked a few hundred yards down a trail lightly dusted with snow. The terrain was unfamiliar to me, mostly flat grassland that rose up into a craggy mountain range. As we neared the base of the range, I spotted a small round opening on a slope dotted with sagebrush. A large, snow-white wolf sat guarding the entrance.

"*Sage, I want you to meet Aris, the father of my pups,*" said Tish. The white wolf stood, walked up to us, and we touched noses. High-pitched squeals and yips floated out to us from the depths of the den. Tish and I stepped inside and walked to the end of the small excavation. "*And these are the girls. The two grays are Lily and Aster, and the tiny white pup between them, we call her Sage.*"

I awoke back in the cabin to see the sun beaming through the bedroom window. A splash of rainbows graced the walls and ceiling where the light caught a crystal I'd hung from the window frame. I left Adam in bed, and made my way to the kitchen, where I brewed a cup of strong cinnamon tea with honey.

Still in robe and slippers, I sat down and logged on to the computer. The first new email in the queue had a title related to wolves. I read the message and shivered. The federal government had taken wolf management away from the states. Wolves in the entire United States were once again fully protected under the Endangered Species Act.

The second email was even more stunning. Federal legislation had been introduced that called for a Predator Protection Act. If passed, the act would prohibit all killing of these magnificent animals, except in the most extreme cases.

Maybe, I thought, the coming year will go down in history as the year humans really start to wake up with respect to other life forms and the future of planet Earth.

The wolf ancestors were howling.

The shift was beginning.

Acknowledgements

Many people helped me with this book—both directly and indirectly. I thank you all, as do the wolves.

Deepest gratitude to my husband, Tom, for unending support and patience with my sometimes all-encompassing projects; to my brother, Marc, for being such a dear friend and for teaching me to talk to the animals; and to Mom and Dad for teaching me to love all things wild.

Many thanks to Jane Goodall, Rick Lamplugh, Amaroq Weiss, Todd Wilkinson, Jim and Jamie Dutcher, and Sy Montgomery for their kind words and consistent support.

Endless thanks to Kate Riley, Marlene Gast, Nan Perigo, Carolee Bull, Julia Lynn Huffman, and Peter Riva for moral, energetic, and literary support; to my shamanic community friends, including Hank Wesselman and Jill Kuykendall of Shared Wisdom, for helping me see the world in new and wonderful ways; and to Robert Redford, Jane Goodall, Aldo Leopold, Barry Lopez, Natalie Goldberg, and Terry Tempest Williams for inspiration on so many levels.

I'm deeply grateful to Marlene Gast, Nan Perigo, and Kathleen Marusak for their thoughtful and very helpful editorial assistance; to Jessa Tucker Riley for the beautiful cover design and marketing tools; to Janica Smith for her patience and for pulling it all together; and to the family dogs, cats, and horses—especially Kodi, Angus, and Leo, who were at my feet in the office during most of my writing time—for serving as muses across time and space.

And a very special thank you to all of the dedicated wolf advocates all over the world, who are tirelessly doing everything they can to ensure wolves have wild and safe lives and futures.

Suggestions For Further Reading

Numerous books have been written about wolf behavior, ecology, management, and conservation. The following list presents a small sample of what is available.

The Ninemile Wolves by Rick Bass

The Hidden Life of Wolves by Jim and Jamie Dutcher

Among Wolves by Gordon Haber and Marybeth Holleman

In the Temple of Wolves: A Winter's Immersion in Wild Yellowstone by Rick Lamplugh

Of Wolves and Men by Barry Lopez

The Wolf: The Ecology and Behavior of an Endangered Species by L. David Mech

Wolves: Behavior, Ecology, and Conservation by L. David Mech and Luigi Boitani (editors)

Never Cry Wolf by Farley Mowat

Decade of the Wolf: Returning the Wild to Yellowstone by Douglas W. Smith and Gary Ferguson

Made in the USA
Coppell, TX
07 November 2020